lost angel

marilyn wallace

bantam books

new york   toronto   london   sydney   auckland

This edition contains the complete text
of the original hardcover edition.
NOT ONE WORD HAS BEEN OMITTED.

Lost Angel
A Bantam Book / Published by association with Doubleday

PUBLISHING HISTORY
Doubleday hardcover edition published February 1996

Bantam paperback edition / December 1996

ISBN: 0-553-56839-6

Published simultaneously in the United States and Canada

Bantam Books are published by Bantam Books, a division of Bantam
Doubleday Dell Publishing Group, Inc. Its trademark, consisting of the
words "Bantam Books" and the portrayal of a rooster, is Registered in
U.S. Patent and Trademark Office and in other countries. Marca
Registrada. Bantam Books, 1540 Broadway, New York, New York
10036.

PRINTED IN THE UNITED STATES OF AMERICA

RAD 10 9 8 7 6 5 4 3 2 1

For Jean Kimball and Joan Cupples, angels.

acknowledgments

Thanks, once again, to Molly Friedrich, one of the 100 dearest people in New York, and to Kate Miciak and Judy Kern, two of the best editors anywhere. I'm grateful to Judy Greber for (among other things) reading and righting, and to Jackie Park for the gift of magic pencils. Special thanks are due my husband Bruce for being fiendishly patient and devilishly supportive.

She's not going to escape here either.

Unless a great, salty wave smashes into the library and sweeps the television set into the Atlantic, Valerie Vincent is doomed to spend the weekend in talk-show hell.

"Well, certainly she's got problems. *He's* her problem. That man loses his temper so often because he drinks too much. And she has no self-respect, it's obvious. Can you imagine? A middle-aged woman dashing into the street because her husband tossed her high school yearbook onto the road. Total lack of restraint." Antonia Carrera adjusts her dark glasses and leans forward in her wheelchair, the way someone might who can actually see the screen.

If only they were back in Brooklyn, or sitting on the damp sand tossing crumbs of dry bread to the gulls scuttling away from the hissing surf . . . but Valerie is pouring a Bombay martini for Antonia Carrera and marveling that the woman devours all this televised misery with such enthusiasm.

Even in her sprawling East Hampton beach house, with six guests upstairs preparing to offer sophisticated banter and precious, useless birthday gifts as payment for the weekend's pleasures, Antonia won't change her routine. She insists on tuning in to her regular shows, as though she'll starve if she's deprived of her daily serving of the grotesque and unbelievable, the *bizarre du jour*.

"She might have kept a letter from some old boyfriend hidden between the pages," Valerie suggests. But that's as far as she can take it. She simply can't come up with speculations about the poor woman and her silly yearbook to entertain Antonia.

Eight hours a day, five days a week, sixteen weeks—at least six hundred and forty hours she's spent working for Antonia at the brownstone overlooking Prospect Park, plus six more hours in East Hampton, amusing the woman with endless stories, reading to her—and now she's hit a wall. Maybe she's been hypnotized by the crash and roll of the waves and the clean expanse of beach, the first landscape she's seen in months without litter-strewn sidewalks framing the scene.

"Only about twenty minutes of sun left on the terrace, Antonia. Why don't we go outside before your guests come down for cocktails?"

"Not yet." Antonia holds up her hand to stop the conversation.

"—a tale of envy and desperation ends in tragedy." The voice-over drones as the camera zooms in on a paunchy, agitated man patting the arm of the gray-haired woman sitting slack-jawed and immobile beside him. "If Eddie Kilmer had seen the speeding car destined to end Rose's normal life, perhaps he wouldn't have taunted his wife and thrown that yearbook onto the blacktop in a fit of jealousy. And now, in a late-breaking story that will touch your hearts, we go to Arthur Gonzalez in Brooklyn."

"I don't want my heart touched by a story about Brooklyn. I came to East Hampton to get *away* from Brooklyn." Antonia gropes for the remote control wand, her fingers brushing the table surface. Too late, Valerie sees the crystal martini glass wobble and then tip. Startled, Antonia pulls her hand back; the remote clatters to the floor.

"It's all right. I've got it." Stooping, Valerie retrieves the remote. She's about to press the OFF button when her attention is drawn to the flickering television image.

A child's face fills the screen, pink mouth half parted, hair a nest of snarls and tangles, skin transformed by the camera into a coarse, dirt-streaked mask. The little girl gulps a few short breaths and her chin quivers, the way it does when she's trying not to cry. Cry again, from the evidence of the glistening tracks on her smudged cheeks.

She's hurt herself, Valerie thinks. *What happened to my daughter?*

Never in her life has she believed that time really can stand still but it does, then, for her. The odd sensation of not being anywhere, of having no substance, is swept away by the need to hold her daughter in her arms and touch her lips to every inch of Joanna's face.

The questions in the little girl's eyes brim over into fresh tears that run down her cheek toward the edge of her mouth. Valerie reaches out to blot the trickle.

Static leaps across the screen, a crackling rebuff that makes her jerk her hand away.

Suddenly she's tossed back into Antonia Carrera's East Hampton summer house. Antonia turns her head toward the steady drip of the spilled martini, but Valerie ignores the unspoken inquiry.

Joanna needs her.

Nothing else matters.

friday

one

She presses a linen napkin onto the spill, rights the fallen glass, and sends silent messages to Joanna. *It's going to be okay, baby. I'm coming. I just have to figure out how to get there.*

How to get where?

She has no idea. The reporter's words tumble around the book-lined alcoves of the elegant room like grains of fine sand in a high wind.

"Since New York City police found her, Baby Jane Doe has clung to her dump truck, playing quietly with the contents of its hopper: two seashells, a porcelain thimble bordered with painted roses, and a pewter pin in the shape of a woman sitting in a crescent moon." The camera lingers on Joanna's plump hand, then pans to the cab of the bright yellow truck.

Antonia stirs in the wheelchair. "What's on the screen, Valerie?"

But she can't reply, can only listen as the reporter's voice fills the room. "These objects are reminders of happier days for this pretty child police are calling Baby Jane."

"Joanna," Valerie corrects. In a bright flash of memory she sees the OB nurse grinning at her eighteen months earlier in the delivery room. Hears her own voice say *Joanna Claire*. Watches herself push the damp hair off her forehead and look down at the slippery, wriggling infant whose eyes are squeezed shut against the sudden light. Remembers how her momentary sense of loss for the cumbersome creature she had been was replaced by giddiness at the wonder of this child whose perfect, tiny fists explored the air.

She remembers, too, how reluctant she'd been to accompany Antonia on this weekend trip. She'd been sure she'd miss watching Joanna line up Cheerios on the high-chair tray and adorn the tips of her fingers with cereal rings and then pop them into her mouth, knew there would be moments she'd wish Joanna were in the next room, sleeping with her Babar book beside her dimpled cheek.

But nothing has prepared her for this.

For what? What's going on? She must make sense of that droning voice.

"From the condition of the Klein apartment, police theorize that sixty-five-year-old Esther Klein may have interrupted a burglary in progress. Take note of the special number displayed on your screens. Viewers are asked to call with any information about the murder of Esther Klein or the identity of Baby Jane."

Esther . . . murdered. That's wrong. Esther cannot, cannot be dead. But he's said it. It sounds as if the bastards have finally won.

Two burglaries in two years. Esther had told her how the police teams strolled in after each break-in, heads bobbing in sympathy, clucking about how Brooklyn wasn't what it used to be. "They maybe thought I should move to the suburbs or, God forbid, Florida," Esther had said, rolling her blue eyes. She'd bought bars for the windows, a chrome whistle for her bedside table, another to hang on a hook near the kitchen stove. In the end, they were only talismans.

Esther Klein has been reduced to a tick in the tally, just another urban statistic.

"What is it, Valerie? What's on the screen?" Antonia insists. It's the pampered Antonia speaking now, the Antonia annoyed by her dependence on others.

Antonia Carrera will have to survive a few minutes

without her. "I'll be right back," Valerie tells her, easing toward the doorway and peering down the shadow-filled hall.

She won't use the phone on the rolltop desk and give Antonia the chance to pepper her with questions. The kitchen phone won't do either, not with the caterer's staff twitching about in the final preparations for the grand birthday dinner. If she wants privacy, she'll have to make the call from Antonia's bedroom in the west wing.

She skids across the polished wood floor and runs down the hall, repeating Joanna's name like a mantra until she pulls the door shut behind her. The gardenias Antonia insists on floating in a black lacquer bowl fill the room with a perfume so sickening it nearly takes her breath away as she lifts the receiver, punches out the number.

A busy signal jeers at her.

So many people with something to say about Esther and Joanna. Five, six times, she hits the redial button and hears only a maddening beep. Finally, *finally* someone answers.

"Seventy-eighth Precinct." The voice is young, male, sharp with irritation. "Detective Russo's office. Weinstein speaking."

Relieved, Valerie lets go of the handful of white cotton coverlet she's been clutching. The Seventy-eighth Precinct. Okay, she knows where that is. A few blocks from Prospect Park. Not far from Esther's apartment.

"I'm Valerie Vincent, Joanna Vincent's mother. The child in Esther Klein's apartment. I'm out on Long Island, in East Hampton. I want to talk to my daughter. She's all right, isn't she?"

"She's fine. Joanna Vincent—how do you spell that?"

Through clenched teeth, she spells out her daughter's name. *"Now* can I talk to her?"

"Look, this line is only for information calls, Ms. Vincent. You know of any problems Mrs. Klein might have had with family, neighbors, someone like that?"

Esther—the dearest heart. *Go, go, you need a little vacation,* Esther had urged, *after all you've been through.*

"I said, do you know anything about Esther Klein,

people who might have threatened her or maybe had something against her?"

And Valerie has said she's Joanna's mother but Weinstein, a little person with a little power, apparently can't deal with facts that don't fill in the blank spaces on his form. "Give me a second here, would you? Esther's apartment was burglarized a couple of times in the past two years, but enemies? Esther was the kindest person in Brooklyn. Now, let me talk to my daughter."

"You want to come down here, we're at Sixth Avenue and Bergen. Just ask for Detective Russo."

"I'll be there in two hours. Make sure someone tells my daughter that Mommy's on her way. You can do that, can't you?"

He hangs up with a careless grunt. The dial tone blares into the gauzy, peach-tinted April twilight.

Esther is dead. Not just dead but *murdered*. Such a lovely sound the word makes, like a stream flowing over round rocks or a breeze lifting green leaves. Murdered: at least Esther is a priority for the police.

And Joanna is all right.

She says it again, and then again, and keeps repeating it until her breathing slows.

A spear of light points to the gilt-faced clock on the dresser. Good, just before six. No one will be in the library when she tells Antonia why she's leaving. The truth, this time.

As it always is when she begins to gather stray bits and pieces of reality into a new story for Antonia, the truth will be the starting point. But this time she'll forgo the elaborate descriptions, the inventive little twists of plot to spin out the telling and make the time pass. This time the plain truth will be the whole story.

She'll need a car and some money, enough for a place to sleep for a couple of nights, until she decides what she and Joanna are going to do. But if she just sits here, surrounded by the colored perfume bottles and the ice-blue pillows that Antonia will wedge behind her before she sips her morning coffee, she'll never get to Brooklyn, to Joanna.

Except for the leather-bound books and the sharp

smell of spilled gin mingling with sea air, the library is empty. Thankfully, someone, probably Nadia, has come in to check on Antonia and shut the cabinet door over the blank eye of the television. A salty breeze swirls over the low stone wall onto the slate-floored terrace, then billows up the wheelchair ramp and through the French doors. To anyone who doesn't know better, Antonia appears to be looking out over the deserted beach to the turbulent evening sea and the dimming light.

Valerie crosses the terrace, making sure her footsteps sound smartly on the stones. Antonia hates to be taken by surprise; she won't allow wall-to-wall carpeting or tennis shoes in either of her homes.

Feathery brows form a V above Antonia's dark glasses and her full mouth lifts in an inquiring smile. An old habit, she told Valerie once, to make people think she really can see them.

"Antonia." Valerie squares her shoulders, ready to get on with it. "I have to go back to the city right away."

"What do you mean, right away?" The smile doesn't falter. "I've got all these guests and a fifty-fifth birthday to celebrate." Antonia smoothes her tailored trousers; in a gentle voice she says, "You've been unlike yourself since that news story. This sudden urgency has something to do with that child on the television, doesn't it, my dear?"

"She's my daughter." Grateful that Antonia has made it so easy, Valerie explains in a rush. "It's always bothered me, lying to you about Joanna. But I really needed this job and Kristin Denby said you wanted a single woman. No husband, no kids, or else no job. So I lied."

Even confined in a wheelchair, Antonia can shift her shoulders just enough to indicate that she's drawing herself up in stiff-spined reaction. "You told me you were twenty-seven, and that you left Columbia County because you wanted to live in a city. You said you were divorced, Valerie. Were those lies as well? Your age, your ex-husband's drinking, his disintegration?"

"That was all true." If only it hadn't been . . . but she doesn't have time to analyze her marriage or her former husband or anything else. She has to get to Joanna.

"And I'd guess you knew this poor woman who was killed."

Valerie nods, then, remembering, says, "Esther Klein and my mother sang together in the chorus in high school. Esther stood beside me at my mother's funeral. Antonia, I—"

"Then this Aunt Esther person you mentioned in your interview wasn't a frail old lady who needed you to take care of her at night. You declined to come live with me because you wanted time with the child, wasn't that it?" Antonia pulls off her dark glasses and sets them on her lap.

Kneeling on the flagstones, Valerie takes Antonia's hand in her own, the slender fingers lying like long, tapering opals in her palm. "Yes, that's right. Listen, Antonia, I really must leave. I don't want to disrupt your birthday any more than I already have. I'd like to borrow one of the cars to get to the city. If I can't, I'll take the train."

Wordlessly, Antonia replaces the glasses.

That answer is clear enough. Valerie sees Joanna's tear-stained face, feels her own impatience tugging her toward the driveway. "I'm sorry, then, but I have to go."

Across the damp air, Antonia reaches for Valerie's sleeve, fingers sliding along the shoulder seam of her blouse and then moving to her collar. She traces the curve of Valerie's jaw with the reverence of a lover's touch, or a mother's, lingering on the planes where bones protrude—chin, nose, cheeks—skimming over her lips, along the ridges above her eyes, sending confusing ripples of sensation through her.

"You're trembling, my dear." Antonia's hand drops gently to the leather pouch hanging inside the arm of her wheelchair. "I do wish you'd told me the truth right off. I'll have Carl bring a car around for you. You and the child can't go back to that apartment. You must stay at my house, I insist. I'll call Kristin and have her bring over some milk and bread. And orange juice. Children need orange juice. Go on now. Here, take this." She presses a bundle of bills into Valerie's hand. "And, Valerie—be sure to phone me as soon as you can."

· · ·

"You're Valerie Vincent?"

She's been pacing in the dingy light of the precinct entryway for so long now, has memorized every flaking spot of pea-green paint with such concentration that the voice startles her. The question has come from a stocky man with a pearly scalp shining through his bristle-cut hair and the wary reserve of a lifelong skeptic. She makes herself look away from the rust-colored splotch on the cuff of his white shirt. She focuses instead on the cleft creasing his chin.

"Yes, yes, that's me. Where's Joanna?"

"I'm Detective Russo. Come with me, Ms. Vincent." He starts down the hall, hitching his pants as he leads her toward an elevator. They ride to the second floor in silence and in darkness, and she's startled when the car lurches to a stop.

Light spills from an open door onto the torn and blackened asphalt tiles, and she knows this is where they're headed, strains to hear Joanna's baby voice or her steady, regular sleep-breathing, perhaps smell the citrusy scent that always seems to cling to her—and she walks faster, passing Detective Russo, breaking into a run.

Empty desks, telephones, hard chairs. That's all.

"My daughter—where is she?" Valerie asks, fighting the feeling that she's being punished for breaking a rule nobody's ever taught her.

"I need to ask you a few questions, Ms. Vincent. Have a seat." Detective Russo's brown eyes are tired, intelligent, and unable to meet her gaze as he points to the chair beside the desk nearest the door.

She's familiar with that bureaucratic distance. It's a cloak that weary high school teachers and county social workers wrap themselves in as a protection from other people's misfortunes. She grips the edge of her chair to keep from shouting: *The City of New York is not paying you to keep my daughter from me.*

"Where were you this afternoon, Ms. Vincent, between three and four o'clock?"

"This afternoon? In a car with three other people, on the Long Island Expressway, headed for East Hampton with my employer, Antonia Carrera. She's blind, confined to a wheelchair, and I—" Valerie stops herself. She doesn't have to justify herself to this man, even though he probably disapproves of women who leave their children with family friends to go off to the Hamptons for a birthday party. "This is ridiculous. A dear friend has been murdered and my daughter has spent several hours alone and scared and I want to—"

"Write down your employer's name and her telephone number, please. And the names of the other people in the car." The detective slides a piece of paper across the desk, hands her his ballpoint pen.

Antonia's East Hampton number . . . she'd scribbled it on a pink Post-It the night before, stuck it on Esther's refrigerator with a magnet, a little plastic apple, crimson and shiny, but she doesn't know it, not from memory. "Look, I don't remember the number, but it should be listed. Is this really necessary, Detective Russo? Why don't you—"

"Write down the names," he says, impatient, as though he assumes she's trying to trick him. "The people you were with in the car."

He thinks I killed Esther.

That's why he's asking for their names, for Antonia's phone number. This expressionless, sturdy man sees her as a suspect, and before she can touch Joanna's soft skin, whisper that everything is all right, she has to prove to him that she was nowhere near Brooklyn when Esther was murdered. Her jaw clenches as she prints Antonia's full name, then Nadia's and Carl's. "Check with them. They'll tell you where I was."

Russo watches her, measuring her truthfulness with his eyes.

"You call them, but I want you to understand: Esther Klein was my mother's closest friend. I've known her all my life. I could no more hurt Esther than I could my own daughter. . . ." Valerie swallows hard. "Detective Russo, I can answer these questions with Joanna on my lap. Will you please—"

"Does your daughter have any special marks—you know, moles, scars, anything like that?"

Russo is following form; she has to go along. "No

scars. A mole, yes, beside her mouth. Another one on her right thigh. And a very pale birthmark, the doctor called it a port-wine stain, but since her hair's grown you can hardly see it, on the back of her scalp low down, near the nape of her neck. Okay, do I pass? Do I get to see my daughter now?"

He sighs and looks at the wall behind her, runs his hand along the top of his head. "Do you have identification, Ms. Vincent? A driver's license, a bank card, whatever."

Nothing, unless a Taconic Hills library card counts. She passes the card to Russo, watches as he studies it, frowns, and hands it back to her.

"I lived in Taconic Hills until five months ago when I—" Of course. He needs proof that she's Joanna's mother. The photograph. She slides a black and white snapshot from its compartment in her wallet and holds it out. "I leave the rest of my papers at Esther's when I go to work. I know this isn't a driver's license or anything like that, but it should be what you're looking for."

For months the picture has been her touchstone, a chance to grab a minute with Joanna in the middle of a workday at Antonia's. Joanna's face pressed against hers, both of them smiling on the porch of the Taconic Hills General Store, the same crinkles at the corners of identical green eyes, the same unruly chestnut curls sneaking onto their foreheads. Early October. They'd just bought brownies for a picnic with Rosie and Andrew Cooper near the pond at Vixen Hill Lodge. The leaves had blazed with color. . . .

For a moment, everything she's worked so hard for comes at her in a torrent, and she misses that other life terribly. Only some of it, she realizes at once. Not the bad marriage. Not her former in-laws.

The detective holds the photograph between two fingers, glances at her. "I need to hang on to this for a while." In his doughy face, the gray shadows beneath Russo's eyes look like indentations left by a pair of dirty thumbs.

Why does he want a picture of Joanna? And why isn't he getting up and calling whoever has her baby, ordering them to bring her in now? Joanna needs to hear her mother's voice, feel her mother's arms around her. It's been nearly three hours since she first saw her daughter's face on the television screen. Enough waiting, enough questions, *enough*.

You have to face some people down to keep them from plowing the same field over and over.

"Detective Russo, it's late and I want to take my daughter home." Valerie Vincent pushes her chair back, reaches for her purse. "If I have to call my lawyer, I will. Now, let me see Joanna."

Russo shakes his head. He runs a square-tipped finger along the edge of the photograph. "I'm afraid you can't do that, Ms. Vincent. We released Joanna to another woman. About twenty minutes before you got here."

two

Control.

Mitch Russo understood now that he'd awakened this morning with Allie Spinella on his mind to remind him about control.

He'd untangled his fingers from Cissie's hair, propped himself against the pillow, tried to figure out what it meant that he'd been dreaming about that August afternoon . . . how long ago?

Thirty-five years. He was twelve. His brother Tony, a year younger and a head taller, had burst into their bedroom, wiping blood from his nose with the edge of his torn polo shirt. The sound of Mama chopping garlic and talking to her long-dead mother in the kitchen down the hall meant that Tony had managed to escape her notice.

"Hey, big shot, you run into a lamppost?" The balsawood Fokker wing strut he gripped between Mama's tweezers slipped into place; he'd have to hold perfectly still until the glue dried.

Tony snuffled and wiped his nose with the back of his hand.

"When you learn to talk, moron, let me know." Mitch brushed the hair out of his eyes, ashamed that even with his brother standing there and dripping blood like a goddamn underdone steak, he was thinking that he wanted wavy hair like Tony's.

Tony rummaged in the closet until he came up with a baseball bat. "Allie Spinella. Bastard was losing the fight so he hit me with a board. I'm gonna get him back—"

"Sit down, jerk." Mitch pressed a balled-up white sock against Tony's blood-smeared nostrils. "Mama will kill you if she finds out you've been fighting again. Press, jerk."

Losing was one thing; it happened. But losing a fight because Spinella, the fat porker, had cheated . . . that was dirty. Mitch felt something speeding up inside him, a runaway train of anger hurtling through his chest. The clanging in his head got louder, louder, and he'd tossed the bat back into the closet and run out of the apartment onto Kings Highway, pounding along the hot pavement toward the schoolyard.

He found Spinella shooting hoops with the guys. He grabbed him from behind by the hair, so fast and so hard they both hit the asphalt with a splat. Later, Mickey Katz told him he'd smashed old lard-belly until his eyes rolled back in his head and his face crumpled, but Mitch didn't remember that. Didn't remember much until he found himself leaning over a knee-high iron fence behind an apartment building, crying and puking until his stomach hurt and his throat burned.

Mitch Russo had learned in all these years to control that anger.

He'd have her checked out, this young woman whose hands held on to the edge of the desk as though she were afraid she might fly away if she let go. He'd have Gallagher call East Hampton, get the local cops to talk to those three people, to verify that Valerie Vincent was sitting in some rich woman's car on the LIE when Esther Klein was murdered.

But he knew what Gallagher would find.

Which meant that the person who had claimed that child, not an hour ago, had fought dirty. Only this time he wasn't going to find her standing at a foul line trying to make a basket, bragging and waiting for him to teach her a lesson. And he wouldn't hit anyone, and afterward he wouldn't get sick from an excess of regret and adrenaline.

He reached for the phone, buzzed his partner, passed

a tissue to Valerie Vincent. "I'll be right back, Ms. Vincent. One second."

By the time he reached the doorway, Teresa Gallagher was standing there. "Ms. Vincent, this is my partner, Detective Teresa Gallagher."

The two women nodded at each other, and Gallagher backed into the hall, her delicate face bunched into a quizzical frown. This mess could put her career, his own—hell, everyone's including the commissioner's—right in the toilet if the press really got going.

"We're screwed, Gallagher," Mitch Russo said. "I'm going to check it out, but I'd bet my kid's college tuition money we sent that baby home with the wrong woman."

Gallagher, who had been trying to get pregnant for a year, paled. "The baby called her 'Mommy.' She did that, didn't she? Said 'Mommy' when the woman picked her up?" Her voice was hoarse, her eyes wide. "Sure, she said 'Mommy.' After the woman whispered something to her. After she walked to the other end of the room with the kid in her arms and kissed her face and whispered to her, the baby said 'Mommy.' Shit."

They'd both heard it. They'd both assumed the kid was glad to see her mother. Hell, it made them both feel good to be part of the happy reunion. "She could have asked the kid if she missed her mommy. Maybe she said she was going to take her to see Mommy. Maybe she just asked her to say the word. And we bought it, Teresa, the whole damn act." Russo's jaw clenched so tight it hurt.

"So who do we have in there? Oh, Mitch, the real mother—" Gallagher clapped a freckled hand over her mouth, then frowned. "You're sure, right? Why couldn't this one be lying? Why do you think she's for real?"

Russo handed her the paper. "I just do. But we're going to find out. Call Suffolk County, have them send someone out to see these people," he said, tapping the neatly printed list, "and check Vincent's movements this afternoon."

"But the mole on the baby's thigh—the woman we talked to before knew exactly where it was." The color returned to Gallagher's cheeks. "Yeah, anyone who was in the Klein apartment when the baby was there might have seen the mole. She stole all that ID, didn't she? From Klein's apartment. She's our perp. Shit."

Mitch Russo would stake his tickets to the Mets' opener that his partner was right. "Pull her prints. We did at least print her, didn't we?"

"Sure, and then we did everything we could to help her get away. Hustled her out the back so she wouldn't have to face reporters. Called for car service and sent her on her merry way." Gallagher wouldn't let go, kept picking at it like some kid with chicken pox. "We even made sure nobody'd stop her and ask questions. 'At the request of the mother, to protect her child and allow the family to recover from this terrible tragedy, we are not releasing the name of the child at this time.' Christ . . . we really did a number."

It wasn't going to do him or Teresa Gallagher—or that baby—any good to go on beating themselves up. "We *were* careful, Teresa. It all added up—the papers, the mole, the kid saying 'Mommy.' She even squeezed out a couple of tears when she talked about the Klein woman. See if you can get hold of that car service dispatcher and find out where they took them. She said something about staying with a friend in Queens, didn't she? Pull in Siroken and Sullivan and Amato, whoever you can find, and let's get pictures circulating. You're right, she's probably the one who bashed Esther Klein."

Gallagher pivoted and ran down the hall. Russo hung in the doorway, trying to compose himself so he could face the young woman inside. Shit, shit, *shit*. How could this happen?

The other one had been cool. She'd strolled in with her summery dress and her long, dark hair tucked up in that baseball cap, talking about how she was out shopping—for a Dustbuster, for Christ's sake—when she passed the electronics department and saw her daughter on a display television. Gallagher had made copies of every piece of paper the woman had produced from her handbag—bank cards, credit cards, one of those printed forms pediatricians give out with a list of a kid's shots, an old high school graduation picture. Could have been her. *Looked* like her face might have ten, twelve years ago.

And it could have been Valerie Vincent.

The baby only said it once. *Mommy*. Excited. Happy. Then she wrapped her arms around the woman's neck and fell asleep again.

Gallagher had sensed the child's reaction was off, but he'd talked her out of it. *"You just don't want to let go of the kid,"* he'd said, knowing how easily he'd been able to read Gallagher's face each month when she got her period. Knowing how she snapped at him and told him to count his blessings whenever he complained that his kids only called him when they needed money. Teresa Gallagher, who was always saying she wouldn't let her feelings get in the way of her work, had caved in to his insistence that Baby Jane Doe was upset by all the commotion at the crime scene and at the precinct.

Bad enough he had to live with the memory of that poor woman lying on the floor with her head in a pool of blood, looking so much like his own mother he'd had to go out into the hall to pull himself together. Bad enough he let the beat cop hand him the child they'd found huddled in the corner of a back bedroom, let himself hold her, touch that baby-fine hair, try to shush her with the silly things he used to say to his own kids whenever they were scared and crying.

As Mitch Russo roused himself and reached for the door, Gallagher stuck her head in the hall.

"Suffolk County is going to follow up. They'll call as soon as they're done, so keep her talking for a while. About an hour, they said."

An hour. In that time, he'd ask Valerie Vincent hard questions and hope that something she'd say would help them figure out who had walked away from the precinct with her child.

Find the woman with the baby and they'd have Esther Klein's killer.

three

Standing in the doorway with his elbow propped against the wood frame, Detective Russo looks like her father. Or, at least, like the picture her mother carried from house to small-town house, setting it out first thing whenever she unpacked. Her late husband, Emily Vincent would explain to each set of new neighbors in her lost, sad voice, a pit mechanic who had the bad luck to be standing at the end of a straightaway when a Formula One hit the wall and burst into flames.

"Tell me again: you sent my daughter off with this stranger because she had my credit cards and Joanna's inoculation record? I called from East Hampton—it couldn't have been more than three minutes after I saw Joanna on television. I told the officer, the one who answered the phone, that she was my daughter. I said I was coming to get her. Didn't that mean anything?"

"Ms. Vincent, I told you. We logged thirty-seven calls—mothers, fathers, grandparents, assorted aunts and cousins and uncles. Four of these so-called relatives actually showed up here."

Thirty-seven calls and four impostors. Some people need to attach their sickness to tragedies—okay, Valerie isn't such a country girl that she can't recognize that. But Russo's the professional, he should have known, should have been more careful.

"And one woman had papers. Like I said, credit cards and doctors' records, and an old high school graduation photo which, I have to tell you, looked enough like her to convince us. She knew about the baby's mole. And the little girl said 'Mommy' when the woman picked her up."

"You're lying." Her cheeks flame with anger. Joanna knows. Even if he doesn't, Joanna knows who her mother is. And who she isn't.

But Russo shakes his head. "I don't know, maybe she tricked the kid into saying it. I swear to God, that's exactly what she said." He looks as though he's going to go on, but he only shifts his weight and leans against the wall.

Mommy. Joanna wouldn't call anyone else Mommy.

"You take a second," Russo says, "and get yourself together. Then I have some questions I need to ask you. We have to move on this, you understand? We check out Esther Klein's past and yours and maybe something stands out."

"My *past*. You're joking, right? Someone has my baby and you want me to hang around here while I tell you about my past?" She bolts from her chair. The room is stuffy, confining, and she can't sit around chatting. She needs space, air, and she has to be free to . . . what? Run into the street and call her child's name and wait for her to come toddling home?

Russo grabs the scuffed wood of the doorframe, blocking her way. "Listen, I got every available cop out there. You never know what's going to turn things around, so you look under every rock, understand, Ms. Vincent? I got kids—they're older but I know, believe me, I *know* what you're feeling."

And that's supposed to be a comfort? What does it matter if this man has children, older children, younger children, children at home or living on another continent? "No. No, you don't know what I'm feeling. You still have your children. I don't have mine. And you let it happen."

His face twists as though he's been jabbed. "Please, help me fix this. Help me out here."

"You're kidding, right? You're asking me to do this for you?" She spits the words out, but the bitter taste won't go away.

Help me out here.

She should help him. The mistake that sent Joanna away—that he could do on his own.

Her fists flail at his chest. She cries out her daughter's name and is shocked to feel arms around her, tight and restraining. She cries until the dampness of his shirt becomes cold against her cheek and when she pulls away she sees tears in his eyes.

"I'm sorry," Mitch Russo whispers. "I want to find her for you. Someone else has your daughter and I want to get her back."

Someone else.

If she can silence the million buzzing sounds in her head maybe she'll be able to think. Think who might have a reason to kill Esther Klein. Think who might want to take Joanna.

Martha and Lucas Starr.

The straw may be flimsy, but she grasps it and holds on. Maybe Martha and Lucas saw Esther as an obstacle to finishing what they started months ago. If they found someone who looked enough like her to fool Russo with that old photograph . . .

Valerie wipes at her face with the back of her hand and settles into the chair, watching as Russo sits down across from her and fumbles with the folder. "This isn't for you, you understand," she says. "It isn't for me, either. This is for Joanna. And for Esther. My divorce came through six months ago and—"

"Your former husband—spell his name, please." Russo pulls the cap off a pen, slides a clean piece of paper out of the folder.

"Johnny Starr. S-T-A-R-R. Look, this isn't going to help find—"

"Please, Ms. Vincent. We don't know yet *what's* going to help. Where's Johnny Starr now?"

Maybe he's right. And the answer won't take much time. "Who knows? I haven't seen him since a month after Joanna was born."

"What kind of work does he do? Any hobbies, interests, groups he belongs to?"

"Johnny gave up painting pictures for painting houses

and then he gave up painting houses for drinking. He used to have hobbies and interests but he drowned them in alcohol. Bourbon, by then. Wild Turkey, and a lot of it." Good ammunition; the name had come up in one of their blazing arguments and she'd relished using it. Johnny wasn't even sober enough to be insulted. "This is a waste of time, talking about Johnny. It's his parents we should be discussing. Martha and Lucas Starr. Right after the divorce, they threatened to sue for custody of Joanna."

"Custody? On what grounds?" He's looking at her straight on, the sympathy in his eyes frozen out by the chill of suspicion.

"Grounds—they didn't have any, so they created some." Created them out of light and shadow and carefully selected props. "They set me up. I didn't realize what was going on at first. Trick or treat, right? They chose Halloween to pull their stunt."

"Tell me about it," he says. "Everything. I mean, I don't need to know how much milk you poured in your cereal that morning but if it helps you remember . . ."

Exhuming the events of that day won't be easy. It's taken a lot of effort to bury them under layers of work, trips to the park with Esther and Joanna, all those long afternoons with Antonia.

For Joanna. This is for Joanna. Valerie arranges herself in the seat and slips into the storytelling rhythms that shape her time with Antonia.

"You know how sometimes it feels like the gods are kind of toying with you so they can watch you squirm? Well, that day started with Margaret Clarkson, my history professor at the State University in Albany, delivering an ultimatum. She had to have the outline for my final paper on her desk in a week, the finished paper by the end of spring semester. I needed this one last course to get my teaching credential, and I wasn't about to let her mess up my plans."

"Which plans do you mean?" The pen is poised above the paper but Russo hasn't written anything except the Starrs' names.

"To teach history in some small country high school. To be the best parent I could be for Joanna, even if it meant smiling and tossing nice words I didn't mean at the Margaret Clarksons of the world to do it. I learned something from my mother—about waiting tables, clerking in discount drugstores, how those jobs wear you out, don't leave you anything for yourself or for your child.

"I was determined to make a good life without Johnny. Without having to share anything with him—not my house, not his crazy outbursts, and certainly not Joanna."

Russo scribbles on his pad, doesn't look up when he prompts, "So after the interview with the professor . . . ?"

"I went home to try to make sense of the transcript of the trial of Dorcas Good. That was the topic of my paper—the Salem witch hunts. How a couple of families turned some land disputes into an economic war. How no one cared that they were destroying innocent women and forever scarring the children of the village. I don't know if you remember your American history but Dorcas Good was four years old when she was forced to testify against her mother. Then they accused *her* of witchcraft. Her mother was executed and Dorcas was kept in prison until she was eight. Grew up to be a crazy, raggedy beggar woman wandering the streets of New England. Big surprise, right?

"I sat for a long time, thinking about Dorcas Good, thinking that she might have looked like my Joanna. I picked up the photograph on my desk, this perfectly beautiful little girl sitting on the floor trying to catch the sunlight in her hands. Joanna was going through that phase where she hugged things. Like she was memorizing the world by its feel, by its weight and temperature and texture."

And now someone else will be watching her learn about the world, if she's still . . . No, she can't let herself think that way.

"Take your time. Whenever you're ready. You need a glass of water?" Russo pushes away from the table, fills two small paper cups with water from the cooler, and returns to his chair.

Concentrate on the details, Valerie reminds herself.

Make it so clear he'll understand and know exactly what to do.

"I was restless so I decided to get ready for the trick-or-treaters before Joanna got up from her nap. I put some chocolates in a bowl. And then I got the pumpkin from the coffee table, to put it on the porch. I was whistling 'Teddy Bears' Picnic,' I remember, and not paying much attention to anything else, certainly not outside noises. So I was startled when I pulled the front door open.

"Martha and Lucas Starr, the doting grandparents, right? I used to think Johnny's parents were like stones. You know—hard, sharp, annoying, always turning up underfoot to interrupt my life and comment on Joanna's pacifier or her toilet training. Scattering their judgments like grit all over my little house. But when I saw them standing in the doorway, Martha with her hand stretched out about to ring the bell and Lucas behind her, sort of skulking in her shadow, it felt more like they were an avalanche about to bury me.'"

four

Mitch Russo tugs at his cuffs, glances at the bloodstain, then drops his hands to his lap. "You need to take a break?"

"No, not yet. You said you wanted to know about my past, that it might help." She's about to revisit a memory she's kept shut away; the only way she can do this is to go right through to the end without stopping.

"I could tell Martha was really nervous by the way she clutched the fringed ends of her scarf. She told me they'd come to talk about Johnny. Actually, what she said was, 'It's time you told us where John is.' As though I'd been hiding something from her."

"Johnny, they hardly knew ye." Me, too. A knot of fury tightens in her chest. The last time she saw him, she'd almost felt sorry for him. Poor, indecisive, alcohol-impaired Johnny, trying to make himself feel good by making her feel bad.

"I told them I didn't have any idea where Johnny was, but they just stood there in the cold. Finally I motioned them in. They didn't even take off their coats, just sat down and started right in."

"Started in? What do you mean?" Russo has set the pen on the table beside his pad; he's watching her face.

"Started in with a critique of my life. Mine and Joanna's. Martha pointed at the yellow dump truck on the floor and asked me if it was 'the child's.' Then Lucas reached for a doll Joanna had scribbled all over with her crayons—she loves bright colors, reds and yellows, especially—and announced that she could use some new toys."

If Martha and Lucas were stones, then she knew she had rocks in her head when she let them in. They'd pulled this inspection routine before.

"And then I heard a noise. I couldn't tell what it was, just a rustle and a creak, really, from somewhere near the back of the house. I thought maybe their voices had awakened Joanna. But she didn't cry or call out, so I decided it must have been the wind. Martha and Lucas were kind of hovering on the sofa. They even *sat* rigidly, like they were afraid to touch their own bodies."

Russo appears confused. "So, they came just to check up on the kind of toys you let your kid play with?"

"What they wanted was Joanna. But they couldn't come right out and say it, of course. Lucas told me they'd been thinking about the child's welfare and praying over their worries. Me with no real job and all—how would I pay for medical care if she needed it? Would I be able to provide her with proper clothing? And he reminded me that she'd need a bed soon."

What he'd actually said was, "Two, three months from now, the child is going to outgrow that old crib." Not even *Joanna*. Just *the child*, generic, interchangeable with a hundred others. And Martha sat there, fiddling with her wedding band, twisting it back and forth, back and forth, as though she were winding herself up.

"Finally Martha said it right out. 'A child needs two parents,' she told me. As though Johnny were capable of doing anything for his daughter. So I reminded her that she'd said they wanted to talk about Johnny.

"Lucas said that John, that's what they called him, never anything else, always John, that John was a child of God, and they hoped he'd join them on the good path someday. He said they were prepared to stand in for John until they found him. What with me going to school and when that was done going off to work, they said it was bound to be easier for me if *the child* lived with them."

First Lucas and Martha Starr had taken over her living

room and turned it into a place of hard surfaces, dark colors, and antiseptic odors. And then they offered her a Trojan horse. The memory makes her jaw clench.

"Joanna was *my* child; they'd already had their chance with Johnny. I warned them that if they wanted to see their grandchild at all they'd better stop threatening me and calling it charity. That seemed to be some sort of signal for them to raise the stakes."

"So, now they've told you they wanted to take your child, is that right? They actually said it, as clear as that?" He scribbles on the pad, nods. The pencil taps against the table as he waits for an answer.

"That's what they said, but they weren't finished. Martha crossed the room and stationed herself in front of my desk. She started to read the notes pinned to the corkboard. I couldn't believe it: the woman had no sense of boundaries. She asked me about one of the pictures. Was this a pilgrim person standing by a gallows? she wanted to know. Said it like a challenge while she pointed a fat finger at one of my seventeenth-century woodcut reproductions and asked if those pictures were new."

Those pictures were indeed new . . . as was Martha's interest in the corkboard. The only way to reclaim the territory Martha had invaded was to answer her opening volley and participate in the undeclared war.

"I said it was a scene from a hanging in Salem village, a copy of one, and that I really didn't have time to discuss art. I assured them that Joanna and I were doing fine. I told her I had to get back to my studies."

Russo is listening intently, but she has to stop, take a sip of water from the paper cup. She doesn't want to relive the rest of it, doesn't want those images in her head again, but she knows she'll go on.

"Martha said, 'Ah, your *studies*. And that's what all these books are for?' She flipped through one, pointing to pictures, asking me if everyone read about witches and Black Sabbats and familiars of the devil for school. And then she pulled a camera from her purse and pointed it at the books and pressed the button. The flash blinded me for a second, but when Martha aimed the lens again, I understood. I was being accused."

Accused. Dark powers and evil practices. Tossed onto the worn planks of a village courtroom and surrounded by the writhing, screaming afflicted, who pointed their fingers and rolled their eyes.

"Accused of what?" Russo frowns.

Lucas had stepped so close that his breath left puffs of medicinal dampness on her cheek. He'd stood in front of the glass elephants on the mantel and called them images of the demon Behemoth, had gone to the window and waved at the circle of rocks in the yard and declared that he knew all about the secret ceremonies.

"Lucas was the one who said it first. 'Thing is,' he said in that nasty, soft voice, 'we can't allow our flesh and blood to be raised by a disciple of Satan.' Then Martha chimed in. Maybe it wasn't really true, maybe I didn't really have a black altar in my bedroom, maybe I wasn't getting ready to worship the Lord of Darkness. 'All Hallows' Eve, big holiday for you people. Do you have an altar back there, Valerie?' she said. And I fell for it."

How stupid it had been to think a show-and-tell tour of her bedroom would satisfy them and send them on their way.

"You fell for what?" Not even Mitch Russo, with all his experience, with all that big-city wariness, can tell what's coming.

"They followed me to the back of the house, and when I pushed my bedroom door open a crack, I swear, I felt a chill seep into the hall. I ignored it and stepped all the way into the room. It took a while for me to really see everything.

"My antique hat forms, all five of them, gouged with inverted crosses. Horrible, ragged channels carved into the beautiful old wood. Feathers all over the floor, as though some huge bird had flown into the blades of a giant propeller. Red slimy stuff was splattered on everything—my Russian nested dolls, a jar of pennies, the fat white candles arranged in a circle on the lace runner."

Now the light of understanding shines from the detective's eyes. "So those noises you heard and all that talk in the living room . . . they were distracting you while someone broke into your house and set you up?"

She nods, grateful she doesn't have to explain. "Above the candles, there was a smudged, lipsticked 666 on the mirror. The final touch. Mark of the devil. I was furious. I told them to get out. I threatened to call the police. Lucas informed me they were going to take the pictures to a judge and use them to prove I was an unfit mother. That if Joanna was exposed to my teachings she'd be beyond redemption."

Beyond redemption—last summer, standing in the cottage kitchen, Sarah Hoving had said that the scarred counters were *beyond redemption*.

"Lucas told me I had two choices. I could tell them where John was or I could turn Joanna over to them. That I had the weekend to think about it."

And then they'd barreled out the front door and sailed onto the porch. Drove away so quickly that the blue exhaust fumes hanging in the air—and the wreckage in the bedroom—were the only confirmation that someone had been there. She'd raced toward the back of the house and yanked open the door to her daughter's room.

"Mommy, *thirsty*," Joanna had whispered in her waking-up voice. The air was perfumed by baby smells, a lingering, milky sweetness that clung to everything in the room. She'd held out her arms to be picked up, damp curls drooping onto her forehead and beads of sweat glistening along the folds of her neck.

Valerie had whispered reassurances into her daughter's hair. And Joanna had laughed and nuzzled her neck. "Mommy, tickles," she'd giggled.

Valerie slumps in the chair and fills her lungs with sour air. The days at Antonia's, the nights and mornings with Joanna and Esther, and the growing pile of pages she's accumulated for her history paper have lulled her into feeling safe. She's been foolish, and now she has to get smart fast.

"So then they filed for custody?"

She's exhausted, but if she has to use her anger to fuel her through a night of talking, she'll do it. For Joanna. She rubs her burning eyes.

"No, they never got that far. That night, I spoke to my attorney. She assured me I'd win . . . after a long, messy fight. I *had* to finish school so I whipped out an outline for Professor Clarkson, packed up the house, paid in advance for eight months' storage for my stuff, and took off with Joanna and my research notes. We went straight to Esther's, in Brooklyn. I didn't tell anyone, not a soul, where we were going. No one in Taconic Hills knew where I was."

Sometime during her telling, Russo has unbuttoned his cuffs and folded back the stained shirtsleeve. "I know a guy who has experience with this kind of thing," he says as he straightens papers noisily. "The accusations of devil worship, I mean. I'm going to check in with him. And I want to talk to your in-laws and your husband—sorry, *ex*-husband. You leave me an address and phone number where I can reach you. You can't go back to the Klein apartment, not until the techs are finished there." Thick ridges furrow his forehead. "You do have someplace to go, don't you?"

She does, but that doesn't mean she'll slink away. Maybe he expects her to hunker down and confine herself to slow, unthreatening gestures until the danger is past, the way she did twenty years ago in Rhinebeck, when a mangy German shepherd with one milk-eye chased her after she'd cut through old Mr. Kennedy's yard on the way home from school.

Maybe, instead, she'll surprise Detective Mitch Russo when he discovers she intends to be the one doing the chasing.

Perhaps the world hasn't really gone bright and silent while he's been talking, maybe time hasn't slowed again, but *something* has changed. Valerie lays her hand on the folder, across the words "Baby Jane Doe," and says, "I'm not going anywhere until I have Joanna back. I'm staying right here. I'm going to call my lawyer and then I'm going to call the press, everyone from *The New York Times* to the *Daily News* to CNN and the networks. I'm not going anywhere."

five

The world is coming into sharper focus, the way it did the day she walked out of the stand of birches bordering Rosie Cooper's stream and headed for a field that seemed to be a blanket of solid green. The closer she came the more she saw—the white clover flowers and the timothy, all bearded and tall and bending in the breeze, then the lace-winged grasshoppers and the smooth white pebbles, and finally the crumbly, dark soil.

She's emerging from the shock of the last few hours; the clarity is exhilarating.

"If you can put her on television and lose her, I can do the same thing to get her back." Valerie reaches across the table for the telephone. It's time to shift her daughter's personal history into the public domain. If that's what it will take to get her back, no problem.

Russo covers her hand with his own, warmer than she'd have expected, dry, solid. "Maybe you shouldn't do that. Too much publicity could scare whoever has her into doing something . . . drastic."

The hand lifts; the word leaves her chilled.

"I don't mean to scare you, Ms. Vincent. But if that woman killed Mrs. Klein, and if it looks like we're closing in, she might feel cornered. Maybe she's thinking, 'Jeez, I better get rid of the evidence.' She knows she's already bought herself a murder charge so what's the difference?

I'm sorry to say it like that, but I don't want you to do anything you'll regret."

Even if he's only trying to keep his name out of the headlines because he screwed up, that doesn't mean he's wrong. She has to talk this out with someone she trusts; sadly, her confidante won't be Esther.

That leaves Rosie Cooper, who doesn't need any more middle-of-the-night phone calls than she had last summer when someone was terrorizing her own family, and Lynn Hammond, friend, lawyer, and unfailing source of sanity when Valerie decided to cut loose from Johnny. Just the thought of hearing Lynn's voice makes the claw that's squeezing her chest loosen its grip a little. But she won't have that conversation with Russo watching her, examining every twitch.

"I want to make a phone call and I'd like a little privacy. Ten minutes, that's all. Alone."

He has the decency not to question her, except with his eyes. A corner of his mouth turns up in acknowledgment and he gathers his papers, his free hand suspended in the air above her shoulder as though he'll touch her again. Instead, Mitch Russo pushes his chair neatly in place and walks her past empty desks to an open door.

"Use this one," he says, pointing to a telephone in the corner of a Formica table that seems too big for the small room. A food-spattered microwave oven rests on a shelf, a dark television set hovers on a metal utility cart, and a single stalk of forsythia, drooping and dusty, tilts in a Snapple bottle. "Real homey, isn't it?" Russo mumbles as he disappears into the other room.

She can dial Lynn's number in her sleep, had done it the time Johnny rolled in at one in the morning, yelling that he was hungry as he stood in front of the open refrigerator grabbing bottles and jars and smashing them on the floor. The familiar pattern of tones as she presses the numbers is the first comforting sound she's heard in hours.

"Lynn, hi, it's me. I'm sorry for calling so late."

In the background, a dog yaps. "Hush up, Poppy," Lynn growls. "Oh, God, Val, I'm so glad you called. I saw this news bulletin at nine. I wasn't sure at first it was Joanna. I mean, babies change so much in just a couple of months, but when she smiled . . . Anyway, I was desperate to reach you but of course I had no way of getting in touch. I ended up phoning the police. They told me Joanna was fine, that you'd already come for her. How is she? You must have been—"

"She's gone, Lynn." Her composure terrifies her.

"Gone?" Lynn's voice falters.

"The police gave Joanna—sent her away with another woman. Someone who had all my papers, a woman who looked like me." Unreal. It can't be happening. She isn't sitting in some decaying old police station saying these words aloud.

"Another woman? What do you mean? Who?" Lynn is suddenly stern and demanding, her courtroom voice asking the questions.

Valerie offers her friend the few available facts. When she says Esther's name aloud, she's sucked into a vacuum that pulls words, heat, plans, everything from her until only an icy numbness remains.

"So, maybe Johnny's parents decided to sidestep the legal system entirely," Lynn says softly. "Okay, what happens now? What are the cops doing? What are *you* doing?"

"I thought at first it would help to call in the press." Maybe she will, maybe that's still her best chance to get Joanna back. If everyone is looking for a beautiful little girl . . . "But Russo, he's the detective in charge, said maybe the publicity would scare this woman and she might hurt Joanna. You think he's right?"

She pictures Lynn in faded jeans and her old Mick Jagger sweatshirt, her bare feet stepping off the distance from the kitchen counter to the pine breakfast table and back as her forehead wrinkles in concentration.

"Possibly. Oh, Val, honey. I wish I had an answer. I don't have any professional experience with kidnapping. If it were me . . ."

As the silence stretches on, she knows that Lynn is thinking about her son, feeling the hollow emptiness in her own chest.

"Your detective might have a point about publicity. I'd go along with him for now. On that, anyway. But make sure Russo knows you're keeping the option open, in case you need it."

"Anything else, Lynn? There must be something I'm missing, something—"

"Yes! God, why didn't I think of this right away? Listen, Val, you know that church of Lucas and Martha's, outside Taconic Hills? I nearly ran my new station wagon up a tree last week because I thought I saw you standing outside talking to them. This woman was your height, curly hair, the whole thing. Maybe I was just hoping it was you. I *was* driving, so I didn't get a really good look."

If she can gather enough straws, she just might be able to build a raft. "Maybe Martha and Lucas recruited the woman," Valerie ad-libs, "to be a soldier of righteousness. Maybe they convinced her to take part in some divine mission to save their poor, endangered granddaughter."

And maybe the stranger Lynn saw will turn out to be a distraction to give whoever *really* has Joanna time to get farther and farther away.

"I hate to say it, Val, but it sounds as though anything's possible right now. You're not going back to Esther's, are you?"

Someday she's going to have to return to the apartment, but not tonight. "I'll be staying with the woman I've been working for, at least for a while. Antonia Carrera. On Prospect Park West in Brooklyn."

"Okay, but when this is all over, you and Joanna come on up here and stay with us. Work on your paper, take long walks, whatever. If you need me, I can be there in two hours max. You remember to breathe, Val. And tell your Detective Russo about this lady I saw."

Lynn has given her not only energy and hope but a concrete piece of information, one that Russo, in the adjoining room, should know how to use.

It's not Mitch Russo who rises to greet her.

Detective Teresa Gallagher nods at her partner, hunched over the phone, and strides to the doorway. "I was about to come see you, Ms. Vincent. The car service says the woman insisted on being dropped off at the D train on Flatbush Avenue. We're canvassing the neighborhood. And I just spoke to the guy who made the nine-eleven call. He lives right below the Klein apartment. He says he heard this ruckus, took a broom handle and banged on his ceiling because the noise was disturbing him. When he opened his door, he saw a woman with dark hair running down the stairs. We're going to interview him again. Maybe we can help him remember some more details, were they arguing, what did he hear, that kind of thing. This might be a break."

And it might fizzle into nothing. Hope could be dangerous. She won't let herself float on its updraft until a wind shear sends her crashing to hard ground. At least Lynn's information about her double is tangible, and she passes it on to Gallagher.

"We'll have the Columbia County sheriff's office check on that. Listen, Ms. Vincent, I . . ." Gallagher's voice fades. "I'm sorry for what you're going through. I wish I could . . ."

Is this what she's in for, sympathy and unfinished speeches about how they wish they could have done more? Before Gallagher can find the words she's searching for, Russo interrupts.

"Ms. Vincent? I just spoke to this journalist who lives in the city, his name is Kevin Murchison. I want you to talk to him."

"A few minutes ago you told me *not* to talk to writers."

"Murchison's a good guy. He's spent years writing about people like you. People who've been accused of devil worship. He figures that ninety-nine percent of the time it's a setup, you know, to make someone look bad. Like your former in-laws tried to do with you. You ever hear of this group Deliverance And Safe Haven? They hardly ever use the full name. Refer to themselves as DASH. Anyway, Murchison's got the goods on them, including how they help people develop cases against relatives."

"And what will talking to this writer do for me, Detective Russo? Maybe it will help him write a better story. Maybe it will even help you keep me off your back. But I can't see how it's going to help me find my daughter."

"*We're* going to find—" Russo sighs noisily. "Murchison wants to talk to you, to see if he can figure out whether DASH might be behind this. If they are, he's the man who knows how they operate, who can maybe tell us enough to help us find your daughter. He says to tell you . . . he says you're probably in for a long, hard trip—and he also says I wasn't just crying wolf when I said that too much publicity might put your daughter in greater jeopardy."

Lord, how she needs to trust someone. Hope might have its dangers, but despair and delay are even worse. Joanna's probably hungry, scared, confused. . . "Fine. Okay. I'll go see him. He's in the city, you said?"

"Not now he isn't. He's at the airport in Denver, about to fly back from a conference on family law. He says you can come to his place. Ten o'clock tomorrow. That's the best he can do."

Ten o'clock tomorrow—Joanna could be thousands of miles away by then. "My daughter has been stolen by some stranger, Detective Russo. I can't do nothing until tomorrow morning. I'm scared and I—"

"Please, go see Murchison at ten. I know you're frightened. What he said, if it's any help, is that if DASH *is* involved your daughter will probably be all right."

Probably. That will have to do for the moment.

six

Martha was letting the situation get to her. Or maybe it was all that excitement on an empty stomach, skipping dinner and still being awake at eleven, an hour later than usual.

Lucas Starr looked away from his newspaper and caught his wife shaking her head. She was upset, that was why she wasn't nattering. Woman was never quiet longer than two minutes, and it had been half an hour now. Martha was shivering, clutching her bathrobe and staring down at her eggs, the smeary yolks drying in the over-heated kitchen. Shivering? It was April, for Chrissake, and the room was stuffy, all that hot air pouring from the floor vents and drying his sinuses.

"You're not going to back out on me, are you?" He hated that whine in his voice, the pleading sound of it. He swallowed hard, then cleared his throat. "Can't anyway, even if you want to. It's gone too far already."

Like a child, that way Martha had of looking down and half smiling. "I know how far it's gone. We're doing God's will, yes, I know. I was only thinking how strong the forces of evil can be. It puzzles me sometimes that God would want to test us like this. I wish John were here with us right now."

It was Martha who sounded all whimpery now, but she always did when she talked about their son. "Well, so do I, Martha. You know that." Lucas smiled indulgently across his teacup before he rose to get the sugar bowl. On the way back to the table, he turned the thermostat down a couple of degrees. Wasn't that one of the strange things in this life, thirty-six years after their wedding night to be playing this game still, her turning the heat up, him tapping it down a notch, neither of them saying anything? What would be the point, anyway? Couldn't change your own body temperature, could you? "I'm going to call her, make sure she's still with us on this. I'm finished here," he said, pointing with his cup at his crumb-specked plate.

Martha took their plates to the sink, ran water over them. Not like her to leave food. They'd have to have it out tomorrow, if she didn't straighten up. Good Lord didn't mean for people to go around all empty-headed like that. Made it harder to do His work.

Lucas fished a scrap of paper and his reading glasses out of his shirt pocket and squinted at the phone number. "This a six or a naught? You ought not be so careless writing things down, Martha."

Her jaw set and her eyes narrowed, but she cocked her head to see the paper. "Six. That little tail at the top, it's clearly a— Oh, you can see it just fine, Lucas." She turned away and started the water running in the sink again.

Woman was not only getting soft, she was forgetting her manners. He tried the number, let it ring nine, ten times, slammed the phone down. "No one's home. Or at least she's not answering the phone. Where do you think she's off to, eleven o'clock on a Friday night?" He snorted. "It's too late for church, she knows that."

"Try her again in the morning, why don't you? Maybe she unplugs the phone at night or maybe she's taking a shower." Martha kept her back to the room, scrubbing the dishes with short, jerky motions, as though she were mad at them. Or at him. Or keeping something from him. It always felt like Martha had secrets, even when they were young and she would stare up at the sky, or down at John in his crib, not saying anything, that look on her face making it seem like she knew something she would never tell.

"You sure you don't know why she isn't home?"

A cup shattered in the sink. Martha gasped, then raised a soapy hand to her mouth.

If she thought she could keep some secret from him . . .

"Of course not. She's the one came to us. She's the one said children have to be saved by working together."

"Get finished here, Martha. First thing in the morning, we're going to pay her a call. If she's gone, we'll find her. Now, come on, stop that staring and clean up that mess."

She turned away and bent over the sink, gathering splinters of pottery into a pile in the sink. A good woman, she really was a good woman. Knew that watching out for the children was important. They had to be careful, not show the world a face that would make people dig in and put up a fight, the way they had with those abortion clinics. There was a right way to do this, and they couldn't afford mistakes.

"Lucas? Did you hear that?"

Now what? She'd cut herself if she stood there with those pieces of broken cup in her hand. "Throw that in the garbage, Martha."

"Lucas, I heard a car outside. Who'd be coming here so late?" She lifted the lid of the trash can and dumped the shards into the bag, stared down at a thread of blood that brightened the center of her palm.

A car? He hadn't heard anything, but better to go check than sit here and watch her look at the blood seeping from her hand. Sighing, Lucas Starr pulled himself out of his chair and crossed the kitchen, walked to the front of the house, stood beside the living-room window and peered through the curtains. Headlights—and a row of three others on the roof, the Columbia County sheriff's insignia clear as day on the door of the car.

Damn. She was right. They didn't need this, Riley Hamm snooping around here in his too big uniform, asking questions in that tight-lipped mumble of his. But they'd talked about how to handle him, prepared for it in those meetings, practiced. All Hamm or any of them outside the group needed to know was that Martha and Lucas were good neighbors, churchgoing, God-fearing people who went to work, paid their taxes, kept their yard tidy.

Lucas Starr could handle the sheriff's deputy, that was for sure. "Go on upstairs, Martha. It's Riley Hamm. I'll take care of it."

Lucas stepped outside, blinking back the glare of the lights. The sheriff's deputy looked like he was determined not to bend anywhere, not his back or his legs or even his arms, which swung like pendulums fixed to his shoulders as he scurried up the gravel.

"Evening, Lucas. Sorry to disturb you so late but I need to ask you and Martha a few questions."

He knew something. It wasn't possible but there was that look on Riley's face, and Lucas Starr didn't like it one bit. "Martha's upstairs. It's night, Riley. Can't this wait?"

Nodding, Riley shifted his hat from one hand to the other, his legs spread wide apart. "I know it's late but I have to talk to you. Why don't we go inside?"

"Now, Riley, aren't you going to tell me what this is about? Martha didn't get any tickets for illegal U-turns, did she?"

But Riley's mouth didn't turn up at one corner the way it did when he was marking his grudging admiration for a joke. "Whyn't we go in, Lucas? It'll be better that way."

If he objected, Riley would get ideas. More ideas than he had already. Lucas restrained the impulse to wipe away the sweat pooling beneath his shirt collar. "Okay, but we go to bed early around here."

"So you can get up for morning prayers. I know." Riley's nose practically twitched as they stepped into the living room. His eyes darted around the room. Looking for signs. The man wasn't being subtle about his examination of the coffee table, the carved Amish chest in the corner, the sofa, Martha's old rocking chair.

"What you looking for, Riley?" Best thing here would be to let the man know he was no fool whiner ready to go all to jelly in the presence of a county cop. "What's this about, anyway?"

"How's Joanna? Haven't seen her around lately."

The room went dead still.

His own breath sounded loud, snorty, and Lucas Starr pressed his teeth together so hard a sharp pain cut through his head, just behind his eyes, the way it always did when anyone mentioned the child.

Lucas inhaled, shrugged. "Dunno. Her mother took off early November and we haven't heard from her. Why you asking?"

"Can you tell me where you and Martha were earlier tonight?"

All right, that was the way he was going to play it. The quickest way to find out what Riley knew was to look like he was going along with the program. "Church meeting. Up in Gallatinville there, at the Westerby house. We were planning a church event." One that not a whole lot of people would be invited to. Certainly not this skinny man with a face like a whippet and eyes that never landed on anything long enough to really look at it.

"Who else was there, Lucas? When'd you arrive, when'd you leave?"

"Jim and Nancy Westerby. Rick Decker, the father, not the kid at the garage. Some fellow and his wife from up near Chatham, name of Magnuson, Bob and Zena Magnuson. A new woman, I think she's from Vermont, works over at Taconic Telephone. Oh, and Will and Berta Hotaling." *And George Perry, come all the way from Jersey, but you'll never hear that name.* Lucas heard Martha's tread creaking the floorboards overhead. Woman at least had the sense to stay away and let him do the talking. "We got there, musta been around seven, got home about a half hour ago. Now you going to tell me what this is about, Riley?"

Riley Hamm set his hat on the banister post and peered up the dark stairway. "You try hard to think of that new gal's name. It's important to me you recall it, Lucas."

"I'm getting the feeling you think we got something to hide. Well, we don't, but that doesn't mean I want you poking around my house like Martha and I are some kind of criminals." That ought to be about right, that was the way they'd planned it. *If* had become *when* now, and it felt good to be ready for this. "Woman's name is something like Felix or Phillips. Ann Phillips, maybe." Ann

Phelps wouldn't like it much, but he'd done the best he could to protect her without outright lying.

Riley was already headed for the kitchen, talking over his shoulder. "Got a call a while ago from a fellow in Brooklyn. A detective working on a case down there." He stopped in the doorway, did that scan again, eyes jumping all around the way they had in the living room.

"Brooklyn? What's that got do with Taconic Hills?"

"Your daughter-in-law? Valerie? She says maybe you know where Joanna is."

Lucas snorted. "I told you. She ran away with the child right around the beginning of November and now she—" Lord in heaven, that bitch was evil. "Hold on. What do you mean?"

Instead of answering, Riley opened the refrigerator and leaned into the damn thing as though he'd crawl inside. Whatever he was looking for, he wouldn't find it, that was for sure. When he straightened, Riley pushed the door shut and wheeled around. "Come on, Lucas. We've known each other since my daddy brought me into your hardware shop to buy a new chain saw. Must be thirty-one, -two years now. I don't want to give you a hard time. You don't want to give me one, either."

There it was, that sound that turned the meaning of Riley's words into a threat. This wasn't going right. He had to change the tone of things and fast.

"Your daddy still working that woodlot over by Polly's?" Lucas Starr knew better than to smile; that would be going too far.

But Riley sidled passed him and headed for the stairs. "Martha, it's Riley Hamm. You decent? I need to come up and see you."

"Hold on." Lucas grabbed a fistful of Riley's shirt-sleeve, let it go when the deputy wheeled around, eyes slitted and brows raised. "Sorry. I just didn't want you going up there and walking in on my wife all in her lingerie or something."

Before he could think of the next thing to say, Martha appeared at the head of the stairs, hairbrush in hand. "It's okay, Riley. Matter of opinion whether a woman's really decent when she doesn't have her makeup on."

Riley shot up the stairs two at a time, as though he were being chased by a swarm of Sarah Hoving's bees. Lucas kept close, following from John's old room to the bathroom, where the smell of that lilac powder Martha slapped all over herself hung in the air, to the big bedroom overlooking the front yard. Martha stood in front of the mirror brushing her hair, her lips drawn out in a thin line.

"You never answered me about Joanna. Doesn't her own mother know where she is?"

Riley shifted his heavy belt. Then, as though he'd just made a decision he didn't much like, he sighed. "Valerie works for this woman, Antonia Carraris, Carrera, something like that, down in Brooklyn. She went out to Long Island with this Carrara woman and left Joanna with a family friend. Seems the friend was murdered. The cops didn't know who the baby was, put her on the television, and a while later someone came with Valerie's identification papers. She took the baby away and now the New York City cops are searching for this woman, and for Joanna. We're helping them out, asking around."

"Asking around *here?* You think I got something to do with this? You better be careful who you go accusing, Riley."

"I'm being real careful, Lucas. I'm also going to check with those people you said were at that church meeting tonight. Now, I'm going to look into that other bedroom there, and if everything's the way I expect it to be, then I'll be leaving."

Lucas stepped aside, and Riley brushed past him. "You're gonna be disappointed. But go ahead, Riley. You go on ahead. Whatever it is you think you're gonna find, it's not gonna be here."

Not tonight, anyway. Lucas Starr started making a list in his mind of all the people he had to call.

seven

She almost didn't recognize him without his brown UPS uniform, but he knew her.

Cameron Zax was still a little bit in love with Kristin Denby, she could tell by the way he stopped her, wanting her to stand there in the sputtering gaslight in front of the carved brownstone façade of Antonia's house and chat about her life, curious about what had brought her back to Prospect Park West.

Kristin shifted the bag of groceries on her hip, impatient to complete her task so she could get back to the apartment, wary of offending by appearing too anxious. "An errand for Mrs. Carrera," she explained, glancing at her watch.

"Oh, sure, I was just surprised to see you after all this time. And glad. I mean, it's been, what, four, five months since you quit working for Mrs. Carrera? And here it is eleven-thirty at night and you come down the street all decked out in this buttercup-yellow jacket that looks like it came from one of those forties movies starring Katie Hepburn or Claudette Colbert, and I think, 'See where she comes apparell'd like the spring.'" He blushed then, and looked down at the sidewalk. "*Pericles,* Act One. I didn't get the part."

"You just keep showing up, Cam. Something will break for you, you'll see." Kristin smiled and patted his shoulder, then whirled away, leaving Cameron Zax and his small disappointments behind.

As she turned the key and tugged on the knob—Antonia had resisted replacing the etched glass door, said it was old and elegant and entitled to be a little difficult—Kristin thought about the call. When the phone rang, she'd been sure it would be Charles calling from San Francisco to go on and on about how much he missed her and how tomorrow couldn't come soon enough, how he needed an infusion of her beauty. Instead, she'd heard Antonia's voice, cool and unruffled, despite the nature of the message.

Valerie's daughter . . . an emergency. No hint of anger at the deception, but then, to Antonia, Valerie Vincent could do no wrong. Kristin started to offer her opinion of Valerie, but Antonia cut her short to deliver instructions. In the background, chatter and tinkling glasses—Antonia had even interrupted her birthday party to make the call.

Kristin closed the door and double-locked it, savoring the feeling that she'd stepped into the real universe again, one from which she'd been banished to prepare to marry Charles Babcock. The mat in the entryway, the color of barely toasted marshmallows and just as soft underfoot, cushioned her first steps as she started down the long foyer.

The white kitchen surfaces glowed pink with reflected city light. Kristin set the paper bag on the counter, stashed the milk and orange juice in the refrigerator, poked among the shelves. Jars of brine-cured olives, fancy mustards, preserves with labels of unnaturally red strawberries, and not a single sign of Antonia's cherished triple-cream Brie. Clearly, Valerie Vincent had made some changes in her absence. Kristin shoved the bread into the drawer, folded the paper bag.

She really shouldn't linger in this empty house; her mission made her uncomfortable.

But when she stepped into the living room and looked out the tall windows, captivated by the way the streetlight at the edge of the park sparkled against the sky, she was overcome by dizziness, and she sat on the sofa to catch her breath.

It had all seemed so severe when she was living here:

the white linen sofa and leather armchairs, the thick, bev-
eled-glass coffee table, the slab of green-veined marble
above the fireplace, even the floor lamp, a soaring brass
tube that stretched like a Brancusi bird toward the ceiling.
The room, with its stark simplicity and spare furnishings,
used to make her feel vulnerable, uneasy. Except for the
angels, of course, the tin planter held up by dancing angels, the pillow embroidered with Caravaggio cherubs, the
watercolor Annunciation angels basking in golden light.

Tonight, the room looked stylish, elegant, *rich*. Even
the air smelled of luxury, as though flowers had been recently whisked into another room for rewatering.

God, she missed this place. For so many years the arrangement had been perfect. Too many years, according to
Charles, and Antonia had agreed when she urged her to
accept Charles's proposal of marriage.

Which meant, of course, that Antonia would have to
find another young woman to keep her company and tell
her stories. It had taken only a week.

But, heaven help her, Valerie Vincent had seemed so
tentative about the whole thing, right from the start. Antonia was sure to play her power cards early; the game was
only worth joining if she was certain of victory.

Did Antonia's new companion spend her afternoons
strolling through museums and parks, searching for just
the right tale to bring back to the cool, white living room?
The woman looked too, well, *academic*, to come up with
anything truly original. Valerie Vincent would never offer
Antonia a man and woman in the sculpture garden of
MOMA, lovers from some Connecticut suburb snatching
a forbidden weekend away from their spouses, or a sullen
student with a backpack and a sketchpad standing spell-
bound in the pastel aura of *Water Lilies*, experiencing a
spiritual transformation and, on the spot, abandoning his
plans to pursue an MBA.

And right here in this grand, high-ceilinged room, did
Antonia, eager to have a bit of a story early in the day,
summon Valerie to her side? "Tell me about the sky," she
might say. Only her hand would lift from the arm of her
wheelchair in a graceful, beckoning gesture.

Kristin used to wonder how long Antonia had worked

on that, on the way those fingers rose in a curve and then
returned. Born knowing. That was how Antonia had described herself. Light would play along her pale skin and
catch in her hair, fragile as spun sugar but still the color of
thick honey, as she listened raptly to Kristin's descriptions
of the street, the park, the passersby.

Of course, it hadn't been a one-sided arrangement.
The quiet little room on the south side of the brownstone
just down the hall from Antonia's small elevator, the
clothes from Saks—they were only the beginning. Antonia
had fed her every day, rich confections of insight and wisdom, teaching her the little tricks of behavior and attitude
that gave her access to a larger world.

Kristin groped her way up the broad stairs to the dark
second-floor hall and headed for her old room, thinking
about Antonia, whose darkness never changed. She remembered how it felt to rummage through the closet,
touching the garments, fingering the slippery silk shirts,
the satisfying stubble of the linen slacks. All those wonderful clothes—subdued colors, natural fabrics, demure, oh
yes, and ladylike.

First Antonia taught her how to dress, then she
schooled her in manners, and finally she invited Kristin to
sit beside her at the weekly dinners to which four or six
carefully chosen guests were invited. Antonia had urged
Kristin to participate in the discussions of art and litera-
ture and exotic travel destinations, saying that she added
zest and charm to a gathering. She'd met Charles at one of
those dinners.

Kristin wandered into Antonia's bedroom. No gardenias. Maybe the beautiful white flowers would reappear
after the weekend—or did Valerie Vincent prefer roses?
She ran her fingers over the ceramic angels perched on the
rim of the planter on the dresser. This was where she'd
been standing when she told Antonia that Charles Babcock had asked her to marry him.

To Antonia, her teacher and her benefactress,
Charles's proposal was proof that she'd done her job well,
as she had with all the other girls who had worked for her.

Girls. They weren't children. They were women, college graduates, young when they came to work at the

brownstone, but still women. Kristin was, what, the
fourth, fifth? Antonia insisted on calling them her girls,
long after they'd married and had children of their own.

*Charles Babcock is kind, thoughtful, prosperous, Kris-
tin, and he adores you. You'll make him a wonderful wife.*
The words had rolled out like a cosmic pronounce-
ment that should have been accompanied by a sign. A
bush burning in the Long Meadow of the park, perhaps,
or lightning striking the clock on the Williamsburg Bank
Building, something momentous and inescapable.

*He worships you, Kristin. You mustn't be upset be-
cause he thinks you're beautiful. And it's no crime to be
rich—his wealth is bound to make your life more pleasant.*
Antonia Carrera spoke from experience: Miguel Carrera's money kept her living in luxury and paid for all the
woman's indulgences, including the surgery that removed
Kristin's old scars.

But Charles Babcock's adoration did upset her.
"Lovely," he'd murmur, unable to take his eyes off her.
Yes, after all those years of longing to hear it, that was
really the right word, yet it made her uneasy. *Lovely.* Her
hair, burnished with auburn and as silky as the blouses
Antonia had bought her; a figure to carry the elegant
clothes that had filled her closet. And creamy, smooth,
pale and perfect skin.

No ridges of twisted flesh along her cheek. No puckers
of hard, lumpy scar tissue from the scalding she'd received
when she bumped into her father when she was ten, sending the shrilling teakettle flying and scalding water streaming onto her face. He'd reached down and rubbed her
cheek, pushing the pain and disfigurement deeper, and
she'd run to her room to sob into her pillow, unable to
sleep and unwilling to expose herself to his wrath by com-
plaining about her agony.

When he awoke the next morning, bleary-eyed and
disgustingly hung over, he gasped when he stumbled into
the kitchen and saw her sitting at the table. From her right
cheekbone to her upper lip, her skin looked as though
scores of tiny worms lay buried just under the surface. He
did what he'd always done when he was stymied—he got
drunk again.

For months she'd turned away from mirrors, windows, even the soup ladle that hung above the stove, refusing to look at her own grotesque reflection. For years she'd insulated herself from the taunts of classmates. Her own company was so much more entertaining than theirs, anyway; she'd overheard enough of their inane chatter to know she wasn't missing much.

Now, thanks to Antonia's generosity, the scars were gone. That had been the bond between them, hadn't it, Antonia's injuries and her own scars?

Kristin straightened a corner of the bedspread and fluffed one of the silk pillows, then lay down and tucked it, cool and yielding, beneath her neck. Just a few minutes more. Then she'd be restored and ready to go back to the apartment, to her new life.

Kristin rubbed her hands along her arms to ward off a chill. The bedroom was filled with ghosts and shadows. She gathered her jacket and her purse, flipped off the light, and made her way down the stairs.

How had Antonia, so strong-minded, so severe, allowed herself to succumb to Valerie Vincent's cheerleader charm? The first time Valerie Vincent appeared, standing in this very doorway, Kristin had seen the lies hidden behind those long-lashed eyes, had known there was a secret.

She wouldn't have guessed, that day, that it was a child.

Kristin Denby didn't want to be here when Valerie Vincent arrived. What could she possibly say to the woman?

saturday

eight

She's never been in Antonia's house later than seven at night, never been here alone at all. The majestic old brownstone has a disdainful air about it, as though her presence is an intrusion, and she finds herself sitting on the edges of chairs or walking gingerly on the wood floors to avoid disturbing anything.

The living room is spacious, calm, except for the city noises that assault her—ambulance sirens, screeching tires, a car alarm braying an unearthly combination of hoots, whines, and shrieks. All that urgent activity—so unlike the deep night silence of Taconic Hills, so deep she used to feel she'd become immune to gravity and had floated into starry space.

Valerie slips off her shoes and sinks back on the sofa, numb and weary, on the edge of sleep. But as soon as she closes her eyes Esther and Joanna appear, laughing, splashing in the bathtub or sitting on a bench in the park overlooking the playground.

Sleep might be impossible; remembering is not.

Through the white drapes that hang beside the tall windows, she watches a snub-nosed Porsche roll down the street, its roof dappled with the shadows of new leaves, a trickle of moonlight slicking all the surfaces. Perhaps the driver has seen Joanna on some deserted street while he was waiting for a light to change.

Surrounded by Antonia's angels, stone and wood and watercolor renderings of seraphim in flight, she offers herself in trade to the powers that control Joanna's fate. She's got to find her own lost angel, but some benevolent, invisible force won't take her hand and spirit her to Joanna's side.

And she won't wait around for Russo and Gallagher, can't sit by while some journalist wings his way across the continent. So, what can she do, shake Martha and Lucas until they confess?

There'll be the devil to pay if she thinks only of her own satisfaction, her own fury vented.

She'll come up with an idea. She has to.

Eventually the sky lightens and a sparrow, like a tiny brown Icarus drawn to the sun's reflection in the living-room window, flies so near the glass she's sure it will crash. But at the last second it veers away and arcs toward Grand Army Plaza. Pink sky turns to red; a swath of brilliant orange stacks along the horizon, and with each bold layer her resolve strengthens.

She'll go upstairs, to the small bedroom at the end of the hall, Kristin Denby's old room. She'll write everything down, as she does when she's starting a paper for school, and maybe then she'll discover something she's missed, even if it means putting words to things she'd rather shove into tiny boxes with tight lids.

She's always thought of Kristin's small bedroom as a haven—soft colors, tiny yellow flowers on the wallpaper, patterned curtains draping the canopy bed like a cloud, even wood shutters on the windows to close the rest of the world out.

The desk lamp casts a consoling light. With a fountain pen she finds in the drawer, she writes Joanna's name on a sheet of paper, looks away from the page, white and black and stark, like the rooms in which Antonia lives. Valerie scans the bookshelves near the doorway for inspiration, a starting place. Tapes of Vivaldi, Bach, Schumann; nineteenth-century British novels; two leather-bound volumes of *A Thousand Nights and a Night*. Nothing triggers a thought.

Instead of solutions or even facts, a jumble of questions fills her head.

Does Joanna think she's been abandoned?

Did Elizabeth Proctor understand or care where it all began when the Salem hangman slipped the noose over her head?

How long did it take Martha and Lucas to plan their Halloween charade? How many others were in on it?

Would it have mattered to Rebecca Nurse to know that she'd be remembered in history books three hundred years later?

Every part of her feels pummeled. She can't keep the demons away and she can no longer fight the sleep she so desperately needs.

She isn't dreaming, and she isn't alone. A muffled conversation drifts up the stairs. Martha and Lucas? Mitch Russo? She's suffocating behind the canopy curtains; they're heavier than they look, and she struggles to push them aside. The pale green quilt holds the impression of her body, as though her ghost is trapped atop the down comforter, but she's free, standing on the cold floor in her bare feet. The clock on the wicker dressing table says seven forty-six. She's been asleep for an hour.

And then she hears Antonia's muted voice, and Valerie remembers: this is Kristin's room, she's in Antonia's house, and no one has called to say they found Joanna.

"Oh, you're awake." Nadia, Antonia's housekeeper, stands in the doorway, one hand smoothing the coil of hair pinned atop her head. "You been sleeping so deep you didn't hear us come in. Mrs. Carrera asked me to tell you that breakfast will be ready in half an hour."

Just the thought of eating makes her queasy. "I'm not hungry, but please tell Mrs. Carrera I'll join her for coffee. Thanks, Nadia."

The woman lingers in the doorway, her broad face flattened out by the light. "An egg, maybe, or a piece of bread, even, *something*. You need your strength, miss." Shaking her head and muttering, Nadia trundles toward the stairs.

What she really needs is a shower and a cup of coffee.

What she really needs is her daughter, sitting in the spray of sunlight that brightens the center of the rug.

The white-tiled bathroom beside Kristin Denby's old room, unused for months, still smells of almond soap. Valerie shucks her underclothes, runs the hot water until the mirror fogs, steps into the shower and begins to lather her body. When her hands touch her belly, she has to press hard to keep the pain away, as though Joanna has just been torn from her.

Better not to stand here exposed and aching.

She rubs herself dry and slips into the white cotton shirt and the print skirt she wore the day before. Joanna will recognize them, will be comforted by their familiarity. Before she heads to the dining room, she calls Russo, demands to know what he's learned in the past eight hours.

Russo is apologetic.

No report from the medical examiner, not for a few days, and there's no point planning a funeral until the body is officially released.

Nothing substantial from the Columbia County sheriff's department. Yes, a deputy went out to the Starrs' house, looked around, checked their alibi and contacted a dark-haired woman named Ann Phelps who had recently joined their church. No, although they seemed edgy, had tried to stall him, the deputy saw nothing, heard nothing at Johnny's parents' house that would indicate the presence of a child, no size 2 coveralls, no toys, no baby aspirin. Yes, he's keeping an eye on them and checking further on the Phelps woman but he has nothing yet.

That seems to be the operative word: nothing.

"Valerie." Antonia sets an uneaten scone on the plate in front of her and dabs her fingers on the napkin in her lap. "Sit here, would you, right beside me. You said you were going to call."

"Sorry." The churning in her stomach stops when she looks away from the glistening, buttery crumbs on Antonia's plate. "I didn't get back here until late, I don't know, maybe two o'clock. I didn't want to wake you and your guests."

Antonia nods. "I spent the whole night wondering

what was happening. I thought if I called here the phone might wake the child, so by five I asked Carl and Nadia to bring me back to Brooklyn. Those other people are terribly boring and they won't even notice I'm gone. When do you think your daughter will wake up?"

The question sounds more like an accusation. Or maybe it's only concern she hears. Of course Antonia has been worried. Valerie tells her about the night before, the story by now reduced to a single, painful line. "Some woman stole my credit cards and Joanna's health record from Esther's apartment and got to the police station before I did and they sent Joanna away with her."

"Oh, my dear, how awful." Antonia's nostrils flare with indignation, as though someone has violated the laws of nature without consulting her. "How stupid. What are they doing now?"

"The detective in charge, Russo, swears they've got every available cop working on the case. He wants me to talk to a man named Kevin Murchison. This Murchison is some kind of magazine writer, I think. Russo says he's done a lot of research, written several articles. About people who've been wrongly accused of belonging to Satanic cults."

In order to explain why that matters, she has to explain to Antonia about Martha and Lucas and the Halloween threats.

"It's really weird to think of telling all that to a total stranger," she says as she brings the story back around to last night's conversation with Russo. "I hate the idea of some reporter turning my life into material. First of all, I can't see how it will help me find Joanna. And it makes me feel, I don't know—exposed. Like I'm standing in the Taconic Hills post office in my underwear."

"But you have nothing to hide." Antonia reaches for her scone and breaks off a small piece. "You don't have any terrible secrets you're afraid this man will discover, do you?"

Terrible? Nothing she'd be afraid to reveal to her daughter when she grows up. "Maybe he'll find out about the time I was suspended from Pine Plains High School. For putting fliers with quotes and pictures from a Jesse

Helms interview about the arts and pornography in certain teachers' mailboxes. Big deal, so I altered the senator's picture by giving him a nice, high, round pair of breasts and a tiny, limp penis."

Antonia laughs appreciatively. "I'd say that's something to be proud of."

"Or maybe Murchison will come up with the Copake Lake incident. It was May, my senior year in high school. There were eight of us, drinking, indulging in a little adolescent groping one Friday night, and then somebody said they were starving. So we made ourselves breakfast in the summer house of a famous *Newsweek* reporter who happened to be in Europe at the time. He backed away from pressing charges at the last minute."

It's been so long, years, really, since she's thought about those events that she might as well be talking about someone else. There's been so little time for looking back.

"I suppose you're right, Antonia. If this Murchison is really looking for a story the only thing he'll find is how I was set up by my in-laws so they could claim I worship the devil."

So they could take Joanna.

Why now? Maybe it's taken Johnny's parents all this time to find her—to find Joanna. Perhaps they've been cooking up new evidence to prove that she's an unfit mother.

Except, without her child, can she call herself a mother?

"Valerie, you mustn't let yourself imagine the worst. You must have faith, my dear, and you must remember to behave with dignity. You're young, but you must command their respect. The police will pay much more attention if you're firm and dignified, I can assure you." Antonia nods in the direction of the silver service on the polished sideboard. "Let's have our coffee."

Valerie pours out two cups of the dark brew, drops a single sugar cube and a dollop of milk into Antonia's cup, sets the cups on the table. The first sip burns its way down her throat.

"Of course, you'll stay here with me. I know you've refused to live here until now, but this is a different situation. And if you need money for anything, anything at all, you shall have it. I'm happy to do what I can."

Strange how it's happened, little by little, first in the darkness and now in the steely light of this spring morning. The unthinkable has become real, and it's drawn Lynn, Kevin Murchison, even Antonia Carrera and her entire household into its orbit. They're all spinning in great, wobbly rings around a powerful, dark core, the way Tituba drew all of Salem into her orbit when she told conjuring stories to amuse her young charges in 1692.

"Antonia, I am sorry to bring my problems into your life. I really am grateful to have a place to stay. Thanks."

"Don't be silly. This is your home now, that's all." Expertly, Antonia sets her cup in the groove of the saucer. "I'm not an easy person to live with, Valerie, I understand that. Quality is important to me, whether it's apples or bed linens or the people in my life. It's one of the few things over which I have some control. I detest shoddiness, and I abhor things done halfway."

Valerie stiffens: is the woman calling her cheap goods?

But, oblivious, Antonia continues. "So you mustn't be too modest to understand that your quick mind, good manners, and generous heart mean a lot to me. I'm not a selfless person, you know that. I simply don't want to lose you. When you get your daughter back, you'll stay on, of course, both of you."

It's nice that someone has written a happy ending to this nightmare. "Thanks. You're kind to offer, truly. But when this is all over, Joanna and I will probably go back to Taconic Hills."

Antonia adjusts her dark glasses, which have slipped down her thin nose again. "I may not be able to see you, but I can tell you're in no state to make such a decision. We'll talk about this another time. In any case, if there's some way I can help you, you must tell me. I have to say, I believe things will work out. Knowing you as I do, I'm sure you've passed on to your daughter a certain strength. Even in so young a child, the important things are there already. She's a sweet-tempered child, am I right?"

Sweet-tempered, yes, she is that. Joanna has put up with all the disruptions in her young life with a smile, apparently unaffected by her father's absence or her mother's busy schedule. Sweet-tempered, and something stronger—confident, that's it.

"Valerie, my dear, I asked about the child."

Before she can respond, brakes grind and squeal as a garbage truck belches to a stop outside the house. Nine o'clock. She can't sit at this white marble table in this ebony high-backed chair and feed little bits of Joanna to Antonia. If she doesn't leave soon, she'll be late for her appointment.

"I'm sorry, Antonia, but I can't talk about Joanna right now. I have to go meet that writer."

The disappointment on Antonia's face is fleeting. "Go ahead, my dear. Take one of the umbrellas in the hall. I'm sure we're going to have rain. Don't worry about me being alone here. Nadia and Carl are staying. You just come and go as you need to."

"Thanks. Thanks for everything." She squeezes Antonia's hand and runs to the foyer, plucks an umbrella from the closet, grabs her purse, and lets herself out.

As the door closes behind her, she notices a young man she's seen before stepping out of a UPS van.

"Hey, it can't be that bad," he says as she passes him.

It can be that bad. It is that bad, but she isn't about to lecture him on the naïveté of assuming everyone's life is as uncomplicated as his own.

nine

Francine rolled over into a shaft of sunlight and groaned. "Nobody's allowed to set the alarm for so early, not on *Saturday*. It's against the law." She pulled the cover over her head—his head too.

Johnny Starr wriggled out from the swaddling and swung his feet to the floor. No dry mouth, no aching head—that was the first victory, the first real pleasure when he gave up drinking ten months ago, and he continued to marvel at how light and full of energy he felt at the start of each day.

"Not so fast, Mr. Starr." Francine's hand was already reaching around, touching him, making him hard. "I'm giving up a whole day of my weekend so you can go to work. That means I've earned a reward, don't you think?"

"And what did you have in mind?" Johnny twisted away from her touch, ducked his head under the covers and kissed the swell of her breast, letting his tongue work easy circles on her sleep-warmed skin.

"Mmm, I'll have to think about it. What are my choices?" She arched under his touch, ribs rising with the sharp intake of breath as his fingers explored between her legs. "That's a good option. I love you, Johnny Starr."

Johnny didn't answer. As he lifted himself above her, she grasped the back of his neck. *The way Valerie used to.* His rhythm was broken, and he frowned at her face. Delicate mouth, strong nose, dark eyes and hair the color of wet tobacco leaves: she was right. He was attracted to a type.

So be it. She was Francine, not Valerie.

At least *she* hadn't taken anything away from him. Just the opposite.

He leaned down to kiss Francine, and the broken spell was mended.

He swiped at the steamy mirror and ran a comb through his hair, thinking, as he did every morning, how smart he'd been to let his beard grow so he could save morning shave time. Francine trimmed it once a month. He liked that she did that, enjoyed the intimacy of her grooming him, like some kind of monkey whose existence depended on acquiring survival skills and on attaching itself to a cozy little group. Family. Tribe. Whatever, it meant connection. People couldn't live without connections.

"You're already beautiful," she said, as though his thoughts had created her, her face ghostlike in the mirror, a peppery grin spreading as she held up her hand and pointed to her watch. "Late, but beautiful."

"You my mother now?" He stuck the comb back on the shelf, turned and kissed her cheek. "Don't worry, I'll make it to work on time." And for his troubles and because it was Saturday, be paid one hundred and twenty dollars for a ten-hour stint of hammering and hauling and breathing plaster dust.

"Your mother? I have enough to think about without worrying whether you've brushed your teeth or not, Johnny Starr. Total selfishness, sweetie pie. I have a lot to do around here." She hooked her arm in his and walked beside him to the kitchen, frowning and shaking her head.

"Such a good little hausfrau. Taking care of your family." He liked using that word, "family," despite her resistance to marriage. Family, she'd said the day she moved into his apartment, was much better when you chose it, infinitely stronger when it was your willingness to stay together and not some dumb piece of paper that kept you connected.

Johnny accepted the coffee she handed him, drank it

down, rinsed the mug, yanked a paper towel from the roll, and swabbed at the puddle on the pitted countertop.

His mother had always stood over him, watching, making sure he cleaned up properly. Maybe if she'd paid a little less attention to his tidiness and a little more to who he really was, to his dreams and his fears . . . He gritted his teeth.

Not this time. That was an old alcohol habit, blaming someone else for things that were his responsibility. He wouldn't use his parents as an excuse. No more props, just taking care of business. In another few weeks he'd have the money saved to move them into a larger space with enough room for him to start working on his own paintings again. He'd see whether he still had it, after all those years of hiding behind the booze and trying to destroy himself because he wasn't the person they wanted him to be.

He'd find a new place in a respectable neighborhood, not some broken-down Lower East Side tenement where people waited for New York City to toss them to the top of the heap and give them another chance or chew them up and spit them out once and for all. Maybe to the young actors and poets who'd fled the burbs, it was chic. But he didn't want to be *Loisaida* anymore.

He was done waiting. He was going to make it happen. *They* were, Francine and him. Buy their own equipment, take out an ad in the *Voice* or something and get twenty dollars an hour for painting people's offices and apartments, still a bargain considering how fast he was, how thorough his cleanup.

"You gonna pick up some milk on your way home?" Francine's breath smelled like the strawberry jam she'd just spread on her toast.

"Jeez, you can't work when I'm around and you can't even take a break to walk half a block to the grocery. Okay, you have an excuse today, but I'm saving up all these chits. You're gonna owe me, you know." He kissed her, delighted that he was starting the day in synch with her, with the world. Most of it, anyway.

Johnny Starr pulled on his sweatshirt and stuffed his wallet in his pocket. This job was almost over; three days, and then when he got paid he'd place that ad. He hadn't felt so excited in a long time. Everything was going well, and he wasn't afraid of the good feelings anymore. He hummed softly, beating the banister with his hand as he bounded down the two flights of stairs.

No sun again today, but that didn't matter. He didn't need fair weather or someone else's approval in order to feel good. Although it would be nice to see Mom and Dad, surprised, shocked even, when he told them he was on his feet again, without their help, running his own business, taking care of his family. And he wouldn't mind seeing Valerie's reaction to the changes in his life.

He skirted around three boys in baggy pants and un-tied sneakers, huddled together in the middle of the side-walk. When he got closer, he saw the reason for their whooping laughter, a black and white girlie magazine they were passing from hand to hand. Skinny, their faces still plump with childhood, they couldn't have been more than nine or ten. Nearby, a group of young women pushed baby strollers and chatted, oblivious to the activity around them.

From the corner of his eye he noticed a toddler step off the curb as a battered panel truck screeched around the corner. Before he could shout a warning, one of the moth-ers raced to the bewildered child and snatched him back onto the sidewalk, yelling and swatting at the child's be-hind.

If she'd been paying attention, the kid would never have strayed into harm's way. Were his mother's licks and her scolding supposed to teach the little boy how to keep himself safe in a dangerous world?

It didn't have to be like that.

Johnny closed his eyes and imagined a green-eyed child in a pink dress, pictured her sitting on his lap as he read to her and explained how the kids in the book looked both ways before crossing the street. There was so much catching up to do, so many things to teach her, so much to learn about her. Did she like peaches, music, dolls?

Joanna.

The cold, dark emptiness nearly swallowed him up again, the way it had for the past year whenever he thought about her.

The pictures he'd been making in his head hadn't been enough. Not *nearly* enough.

ten

Washington and Perry, the western edge of nowhere,
tucked away on one of the angled streets that make Green-
wich Village a nightmare for the uninitiated to navigate.
The man on the corner looks like a turtle, only his head
sticking out from a stained, fraying shell of coats and
sweaters. He's declaiming in what sounds like Italian,
pointing to the thick clouds that elbow their way past the
distant beacon of the Empire State Building.

More people talk to themselves in New York City
than to their neighbors in Taconic Hills.

The building where Kevin Murchison lives squats in
the middle of the block. Soot has turned the cut-stone
façade the color of cigarette ash but cast-iron scrollwork
flows gracefully above the arched windows, a reminder of
a different era. Thick air absorbs the sound of her footsteps like new snow, and she pushes the door open and
then looks around to make sure no surprises are lurking in
dark corners.

When she presses the UP button beside the elevator,
gears groan. Apartment 412. The stairs are broad and well
lit, safer and less menacing than being lifted by pulleys in a
box that will shudder and squeal and inch its way upward.

In the semidarkness of the third-floor landing she
stops to catch her breath. The shadow on the wall looks
like a child curled in sleep. Like Joanna with one hand

tucked beneath her cheek and the other resting against the yellow dump truck.

If she closes her eyes, maybe she'll be able to see the details of her daughter's surroundings. But the only picture that comes to her is Joanna, smiling, playing with the truck. She could be anywhere . . . anywhere except where she belongs. Valerie takes the last half flight of stairs at a run.

She finds the apartment, knocks, hears nothing from the other side of the door. "Hello? Mr. Murchison? You said ten o'clock. It's Valerie Vincent."

"Door's open." The voice sounds muffled, faraway.

A photo gallery of children's faces, a framed square of fabric brilliant with peacock colors, and floor-to-ceiling bookshelves cover one wall of a large, sunny room. Assorted clothing is folded neatly in stacked plastic cubes that flank a yellowing shoji screen. Books and papers teeter on an old fruit crate beside the precisely made bed. A conference table that looks as though it's been liberated from some college library complete with computer, yellow legal pad, more books, sits opposite the Pullman kitchen. The counters are bare.

An odd combination of order and energy, of the ordinary and the unusual: not much worldliness here—but the geometric neatness does reflect a certain discipline, an intellectual rigor. The person who lives here may really be able to help her find her daughter.

Working the top button of his faded denim shirt, Kevin Murchison steps out from behind the screen, thick eyebrows bunched above his prominent nose. Tall, stoop-shouldered even when he straightens, he looks like a director of low-budget movies. The brackets at the corners of his mouth and the web of wrinkles around his eyes deepen as he brushes at his corduroy trousers and studies her. "Ah, the lady from Taconic Hills. Who knows you're here?"

It's his eyes that give him away, hard and dark as roasted coffee beans and set in a perpetual squint. Let him stare; all he'll see now is her resolve.

"No one. Look, we don't really have to do this cloak-and-dagger stuff, do we? All I want is to get my daughter back. I need to know what I can expect from this DASH organization, what they want."

He pulls wire-rimmed glasses from his pocket, adjusts the earpiece beneath his close-cropped hair, points her to a chair at the long table, then sits across from her. "Believe me, Ms. Vincent, I'm not playing games. I've known about DASH and their tactics for eight years, and you wouldn't believe some of the—" He sighs and folds his hands, fingers twined so tight the knuckles stretch thin and white. "Please, I want to help you. How about extending me a little of your trust? And I also need a lot of your background. Russo says your former in-laws tried to scare you into giving up your daughter six months ago, is that right?"

He's not going to do this to her, not going to subvert her question with questions of his own so he can twist things around to suit himself.

"You need background so you can write one of your exposés? I came here at Detective Russo's urging, but before I tell you anything about myself, I want some information. About DASH. And about you, Mr. Murchison. I'm not going to turn my life into fodder for one of your articles."

A flash of anger crackles in Murchison's dark eyes. "Self-interest has nothing to do—" The spark turns to ashes in an instant. He nods and raises his hands. "Fair enough. Here's the short version. You never heard of DASH before last night, right? I'm sure Russo told you that innocuous acronym stands for Deliverance And Safe Haven. DASH boasts of having members in all fifty states. By their own count, three thousand people. Not a lot when you think of this grand nation's population, but even if it's only half that, enough of them to make the whole pisspot dangerous. They claim that kids everywhere are being subjected to systematic abuse, ritual Satanic abuse, perpetrated by adults, usually the kid's own parents or teachers. Adults who—so DASH claims—have joined Satanic conspiracies that reach into the ranks of schools, cops, public officials, you name it.

"Sometimes, all DASH manages to do is destroy reputations, but they've shattered families as well. To date, they've successfully rescued—that's what they call it, *rescued*—at least three kids I know of."

When he gestures at the photographs on the wall, she notices a picture in the bottom row. A woman about her own age, her head thrown back in laughter, her blond hair streaming behind her, not a child at all.

"Those first three kids—they're the ones DASH rescued. Danny, Shavonna, Linda. What they do when they focus all their energies on a kid, and it's been a very young child each time, is to steal it. Kidnap it. The kid disappears and turns up hundreds of miles away with a new identity."

A surge of excitement thumps at her heart. If that's what's happened, then Joanna is alive. And as long as she's alive, whatever it takes, she will find her.

He frowns as though he doesn't understand what he's said to make her smile. "That's why I think it's a bad idea to go to the press. Whenever there's a lot of publicity, they go deeper, move the child around more. The two cases I know of where the parents made direct pleas through the press . . ." He shakes his head. "It's taken much longer to find them, thirteen, fourteen months instead of one or two."

Fourteen months. What happens to the mind of a child who's in a constant state of terror for more than a year, a child torn out of her life for fourteen months?

"Some people think DASH's real agenda is to cover up their own abusive practices. Personally, I think these jerks need to believe what they're saying so they can lay blame for family problems anywhere but on their own doorsteps. Which makes it harder to get them to back off. But I've never, ever heard of them committing murder to get a kid. I don't know, I can't tell if this is an escalation or an accident or just a damn blind alley."

Abruptly he strides to the sink. "Any of this sound relevant?" he demands.

If DASH were a topic she'd chosen for a history paper, she'd consider the context, would examine the lives of key individuals from the perspective of social movements, the political, religious, and economic *Zeitgeist*. But this is Joanna's life, and she isn't an objective observer.

Still, one thing stands out, would to anyone, she's certain. "I'd bet my ex-husband's parents belong to DASH. The narrow-mindedness, the need to shift blame away from themselves—it all fits. To Martha and Lucas Starr, I've always been evil incarnate. I'm not sure why, but they convinced themselves that Johnny went to ruin because I wasn't the type to join the Ladies' Auxiliary or something."

"Ah, the Starr suspects." He waves away his own remark. "Who are they? I mean, what do they believe, how do they live, how have they treated you?"

She tells him about their disapproval of her mother's jobs waiting tables or selling shampoo and aspirin. She talks about how Johnny's parents turned a blind eye on his drinking and then berated her for not letting him heap more and more hostility on her, how they blamed her for the divorce. And finally she tells him again about her All Hallows' Eve encounter with the devil.

"And you were furious and you were afraid they'd use those pictures so you ran away, right?"

"I didn't think of it that way at the time. I was just making sure I could finish my history paper by the end of the semester. Martha and Lucas were so adamant about taking charge of Joanna's life. They'd already decided God was their copilot or something like that, which gave them license to do . . . whatever."

She leans back, glad to be done talking about Martha and Lucas, thinking only, *Say you can help me find my daughter. Tell me you'll help bring Esther's murderer to justice.*

"Here we go again," Murchison says softly. "Maybe the Starrs *are* card-carrying members. I'll do my best to find out. And I'll try to find out if there's any buzz about a new child rescued on the East Coast. I can't promise I'll succeed—those people have charged into the computer age with a vengeance, and they keep changing access codes practically every other day. If they can't win by going through the system, they'll look for a way to hack their way around it. But I do want something in return. I'm working on—"

"I was waiting for this. You want to sell the story of sweet little Joanna Vincent to the highest bidder, right?

Well, I'm not ready to have my daughter cut up into lurid paragraphs for the *Inquirer,* or handy sound bites for 'Hard Copy.' I don't think there's a whole lot I can do for you, Mr. Murchison."

"I'm not after sound bites or smarmy stories, Ms. Vincent." His face is ashen, his mouth drawn taut. "I do want a written account of everything that happens and how you feel about it. Nothing fancy, just a page or two every day, more if you're so inclined. And then you turn it over to me and it becomes a chapter in the book I'm working on. About DASH. I've got an agent and a publisher and a deadline of Christmas. All I want is a little of your soul."

Valerie looks away from his tortured face. She's been so fixed on a concept, on the idea of him as journalist, that she's misplaced Kevin Murchison's humanity. "Why are you so interested in DASH, Mr. Murchison?" she asks softly.

In the tidy, sunlit room, Kevin Murchison seems to be pushing back the curtain of time, and it appears as difficult for him as it had been for her the night before. He plucks a pencil from the jar, jabs at the yellow pad until the point snaps, lets the pencil fall from his grasp and roll off the table to the floor.

"My sister was a guidance counselor in a lovely suburban elementary school. For some reason, she became a target. Maybe those prim ladies and their starched-shirt husbands didn't approve of my sister's pretty, petite live-in companion. Maybe my sister and her lady love were too open about the fact that they liked each other just fine and no men need apply."

The picture in the bottom row, that joyous, laughing young woman . . . It takes all her will to keep her gaze focused on the table.

"Anyway, before the bastards really got rolling on their smear campaign, two, three parents of kids who were getting into trouble—lighting fires in the bathroom, stealing things out of other kids' lockers—went to the principal to complain about her being part of a Satanic conspiracy. She was on her way home from a closed-door Board of Ed meeting. It was raining hard, and her car didn't make it around a curve. A very big tree was waiting to slow her down, and kablooey, road kill."

His clenched fists, his tight mouth—she recognizes how much effort it takes to keep the pain of his loss at bay.

He exhales loudly. "I don't know if she killed herself or if someone forced her off the road or if it was just a goddamn accident. But if DASH hadn't gone after her, if those parents hadn't picked her as a target and an explanation for all their kids' problems, my gut tells me she'd still be alive. I quit my job three weeks after she died. No accountant walks away from a potential partnership at Peat Marwick. No accountant but me. I started doing research on those bastards the next day, Ms. Vincent, and I haven't stopped. Whether you decide to work with me or not," he says as his eyes meet hers, "take them seriously."

"I'm so sorry about your sister." She wants to say more, but words feel empty, useless.

"Look, I need help making a strong case and getting it into the public record. This book is the best way I know to achieve my goal, and I'm asking for your help. If you can't do it, don't worry, we'll work something out." He says it without a leer, and his voice is kind. "You walk in here and tell me your story and say you want advice but you're also asking for reassurance. I could say things that might make you feel better, sure, but I'm not going to lie to you. Maybe DASH has changed the rules. And I need to know more about you. They sent one of their people up here once before, cunning, really, and it's made me take, well, precautions I didn't before that."

Cunning: no one's ever used that word to describe her, but she understands now why this man, even sitting here in his put-together studio apartment surrounded by the things that define his life, feels unsafe. "Thanks for taking the time to see me, Mr. Murchison. And thanks for your honesty. I guess we both have to think about what happens next. I'm not even sure I can do what you're asking."

"If you think there might be a chance this group is connected to your daughter's disappearance, you'll be back, Valerie Vincent. And I already have a pretty good idea of what I'm going to find when I check you out. Here." He slides a large, dun-colored envelope across his desk. "Go ahead. Read it all. Then decide if you want to figure out a way to work with me."

eleven

With a rush of cold wind and the deafening screech of metal wheels against metal tracks, her subway train finally arrives at the West Fourth Street station. She scrambles past an old man in a dark overcoat, apologizes under her breath as she squeezes into the car just before the doors close. Valerie finds a seat and opens the packet Murchison handed her.

His history is right here, source material that will give her a handle on what to expect from him and from DASH. She'll wade through the stuff he's pressed into her hands and examine it with the skills she's picked up reading the three-hundred-year-old court transcripts of the Salem witch trials. And she'll remember that each person isn't just a tidy category, *a colonial settler, a pioneer, a member of a temperance society*. Not just a chapter of a book.

A sheaf of photocopied pages slides out of the envelope and almost falls from her hands. The stories, all with Kevin Murchison's byline, are written with cool detachment, tales of men and women in California, Virginia, Montana whose dreams were stolen, reputations trashed, peace of mind destroyed by the threat of having their children taken from them. If she had come across the articles before Halloween, in the *Taconic Journal* or the *New York Times*, they would have leaped out at her . . . but more for their relevance to seventeenth-century Salem than for personal reasons.

Two more stops. Papers rattle in her hands as the car shuttles forward, and she reads every word.

Invariably Murchison's articles describe the same scenario. The defense lawyer calls friends of local DASH members as witnesses. Despite themselves, those fine, upstanding citizens end up providing alibis for the accused or attesting to their good character. The lawyer offers a calm, reasoned closing argument and then celebrates victory by granting a single interview—to Murchison.

It's the ultimate irony, the perfect punishment for him. Those same mad gods who delighted in watching her squirm in Professor Clarkson's office have provided him with the opportunity to warn the world about DASH. But, just as she can't bring Esther back to life, he'll never be able to save his own sister. Can Kevin Murchison's obsession possibly help her get Joanna back?

She stuffs the photocopies into the envelope as passengers stream past her toward the stairs. Carried along by the crowd, she walks briskly onto the street. The gray sky has lowered; a wind whips scraps of paper, thin as dandelion fluff, in an eddy in front of a newsstand.

Fourteen months. Murchison said it took over a year to find a child whose parents went to the press with their story. Joanna would be almost three. . . .

Has some rabid reporter written a heart-wrenching little piece about Esther's murder, about the fate of Baby Jane Doe? She scoops up the three dailies, tosses a handful of change onto the counter, and hurries past the smell of frying onions and curry toward the park.

Out of habit, she almost turns right at Seventh Avenue, to head for Esther's apartment. She stops herself in time and waits until the tears pass before she starts down Flatbush Avenue again.

As she approaches the huge granite arch in the center of Grand Army Plaza, she looks up at the horse-drawn chariot marching across the top. So much money, so much energy spent to erect monuments that celebrate war—but for the first time she almost understands.

She's engaged in a war too.

Yes, she'll take Murchison's deal. Not much of a burden, really, to keep a journal that makes a little sense of this mess and records the important bits. School habits are still so ingrained she sometimes believes she can't think without a pen in her hand. Maybe the exercise will help her see her daughter's face instead of the hazy picture she tries to hold in her mind as it fades with alarming regularity. She wants a personal payoff—eating breakfast with her daughter, gathering wildflowers to put in a mayonnaise jar on the table. Holding Joanna in her arms would be enough.

What a moment that will be.

She'll kneel and speak softly, maybe hold the Babar book casually in one hand while she asks Joanna if she's hungry. Raisins and hard pretzels. She should have some around so that when—

A horn blares. Cars careen around the traffic rotary, so close she nearly chokes on the oily fumes. She looks up into a driver's face, twisted in anger as he leans out the window, shouts, "Wake up, lady!" and then peels away.

Shaken, she runs ahead to the safety of the sidewalk and clutches the newspapers and the large envelope to her chest to slow her racing heart.

The driver is right. If something happens to her . . . she can't let Joanna return to a motherless world. She must be careful. It's too easy to slip into a dream haven, like the one Kristin Denby created on the second floor of Antonia's brownstone. Too tempting to pretend away the truth.

Before she can escape to the silence of the upstairs bedroom, Antonia calls her name, says it like a summons rather than a greeting, so that it's clear she's expected to make an appearance. Antonia is waiting in the living room, her back to the cold fireplace, her hands running restlessly along the armrests of the wheelchair. This is where she sits in the mornings so she can hear Valerie's key in the door, her footsteps on the polished wood floor of the entryway.

"Oh, my dear, I'm so glad you're back. There's been a phone call."

Valerie can't read the look on the woman's face.

"I can't figure out how he knew to call you here. This is such a hopeful sign."

The woman's words make no sense. "Antonia, I don't understand what you're saying. Please, start at the beginning and tell me what's going on."

"Ten minutes ago, a man called. He sounded, well, the best way to describe his voice is senatorial. Very refined, deep voice, perfect enunciation, as though he were used to delivering orations."

Not Russo, not Lucas or Johnny. Not anyone she can think of.

"When I told him you were out, he almost hung up on me but I convinced him to go on. He said he would talk only to you. He said it was about Joanna."

twelve

It seems to take a century before Antonia continues, time enough for Valerie to recognize the light of hope seeping into the dark tunnel she's tumbled into. Finally, an end to the waiting. Or, at least, a break in it.

"He said not to call the police, that Joanna was all right now, but if you contacted the police, that might not be the case anymore. He insisted he'd talk only to you. He said he'd call back. Just before he hung up, he said the oddest thing. 'It's my burden to protect the children.' It was chilling, Valerie, positively chilling."

To protect the children. She's read Murchison's papers. That sounds like the kind of pompous phrase DASH might dream up.

"Nothing else? No demands, no conditions?"

"That was all. That awful threat about not calling the police, that he'd call back, and that one odd sentence."

Valerie understands for the first time how people can kill with their bare hands. If this anonymous, sadistic caller were standing in front of her . . . The rush of fury almost scares her.

"*You* didn't call the police, right?"

"Of course not. That's not my decision to make, my dear. You must have the final say in this matter. But I certainly wouldn't antagonize this man, whoever he is." Antonia is gentle. "Who knows you're staying here with me? Your lawyer. Your policeman. This writer in the city. Who else?"

"No one. No one who would tell anyone."

Don't call the police. The person who delivered that warning isn't worried about keeping children from harm. He's anxious to protect himself from being charged with Esther's murder.

In her mind, she listens to voices—friends, acquaintances, teachers, colleagues, shopkeepers—but she can't hear one so distinctive that Antonia would describe it as senatorial. A stranger, then. A messenger, perhaps.

"The caller—he could be playing John Alden to Lucas and Martha's Miles Standish. They're trying to bargain their way out of a murder charge. Joanna's their ace. They could be planning to turn her over to me as long as I don't bring the cops or anyone else into it."

Antonia nods. "That's certainly shrewd."

And then it hits her with stunning force.

She hasn't understood until this minute, but it's so right, no question it's the explanation for what they did on Halloween and everything that's happened since.

"Oh, God—it's not Joanna they're after. They want their son. What I have to do is promise them Johnny and find a way to give him to them." That's what they want. That's all they've wanted all along—Johnny for Joanna.

I'll help you find your son. I can get Johnny for you. Fair trade: her child for theirs.

"Valerie, you're not thinking clearly. You can't make that promise and not deliver. Your ex-husband could be anywhere, my dear. From what you've told me about his drinking, he might be one of those pathetic men on the streets begging for change. Sit down and I'll get Nadia to bring you a glass of cool water."

The bell tinkles, rain falling on a sheet of silver. Nadia appears, then hurries away to fulfill Antonia's request.

Valerie paces, wanders to the window, to the table where the telephone refuses to ring. Joanna has been missing nearly eighteen hours now. How much longer will he make her wait for his call?

She goes to the kitchen and into the upstairs bedrooms to make sure the phones are working, that they haven't somehow been left off the hook. And then she remembers the newspapers—the call could have been prompted by a story. . . . She races to the hall, examines every page of all three papers.

Page 5 of the *New York Post*. Page 7 of the *Daily News*. Two paragraphs about Esther, only a single line about the child sent home with her mother, whose identity the police will not release. No photos. No mention at all in *The New York Times*.

Thank God.

Antonia is still in front of the fireplace when she returns to the living room, but she says nothing as Valerie rummages through the drawer of the lamp table, finds a notepad and a pen, then sits down again, her hand tight on the telephone receiver.

Waiting, waiting. That's all she's been doing. If she knew who made that call . . .

"You know what they say about the mountain not coming to Mohammed." The receiver is cold against her hand.

"Are you suggesting you're going to call Lucas Starr?" Alarm pushes Antonia's voice higher, makes her words tight and clipped. "Isn't that risky?"

"It would be a mistake to offer him his son, you're right. But I can find out if he knows anything about the phone call. I'll work the phrase about protecting the children into the conversation and see how he reacts. It would be better in person. I'd have the advantage of seeing his face. But the telephone will do, if I listen carefully."

Of course she can do it. Can judge from the quality of his voice, from his pauses, from his breathing, whether Lucas Starr is her anonymous caller. At last. Something she can *do* for Joanna. Excited, she dials the number. They have only one phone, in the kitchen, but they turn the bell up loud so they can hear it when they're working in the garden.

The hard part will be keeping herself cool, prowling through their secrets like an ocelot stalking a small jungle creature. She can do this. She has to.

"This is Lucas Starr," the voice says, and she knows right away it's a machine.

"This is Valerie." Tears of frustration sting her eyes. She swallows hard and goes on. "I got your message. I haven't told the police or anyone else. Please, call me back. I really want to talk to you."

Antonia is dabbing a finger into a tiny pot of lip gloss, applying the clear red to her mouth with utter concentration. She's turned toward the window, as though she's actually looking the other way to give Valerie privacy. When Valerie has replaced the receiver, Antonia says, "Have you had anything to eat today, my dear, anything at all?"

She can't remember. The gnawing emptiness in the center of her has nothing to do with food, she knows that much. "I'm not hungry," she says.

"Would you like some tea, Valerie? Or perhaps some company for a while?"

She doesn't want company. She wants her daughter. But she mustn't let her pain consume her, can't let time drip like a narcotic into her veins.

Valerie lowers herself to the sofa, her mind veering crazily to the thought that Joanna hasn't had her vitamins in two days. She was like a baby bird with those infant vitamins, opened her mouth in a little O when Valerie squeezed the dropper, an eager nestling craving some delicate nectar.

Vitamins. A year from now, are these the only details she'll have left of Joanna?

"I don't know what to do, Antonia. I'm afraid to call Russo and I'm afraid not to. And I keep getting these crazy pictures of Joanna in my head."

"I'm sure they're not crazy, my dear. It's only natural. You'd be a strange mother if you *weren't* thinking about your child. Maybe you should just talk about her a little. Before you left to see that writer, you were about to tell me about her." The chair backs up, then rolls to Antonia's favorite daytime spot near the window. "You were going to tell me about her temperament, as I recall."

Joanna's temperament. Antonia did ask about that earlier.

"Actually, she's always had this kind of, I don't know, I'd call it a cheerful steadfastness. When I was studying, she used to crawl right onto my lap without saying a word. When I tilted my head, she tilted hers. When I reached for a pencil, she wanted one too."

She'd held it in her fist, pudgy fingers clasped tight as she scribbled happily, giggling with delight and astonishment, filling the paper with coils and flecks and zigzag lines, her sturdy little body warm and relaxed against Valerie's chest.

"We read De Tocqueville and Cotton Mather together. And then we—" *Read about Salem and witches and persecution and hangings*. Valerie can't say the words aloud, not now.

"She's a healthy child, is she not? Physically, I mean." Antonia's still, carved features crowd into a frown as her head turns toward the doorway. "What is it, Nadia?"

Valerie's been so engrossed in talking about Joanna she hasn't even heard the woman come in.

"I'm going out now. To take care of that errand." Nadia peers into the depth of her open purse. "I have it," she says, "so I'll be back later."

Antonia waves her away impatiently. "Well, then, go ahead. Valerie and I are talking."

Nadia, who probably doesn't realize how Antonia hates to have stories interrupted, looks offended at the brusqueness, but she only nods and disappears from the doorway.

"Now then, my dear. You were going to tell me more about your daughter."

Valerie roots around in the past and unearths images. Joanna, eyes wide with surprise as she gets her first DPT shot. Joanna, a year ago, crying and tugging at her ear. This time, the exercise brings her daughter so close she has to blink her eyes against the dazzling white of Joanna's T-shirt.

"Nothing serious, the usual early stuff, earaches and colds. One night she woke up crying, pressing her head to her shoulder. Her skin was so hot it frightened me. Poor thing, she was miserable. When she looked at me through those red eyes, I was sure she was wondering why I didn't stop the pain. I bundled her up and tore down the back roads to the hospital emergency room in Hudson. They gave her an antibiotic and within two hours she was asleep again and smiling."

"And she's a bright child, I'd guess. She walked sooner than other children and spoke earlier, didn't she?" Antonia leans forward, her cheeks flushed with anticipation.

Despite herself, Valerie smiles with the memory. "The first thing Joanna ever said was 'Poppy.' She was nine months old."

She can almost smell the vegetable soup simmering on the stove, can see the way the late afternoon sun slants through the white-curtained window, brightening the tiny room. *Her* kitchen, her sweat that had transformed it. Weeks of scraping cabinets, uncovering layers of yellow and blue and orange—who in the world would paint cabinets *orange*? Applying two coats of Navaho Sand, hanging the carefully matted pictures of fruits and vegetables she'd cut from last year's calendar. And then Sarah Hoving saying, "It's perfect, Val. Small but perfect for a woman who lives by the motto that cooking is terrific as long as someone else is doing it."

Is it possible that Ruth Hoving, Sarah's mother-in-law and one of the movers and shakers in Taconic Hills, knew that Martha and Lucas were planning to rescue Joanna? Maybe she should call Sarah and—

"Valerie, dear. You were saying?" Antonia is smiling, her head propped against her fist.

What *was* she saying?

"Poppy," Antonia prompts.

Right. Joanna's first word.

"She had this game she loved to play, the books all say it's a sign of fine motor skills developing, but Joanna loved the fun of it. She'd pick something up and then drop it to the floor and laugh and squeal. I was supposed to look surprised and then put it back in her reach and then the game would start all over again. One day, we were in the kitchen and all of a sudden Joanna said 'Poppy' and started wailing.

"The only thing anywhere near her high chair was this book, one of those cloth things with bright, textured patches on each page. She must have said it ten times.

'Poppy, Poppy, Poppy.' I gave her the book and she hugged it and said it again. 'Poppy.' As clear as could be, smiling away.

"And then I made the connection. We'd been visiting my friend Lynn the day before. Her dog came to check out Joanna's toys and he picked the book up in his mouth. When he started trotting out of the room with it, Lynn called after him. *Poppy.* He came back, head hanging, and gave her the book. It took me a while to straighten Joanna out that Poppy was the name of Lynn's dog and not the word for book."

"Less than a year—isn't that early for a child to speak? Well, the experts say it helps develop language facility if you read to children and talk to them a lot when they're young. And I'm sure you spoke to her all the time. Her father wasn't there to talk to her, was he?" Head canted and mouth pursed in thought, Antonia asks, "How did you meet him?"

The Johnny Starr she met that day was so different from the man who disappeared more than a year ago.

"At a Fourth of July party in Taconic Hills. Five years ago."

"Fourth of July in a small country town. Ah, I haven't done that in ages," Antonia sighs.

"It was beautiful, more like May than midsummer. You know—sunshine, gentle breezes. I was new in town. The party was at Ruth Hoving's house and Catherine Delaney took me on a tour of the place. Wonderful colonial chests and wardrobes, an old bed that was so high you needed a stool to climb into it. It was like a museum of Americana. Except for one painting in the upstairs hall, a huge canvas full of slashing blood-red lines on a black background. I kept wanting to look away but I couldn't take my eyes off it. Finally, I said something like, 'This really gives me the creeps. I can't imagine wanting to look at this every day.' Catherine kept grinning over my shoulder. I just rattled on and on about how the painting looked like a nightmare or a war zone in a battle that would never end."

"And Johnny was standing on the stairs, wasn't he?" Antonia seems amused. "He heard everything you said."

"Every bit of it. And then he told me he'd never heard anyone describe so clearly what he wanted to say in that painting. We all three spent a couple of hours talking about a million things. Catherine left and Johnny and I just kept talking. I'd thrown on jeans and an old blouse that morning but Johnny made me feel like I was wearing a Victorian summer frock and a straw hat. From that day until the night we were married, I felt like I was starring in a happily-ever-after movie. But then—"

The telephone shrills.

She can't breathe. This is it. The call she's been waiting for. The senatorial voice. She snatches the receiver from the cradle and manages to say, "This is Valerie."

"Mitch Russo," the voice announces, and she nearly cries out in disappointment. "I wanted to check in, you know, touch base with you. How'd it go with Murchison?"

She was in Kevin Murchison's apartment just a few hours ago. Came home at a little after noon, and Antonia told her about the call . . . "Fine. It was fine."

"Yeah, well, he's a writer, not a magician. I told you we took some prints last night? They match the prints we found in Esther Klein's apartment. We're running them against our files and if we don't get a hit, we'll send them on to Washington. Listen, I still want to talk to your husband. You're sure you don't remember where he is?"

"I *can't* remember, Detective Russo. I never *knew*." If only she did. . . . "Did you find out about this Phelps woman in Taconic Hills? Do you know if Martha and Lucas Starr belong to DASH? Did you talk to anyone who might have seen my daughter last night after the car dropped them at the subway?"

It takes him a while to answer. "Look, we're after the same thing here. The only call I got from Taconic Hills since I spoke to you was from the sheriff. To say he recognized you and your daughter from the picture I faxed him. We're checking it all, Ms. Vincent. You're sure there's nothing else, something you thought of that I should know?"

"No. Nothing."

Not that she's ready to tell him. Not yet, anyway.

thirteen

It felt so good to have her scalp massaged, Kristin Denby thought maybe she'd just come in every day and let Marie wash her hair. But she didn't plan to spend her whole life in Park Slope, and Marie was a Brooklyn girl through and through.

"Too hot?" Marie moved the water spray so that it splashed against the side of the sink.

"Perfect." Eyes still closed, Kristin waited for the cascade of water to flow over her again, carrying with it the accumulated tensions that had gathered in her neck and shoulders. Lying back and letting her mind go empty was such an infrequent pleasure these days, and nothing was likely to change any time soon. Not until this situation with Charles was resolved. Not until Antonia understood why she couldn't go through with the wedding plans.

Marie was chattering about something, her voice barely audible above the splash and hiss of the water, not even aware she was talking to herself. Which was a good thing, since Kristin hated making conversation with people whose paths wouldn't cross hers except in a shop or a restaurant or a beauty salon. Antonia always said the key to living successfully in society was to find some bit of common ground with each person you met, whether at a dinner party or the corner grocery. With Marie, that was a stretch.

"Okay, honey, Paolo's waiting for you." Marie blotted the dripping water from Kristin's forehead, then wrapped the towel around her head and patted her shoulder.

Kristin sighed, sat up, opened her eyes to the too bright fluorescent lights of the salon. *Salon*. In Manhattan these days, the advertising copywriters were calling beauty shops *studios*. So, what would they call Charles? Not her sugar daddy, not her gold mine or her power figure. An icon: Charles would like that.

Paolo motioned her to the chair, his full mouth stretched into a grin above the two-day stubble darkening his jaw and the space above his lips. His customary jeans and white T-shirt fit well on his compact body; at least he had the good sense not to dress absurdly. Paolo, with that short, gleaming wave that dipped onto his forehead and those almost stubby fingers, looked more like an auto mechanic than a hairdresser. He even kept a picture of his wife and kids stuck in the mirror at his station. *Stylist*. Wasn't that what he called himself?

"Growing a beard?" she asked brightly as she lowered herself into the soft leather seat.

In the mirror, his brown eyes registered surprise. "You ask a question like that? I thought you were *au courant*, pretty face."

Whenever he called her that, she wanted to call him Paulie, the way his friends must have when he was growing up in Bensonhurst. Instead, she said, "You've been hanging around too many dentists' offices, Paolo."

He frowned and ran his tongue over his front teeth.

"Reading old magazines," she continued. "The grungy, unshaven look is *out*, you know."

"Speaking of which," Paolo said smugly, "when are you going to let me do something with all that hair?"

Why not? Antonia had said countless times, in her arbiter-of-fashion firmness, that Kristin should update her look. A simple bob, chin-length, shiny. *It will draw attention to your intelligent eyes, Kristin, instead of just to your hair*. And then went on and on about simplicity being the hallmark of true style. Never used the word "class," of course, not Antonia Carrera.

Hell, why not?

"Okay, Paolo, but no shorter than here," she said, grazing her jaw with the back of her hand. "All one length, I think, don't you?"

"Ah, finally! I've been waiting for you to say that." His hands were in her hair, lifting it, pulling tendrils forward onto her forehead, folding the mass of it behind her. "Your face is a perfect oval, so we don't have to worry about correcting, you know, flaws of nature. You're right. I see you with a medium-length bob, unlayered except for a little interest around your forehead and temples. Great texture, wonderful body, a little natural curl—it's perfect for you."

She nodded her agreement. "Let's do it. I have to be out of here in thirty-five minutes, okay?"

His eyes sought hers in the mirror. "I passed the test, did I?"

She returned his smile and removed her earrings, held them in her hand. "Part one. Now you have to actually make it look good. I want people who know me to notice that something's changed, and people who don't to think I've looked like this forever. And no conversation today, Paolo. I have a lot on my mind."

He bowed and reached for his scissors. Wordlessly he clipped a mass of hair to the top of her head and began to snip at the length in the back.

Eyes closed—she trusted him, wanted to see only the finished product and not watch the transformation in process—Kristin began to review her plan.

Because she wanted to spare him the jolt of an abrupt departure, she'd send the note in the mail.

Dear Charles, I'm sorry that I've worried you lately. I've tried several times but I can't seem to say the right words when we're together. I'm still not completely comfortable talking about these feelings, but I find myself confused and I value you too much to deceive you. That's why I've written this letter. It's better for you to know a little than to wander about in the dark thinking this silence is your fault. Please try to understand. I need a few days by myself to sort things out. Love, Kristin.

No timetable, of course, and no demands. No explanations or dissertations on his fawning, how that adoration made her feel like some specimen under a microscope, a butterfly trapped in a glass paperweight. Only that sympathetic preparation for what would follow later.

Just to prove her moral compass was still working, she'd send him back his ring and all the other jewelry. Perfect.

In a couple of days, after he'd had the chance to absorb the utterly unchangeable truth of her absence, she'd tell Charles she couldn't marry him. It would be hard on him, but simply disappearing would devastate the man.

She'd find a way to convince him that it wasn't him, oh no, absolutely not him but her own restlessness, her need to discover more about herself. Maybe she'd even say she was dazzled at first by his money and the lifestyle; he'd appreciate that as the truth. The suggestion that they see other people, live their lives separately and without any commitments to a future together would seem, eventually, like a kindness, a realistic, reasonable, and entirely unavoidable kindness.

The real trick in calling off her engagement to Charles Babcock would be to avoid Antonia's displeasure. Antonia, who had so much experience in engineering these matches, had made sure Kristin and Charles sat near each other or across the table, threw them together whenever she could manage.

After all, you're about to turn thirty. He's an ideal companion, don't you think, my dear? Witty, devoted, a man of substance.

As though those qualities were sufficient in themselves and the case was therefore closed. As though her age were a magic number, and she'd turn into a dull, lumpy clod of a pumpkin unless she got married before her thirtieth birthday.

Paolo removed the clip, let another section of long

hair fall against her back, swiftly pinned up the rest. She opened her eyes for a second, saw only his rapt, attentive gaze fixed on her hair, and sank back into thought.

It wouldn't be right to string Charles along and let him go on thinking the relationship was salvageable. In time, he'd find someone else who actually thrived on the kind of smothery attention he paid her, who loved it when he stared at her in stricken, lovesick disbelief. Eventually he'd understand that he was lucky they hadn't gone through with a marriage that could only have ended unhappily.

If they were both lucky, that's how it would work. Even if he insisted on nursing his hurt publicly, she would be able to say she'd done her best. And she'd be free of him. She couldn't wait until the whole Charles thing was resolved to start getting ready for the rest of her life. The last time she'd spoken to her, Antonia had mentioned a couple overseas somewhere who—

"Open your eyes a minute, pretty face. I want to check the length with you before I do the sides."

She glared at him. "I thought I told you just go ahead and do it. That I didn't want to talk."

Scissors dangling in his outstretched hand, Paolo stood frozen behind her. "Hey, hey, sorry. You go back to your daydream."

God, she'd been rude. Unintentionally, of course, but she shouldn't have taken out her problems on poor Paolo. "I didn't mean to snap like that. I guess I'm a little tense."

With his free hand, he massaged her neck, the strong fingers pushing the knots into submission so easily she had to smile with pleasure and relief.

"All right, baby, close your eyes again and I'll finish in silence. You ever try running? Meditation? All those magazines say—" Paolo laughed softly. "Whoops. You sit back and I'll be quiet."

Her train of thought was broken, the prospects too vague to pursue anyway. She didn't have enough information about Antonia's international friends to make any decisions yet.

Besides, she needed to come up with a third plan, one that didn't involve getting help from anyone. You couldn't count on people. In the end, they always did what served themselves best, and she'd be a fool if she let herself forget that.

fourteen

All that plaster work made him thirsty.

Johnny Starr looked longingly at the lanky kid on the corner slugging from a brown bottle wrapped in a brown paper bag. If he were a diabetic, he wouldn't go buy some candy every time he saw some ten-year-old munching on a Snickers bar. The rush of pleasure had a sledgehammer attached to it. Drinking wasn't worth the trouble.

Especially not now, with so much at stake.

He ducked into the corner bodega, grabbed a bottled iced tea, nodded at the tiny woman behind the counter as he laid his dollar bill down. *"Gracias,"* he said, smiling and scooping up his change.

One hand on the door, he stopped. He smelled them before he saw them. Lilacs, the first of spring, most of the flowers still closed tight in dark clusters hidden among the deep green leaves. Francine loved lilacs, and it was definitely time for a celebration. Shaking water from the woody stalks, he walked back to the counter. *"Combien?"*

"Six." She said it without a trace of Spanish accent, and without a smile.

Okay, so he'd work an extra half hour next week. Francine had stuck by him through a hard time. Soon a six-dollar purchase would hardly make a dent.

On the street, he felt a little like a character from some fifties musical, Gene Kelly maybe, courting the girl next door. Well, he didn't really have to prove anything to Francine, but he felt like dancing anyway. God, it was good when things went the way you planned. Luck had nothing to do with it. He'd earned every bloody bit of this and he was going to enjoy it and share his pleasure, too.

Humming, stopping once in the middle of the block to do a little two-step, Johnny Starr hurried home with his good feelings and his lilacs.

"They're so beautiful. Here, I want to get them in water and put them in the sun so they'll open up." Francine had to shout above the racket of the jackhammer in the street below. She buried her face in the flowers again, then leaned forward and kissed him. "This isn't an apology of some sort, is it? And don't tell me these are Valerie's favorite flowers or I'll walk out this door this minute."

"Will you shut up and say thank you? I said once, *once,* that you look like my ex-wife and you carry on as though that's the only reason I'm with you." The jackhammer stopped all at once, and he realized he didn't have to shout anymore. "I don't even know if she *has* a favorite flower. And the lilacs are because I had to work on Saturday and we didn't have any time together and you love lilacs and I love you."

And he did. Loved the way she didn't nag him about painting, as Valerie used to, loved how she surprised him with tickets to a Rangers game for his birthday. And, especially, loved having her share his dreams.

Dark hair cascaded down her back as she stretched to reach the milk bottle she'd picked up a month earlier at a street fair for twenty-five cents. She filled it with water, arranged the flowers. "Johnny, there's something I want to talk to you about."

The air went out of him, as though he'd taken a huge bellywhopper into Stissing Lake. Her face, set in that carefully controlled emptiness, exactly matched the tone of her voice. She was trying to defuse some bomb she was about to drop, working really hard at it, not succeeding.

"I think it's time for us to look for a bigger place."

Johnny laughed, from sheer relief and because earlier

he'd thought the same thing in practically the same words. "You really scared me for a minute there."

"Well, I didn't know how you'd feel if I came right out and told you everything at once."

"Everything? There's more?"

She nodded, unable to suppress her smile. "You remember my friend Ellie from work? She's moving back to Ohio and she wants to know if we want her rent-controlled apartment. It's not huge, two tiny bedrooms, a kitchen Pavarotti couldn't turn around in, and a living room with a little L-shaped dining area. And it's on Carmine Street, in the Village."

This really was a sign that they were on the right track. "That's great, Franny. You scared the shit out of me, you know that? You were so serious. I thought you were about to say you didn't want to do the business, or you were leaving because you met a guy who could buy you roses every day."

"You have to stop that." The pulse in her neck beat rapidly. She planted herself in front of him and tugged playfully at his beard. "That's really insulting, you know? Anyway, you're changing the topic. This is starting to feel like the incredible shrinking apartment and the neighborhood is getting to me. Can we do it, Johnny? Take that place in the Village and get out of here, finally?"

"You're right. Okay, let's make a deal. I'll go see the apartment if you think, I mean *really* think, about marrying me." He touched her hair and bent to kiss her. "Maybe it's just habit, but I get scared every once in a while that this whole plan will fall apart. Promise me. Marry me, Franny. Think about it, at least. We can do it in City Hall or at a church or wherever you—"

The buzzer cut short his words.

They weren't expecting visitors. Suddenly ashen, Francine pulled away, held a finger to her lips.

What now?

He stood unmoving, straining to hear some clue from the other side of the door. Again, the buzzer blared, two short, impatient jabs.

"Mr. Starr. It's the police." The jackhammer started up again, drowning out the voice.

Francine backed away slowly, headed for the bedroom, and pulled the door closed.

The police.

"Mr. Starr, I know you're in there. You came in five minutes ago, carrying flowers. I need to talk to you."

Could someone have followed him? Obviously, and it was someone who knew what they were doing. If it *was* the police and if he didn't respond, it would look suspicious.

A fist pounded at the door, and the voice shouted, "Mr. Starr, open up."

Johnny unlocked the door and stared at the upturned, freckled face of a petite, red-haired woman. She held up a leather wallet containing a shield and a photo ID.

"Mr. Starr? John Starr?" She flipped the wallet shut and slipped it into her purse.

"Yes. Look, what's going on? What's this all about? I'm sorry, I didn't get your name, Miss—"

"Detective. Detective Gallagher. I'd like to talk to you." The heavy equipment battered at the sidewalk below.

Shit, just what he needed. Just when everything was going so well. "What's this about, Detective Gallagher?"

"I'm investigating the murder of a woman named Esther Klein. Now, can I come in or is there something you'd rather I didn't see?" She filled the doorway now, taking up more space than a woman her size could possibly occupy.

"Esther Klein? The lady in the next building, the one with the squeaky shopping cart?" Johnny swung the door open, noticed that the redhead kept her hand on a bulge in the pocket of her blazer. "I don't think I know anyone named Esther Klein."

Her hand dropped to her side as she moved into the living room, walked to the window, then headed for the bathroom and peered inside.

He had the shakes, goddamn racking shakes like he'd never experienced when he was going through detox. The only way to keep his knees from banging together was to sit down.

"Where were you last night, Mr. Starr?" She was cutting him no slack.

"Here, sprawled out on the bed watching the Knicks game." Feeling good because he had a can of cold Sprite in his hand, not the beer it would have been a year ago. Francine hadn't come back yet.

"And before the game? Late afternoon, say between three and four?"

This time it was his hands that started trembling, and he stuffed them into his pockets. "On my way to an AA meeting. I got off work at three-thirty. The meeting starts at four-thirty. I go to that one on the Upper East Side because they don't allow smoking. I can't stand to be in a closed room with ten, twenty cigarettes going at once. Makes me sick."

Detective Gallagher sat down in the chair across from him. Francine's chair. She leaned forward, chin on hands, elbows resting on her knees, and just stared. Kept her eyes locked to his, until he frowned.

"What?" The jackhammer pounded away, and the throbbing behind his eyes swelled to fill his head. "I want to know why you're asking me all this. I already told you, I don't know any Esther Klein."

"And I want to know why Jimmy Gilhooley told me you left before three yesterday."

"Who? Jimmy who?" This was crazy, this cop sitting there and dragging out names of people he'd never even—

"The floor guy, the one who was working at that loft in SoHo where you're doing some painting." She shrugged. "Jimmy says you left a little before three."

"Oh, right. I had to meet a friend who was lending me money. I forgot about that."

Gallagher didn't crack a smile. "A friend? You're going to tell me this friend's name, right?"

Involuntarily Johnny looked at the bedroom door. "Why do you need to know that? Listen, I'm trying to be cooperative here, but I don't have a clue what's going on. Why did you go to all the trouble to find me?"

"When's the last time you spoke to your parents, Mr. Starr?"

She was trying to disarm him with her jackrabbit tactics, jumping all over the open field, hoping he wouldn't figure out what she was up to.

"I can't remember. A long time, over a year. What's this about, Detective Gallagher?"

"When did you last see Joanna?"

"Joanna?" Johnny Starr wished the room would stop spinning and that this woman sitting with her back straight and her hand reaching for her pocket would go away. "My daughter?"

"Yes, Mr. Starr. Your daughter."

"My ex-wife didn't ask for child support. What's going on?"

"This isn't about child support, Mr. Starr. When did you last see your daughter?"

Abruptly the clattering of the machinery outside stopped.

"A month after she was born. A year ago November." This wasn't going well, he could tell from the *Yeah, prove it* expression on the cop's face.

From the bedroom, a rhythmic tapping ticked through the air. Like a deer reacting to a motion in the underbrush, Detective Gallagher's body jerked upright and she bolted for the door.

She wrapped her left hand around the doorknob; her right hand drew the gun from her pocket. In a single clean movement, she turned the knob and pushed the door open.

A torn window shade flapped in the breeze. Gallagher ran to the open window, peered at the rusting fire escape, then hoisted herself up and wriggled outside. Johnny saw only her shoes and the crisp cuff of her pants as she stood at the far edge near the railing, where she could see the alley below.

The detective lowered herself back into the room.

Francine had moved quickly.

Her back to him, Gallagher grabbed the framed photograph from the dresser.

Their day in Rockaway. A stranger had agreed to take their picture. And had done a bad job of it, had stood too far away, had moved so everything was a little blurred, out of focus. Still, Francine had treasured the photo.

"Who's this?"

"A friend. Listen—I have a right to know what's going on."

"All those dark curls," she asked softly, "do they fit under a baseball cap?"

"What does this have to do with Joanna?"

"Sit down, Mr. Starr. I'll tell you about that. After you answer all my questions."

sunday

fifteen

Idly she writes *Joanna Claire* on the notepad, but it's no use. She can't give Kevin Murchison what he's asked for, at least not now. For one thing, she's ravenous. The dark, restless hours she's spent in the tangle of sheets and blankets in the canopy bed have only made her hungry, not wiser, not calmer.

Besides, her mind insists on skittering. She wonders what Russo and Gallagher have been doing, hopes her daughter slept better than she did, replays the phone calls she made last night before it got too late to go on—old friends of Johnny's, his high school art teacher, neighbors in Taconic Hills—dead ends, all of them. The story came easily after the first call: she's a gallery owner trying to find Johnny Starr because she's interested in his work. But no one has any idea where he might be. At least, that's what they tell her.

No luck.

No Johnny.

The house is silent, the kitchen streaked with morning light. A robin struts in the grass between the slate slabs that form a path through the backyard. Still wearing the robe she found in Kristin's closet, Valerie starts the coffee maker, grabs butter, three eggs, two slices of bread, a jar of orange marmalade from the refrigerator, her stomach grumbling with impatience.

The cast-iron frying pan hanging from the rack above the stove is just the right size. Within seconds, the smell of sizzling butter makes her mouth water. "Quick eggs." That's what her mother used to call them, breaking the fragile shells on the side of the pan, dropping the eggs into the butter, scrambling them in the pan until they were just set, the white not quite mixed into the yolk.

She's glad no one's watching as she shakes salt and pepper onto the eggs and scoops a forkful from the pan into her mouth. She alternates great bites of bread with the eggs. The pan is almost empty when she hears the elevator deposit Antonia's wheelchair into the hall.

"Nadia would have made you breakfast."

The kitchen doorway, narrower than the arched entries to the other rooms, is wide enough for Antonia's wheelchair to pass through, but she remains in the hall. She's smiling, already dressed in taupe slacks and a matching shirt. "I'm glad your appetite is back, Valerie. Since you're not sleeping, you need food to keep you going."

"Was I that noisy last night?" She brushes crumbs from the counter into her hand, dumps them into the garbage bag beneath the sink.

"No, on the contrary, you were quite thoughtful. I couldn't sleep either. I only heard you walking around because I had one of my bad nights. By the way, I had Nadia collect your skirt and blouse. She's washing them now and she'll press them as soon as they're clean."

And if her phantom caller phones again and she has to go out? A vise starts to tighten around her undigested meal, until she remembers the pants and sweater hanging in Kristin's closet. They'll fit her if she needs them. Antonia is only being thoughtful. "Thanks. Can I get you some coffee?"

Antonia smiles. "That will be lovely. Why don't you join me in the dining room?"

"I'll be there in a minute."

When Antonia disappears, Valerie dials Russo's office. "What did you find out about those fingerprints?" she asks after the detective identifies himself.

"So far no match. We did talk to the guy who owns that video store near the subway station. He saw a woman and a child get out of the car. He recognized the driver, said he used the same car service himself sometimes. He verified the driver's information. The woman carried the child down the steps to the subway entrance and—"

"Detective Russo, do you know where my daughter is? You don't have any leads, do you?" She won't let him soothe her with irrelevancies, doesn't care about empty information. "I still haven't ruled out making some kind of appeal to the public for information."

"You do what you have to, Ms. Vincent. Murchison tell you he thought that would help?"

No, of course he didn't, and Russo knows it. "I'll talk to you later. I'll *keep* talking to you until . . ." What's the point of saying anything more?

She bangs the phone down, pours two cups of coffee, struggles to recapture the thread of hope she'd woven last night. As she carries the cups to the marble dining table, she reviews the plan she laid out during the long, bleak hours when she couldn't sleep. If Antonia, too, believes it might succeed, then she'll set it all in motion.

"I realized something last night." Valerie pulls her chair closer to the table, reaches for her cup. "If Kevin Murchison is right about DASH infecting people all over the country, then surely New York City must have a poisonous little cell of its own."

A skeptical frown creases Antonia's forehead, but she says nothing.

"Suppose a woman passed through Montana, say. Maybe this woman met a couple who convinced her that everything from the national health care crisis to high interest rates and tight shoes were plots against decent Americans. Plots perpetrated by worshipers of the devil. Worshipers who use and abuse children in their secret rites. And the couple told this woman about DASH and its mission." It sounds even better when she says it aloud than it did last night in the isolation of Kristin's room.

"The woman—who is she? Who are these people she met? I don't see what you're getting at." Antonia doesn't seem to share her enthusiasm for the scheme, or maybe it's just that she doesn't understand yet.

"Let's say she's a teacher who's dedicated her life to

making the world a safer place for children. Somehow, she gets involved with DASH. This teacher might learn about a pretty child who's been taken from her evil mother so her fine, upstanding grandparents can raise her in a good Christian home. She might even find out where the child is. *If* she can find out where DASH meets . . ."

"You—" Antonia can barely get the word out. She shakes her head furiously. "You can't do that. It's too dangerous."

"It might be. But if I don't hear from that caller, if the police don't have any news today, I'm going to contact DASH."

The coffee in Antonia's cup is untouched. She rolls the edge of her napkin between her fingers, presses her shoulders against the back of the wheelchair. "This is a foolish idea, Valerie. You can't put yourself in harm's way in order to protect your daughter. There's no point in that. You cannot do something so risky."

Nadia appears in the doorway, holding two plastic hangers with the shirt and skirt she'd whisked away to the laundry room earlier. "Here they are, Miss Valerie. All pressed and warm." She nods mournfully and then vanishes.

Good timing. Nadia's given her an excuse to interrupt what's beginning to look like a contest of wills with Antonia. "I'll be back in a few minutes," Valerie says as she sets her napkin on the table, "as soon as I get dressed."

The overture to *Carmen* is just ending as Valerie enters the study. Antonia is seated in front of the bay window, hands lying slack against her thighs as though she's letting the spirited melodies swell in prelude to a dance. Then her head turns toward the doorway and she gestures in the direction of the mahogany writing desk. "Hand me that binder in the top drawer, would you? The leather one."

Valerie pulls the binder from below a square ledger with the word ACCOUNTS embossed in gold in the center. Antonia runs her fingers along the first page, a transparent sheet with pockets, like a photo album, except that it's filled with credit cards.

"First thing tomorrow, I want you to go to

MaryBeth's Closet, on Seventh Avenue, next to the pottery store. I'll call ahead to say it's all right for you to use my card. If I were your age, I'd choose something with a little color near the neckline, not too much of course, but young people can carry it off. And while you're there, you might try on some shoes. Yours sound a bit worn down at the heels. It may be dangerously close to a cliché, but plenty of people still believe you can judge a person from their shoes."

"I don't understand. You want me to buy new clothes?" Antonia's generosity is touching. Except for the trinkets Johnny surprised her with five or six times that first year, no one's ever given her gifts, unless it was her birthday or Christmas.

"Of course. Whatever you need. All your things are still in the Klein woman's apartment, aren't they? So you need new clothes, undergarments, shoes. It gives me pleasure to share what I have with you." Her smile is broad; she's already pleased, it seems, by the very thought of Valerie's new attire. "Anyway, I want you to be as comfortable as you can at this awful time. Take the card, go to MaryBeth's tomorrow. When you come back, you can show me your treasures. It will do you good to have a bit of a distraction."

"Thank you, Antonia. That's really very kind." Even at the best of times, shopping has been more a necessary chore than a form of recreation. But it won't do to appear ungrateful, and she takes the card gently from Antonia's fingers.

Nadia, her coat half buttoned and a square black purse tucked under her arm, appears in the doorway. The woman is like a shadow, noiseless, coming and going unexpectedly. Her ruddy face has lost its color and her eyes are tiny brown targets in a sea of white. Valerie knows at once that this is about Joanna.

"What is it, Nadia?" Antonia asks.

"I was about to go out and there was a knock on the door. There's a gentleman here to see—"

Valerie flies from the room to the front foyer, stops mid-stride when she sees him.

Impossible.

She's cast her net for him, but the holes have been so big she's caught nothing. Now he's standing beside the hall table with his hands stuffed into his pockets. Unmistakably Johnny Starr, even though he's grown a beard and lost about twenty pounds of whiskey bloat. He's wearing neat jeans and a dark blue T-shirt, his arms muscled and firm beneath the short sleeves. His skin isn't waxy anymore, his blue eyes are clear, his hair gleaming and just short enough to avoid looking unkempt. He looks like the Johnny she met at Ruth Hoving's Fourth of July party years ago, older, a bit more uncertain perhaps, definitely sturdier.

"Valerie, oh, God." He shakes his head as though he's trying to wake himself up.

Nadia shuffles past them and shuts the door softly behind her.

"You still have amazing timing, Johnny. How did you find me?" she asks finally.

"Some NYPD detective, a woman named Gallagher, tracked me down through the painting contractor I work for. She told me what happened to Joanna. And to Esther. I'm so sorry, Val, I really am."

Someday, hearing Esther's name won't stab at her this way. "And Detective Gallagher told you I was here in Brooklyn?"

Johnny studies the pastel angels perched on an empty candy dish. "Took me a few minutes to realize she thought I had something to do with Joanna's disappearance. It got pretty hairy there for a while. Didn't help any that Francine—she's the woman I'm living with—ran away and Gallagher kind of picked up that something fishy was going on. Poor Franny thought it was the immigration cops after her. She's from Belfast, came here on a student visa and never went back. When she heard Gallagher identify herself, she climbed out the window and ran away. She's staying with a friend, but she's still afraid to come home." He runs his hand through his beard and sighs. "Anyway, as soon as Gallagher finished checking me out, I asked about you. But she wouldn't tell me where you were."

He's going round and round, not really answering her question. If Teresa Gallagher didn't reveal where she was, who did? And why didn't Russo tell her they'd found Johnny? Maybe they aren't compelled by law to tell her, but that's not the only measure of things. What other secrets are they keeping from her?

"You didn't answer me, Johnny." How many times in her life has she said that? But if he hears an echo of the past, Johnny doesn't seem to care.

"I called Lynn. I figured if anyone on the planet knew where you were, it was Lynn Hammond. She wasn't home, and I spoke to one of the boys. Luckily, she'd written your name and then Antonia Carrera's just next to it on a piece of paper and stuck it on the refrigerator with a magnet. Mike, Jr., I think it was. Anyway, he was very proud he figured it out. So here I am. We have to talk, Val."

His story is probably true. Johnny was never good at making things up. Unless that's another thing that's different since she last saw him.

"Let's not talk here. Wait a minute. I'll grab my purse and be right back."

Antonia's wheelchair is closer to the doorway than it had been earlier, near enough to the hallway for her to have overheard that awkward little reunion. From the pinched look on her face, she seems to be working herself up to deliver a speech, one that Valerie doesn't have the time to hear.

"I have to go out, Antonia. It's ten-fifteen now. If anyone calls, please tell them I'll be back by eleven-fifteen."

"Don't you let him fool you, Valerie. Even when I was your age, I knew that they come back full of apologies and promises, but it never works out the way they say it will." Antonia is intent on delivering her lecture, like a long-suffering mother addressing a wayward child. She's composed, unsmiling, absolutely authoritative. "That man out there might know a lot more than he's saying about what happened Friday night. You'd be better off not to go anywhere with him, but I know you will so I have one caution. You must think of yourself. And of Joanna."

. . . .

They sit on a bench, in the weak sunshine that falls between the branches. The cherry blossoms are even lovelier than she'd imagined, an innocent pink veined with white. Because it's the first nice Sunday in weeks, the Botanic Garden's paths are crowded.

"So you went to a little trouble to find me. I'm still not sure why, Johnny." If he's expecting her to console him about his daughter being kidnapped, he's going to have a long wait. She hasn't broached the subject of Martha and Lucas yet, hasn't even said their names in the twenty minutes it's taken to walk across the park.

"Look, Val . . . I'm not going to make excuses for myself. I don't blame you for keeping me at a distance. But there are a couple things I want you to know. I've been sober for almost ten months, I've had a decent job since August, and I've been living with Francine since five months after I left Taconic Hills."

How thoughtful of him to put her through two years of hell in order to straighten himself out.

"I'm glad for you, Johnny, but I have other things on my mind."

"Joanna. Funny . . . I made all those changes for myself, of course, but she's what got me started. I just kept thinking about her all the time, wondering what she looked like, what she was doing."

"We weren't hard to find. At least, not until November. All you had to do was pick up the phone. We could have worked out a visit. Why didn't you call us, write a letter, something?" She's mostly successful at keeping the scorn out of her voice.

"I had this stupid thought that I wouldn't be ready until I'd been clean for a whole year. All that time, I was wondering how I'd fit into her life. I mean, I kept thinking you were moving ahead with school, getting yourself set up for a decent future, and I didn't deserve to see her until I could say the same thing."

It actually makes some sense, what he's saying. She wants to pat his arm, but he's so stiff she's afraid he'd shatter at her touch.

"And now this. Maybe if I tried to see you a month ago, she'd be . . ." His voice trails off.

Her heart constricts; he's suffering too. She unfolds her hands from her lap, reaches for him.

"If I were around," Johnny says firmly, "this wouldn't have happened. That's what fathers do, isn't it, protect the children?"

sixteen

She's reeling with his words. All she can do is repeat, "Protect the children?"

Johnny hangs his head. "Look, I know I haven't done a thing for her. You've had the whole burden. And you've had all the joy, too. I was too messed up to even think about a child. I told you: I didn't want to do anything, to even try to get in touch with you, until I'd had a year sober and could prove that you could trust me to be part of Joanna's life. I've given it a lot of thought, Val, and the thing I see is that the world is full of dangers, risks, traps, big dark holes a kid can fall into. Parents have to teach their kids what those dangers are. I mean, that's only one part of being a parent but it's an important one. I . . ."

While he searches for words, Valerie examines his tidy little speech to see if it's a smooth gloss to cover up his reference to protecting children. Johnny's always been transparent, one of his virtues. He lacks guile, so that his feelings, even if they're childish or vague or magnified by alcohol, are right out there, in his words, his tone, his expression.

She wishes she could stop doing four things at once. Why can't she give up trying to figure out what he's really after, let go of her defensiveness, forget the past, and just deal with Joanna's situation?

"I need you to tell me straight out, Johnny. Are you

holding something back? Did you have anything to do with what's happened to Joanna?"

He fusses at a bottle cap with the toe of his shoe until it skitters under the bench. "Only in the way I said. That I wasn't available to be a real father and take care of my own daughter because I was too drunk or too involved in getting sober and making sure I steered clear of my past—you, Taconic Hills, my parents—while I was patching my life together."

This is the opening she needs, and she'd better take advantage of it before he gets too deep into confession and self-pity.

"About Martha and Lucas," she begins, and she describes what happened on Halloween, her voice sharp with the sting of outrage still undiluted in the telling and retelling of the same story so many times.

When she finishes reeling off the list of horrors they planted in her bedroom, Johnny Starr slams his open hand on the seat of the bench. "Sick! They're really sick, you know that, even more twisted than I thought."

It's still there, that short fuse that connects Johnny to Martha and Lucas, that same bright rage. Gently she says, "Maybe they thought I knew how to get in touch with you. They might have figured I'd try to get you to call them off. Maybe they were worried about what was happening to you and thought they could use me to find you."

"Me. Everything in their lives is because of me. I was always sure it was me, that when my father went off the deep end it was because I didn't do what he expected. He made me feel like I was some fourteen-year-old kid who couldn't sit with the grownups because I hadn't killed my first deer. Did you know that? That I had to sit with the little kids, every Thanksgiving, every Christmas, every time the whole family got together, because I wouldn't shoot a damn deer? That's why I never came home for holidays when I was in college. Until we got married. Even my father couldn't justify it after that.

"Anyway, the last time I spoke to him he said he had a job lined up for me. Working the fields at the Hotaling farm. That I needed to do some real work, sweat all the drink out of me, dedicate my life to God instead of to the pleasures of the flesh. All I wanted to do was hit him in his smug, judgmental face, grab my car keys, and roar out of the driveway." Johnny smiles ruefully. "Not that I had a car."

"So you haven't spoken to him since you left Taconic Hills?"

"I talked to him just after the divorce went through. That was the last time. It was the same old game, my father trying to make me feel guilty because I was upsetting him. I know better now, he can't make me feel anything. I do that on my own. And I'm not the one who sends him into a fury. He does it himself. He *chooses* to make me the excuse for everything in his life."

Lucas Starr is a master at pushing buttons, and over the years he's found all of Johnny's. "Vintage Lucas. He was putting the moves on you to get you to do things his way."

He smiles at her, shy, grateful, it seems, for her understanding. "Val, I don't want to spend all this time talking about my parents. Joanna's out there somewhere. The police haven't found her, but maybe there's something we can do without them. I don't know, some kind of . . ."

Johnny Starr still doesn't get it. "Joanna's disappearance—maybe Lucas engineered it to find you. Maybe that's what your father was after all along."

His head whips around, and he stares at her coldly.

Her words hang between them, and she wishes she could snatch them back. The man sitting beside her is neither the old idealistic Johnny she once loved nor the hostile, self-absorbed casualty of alcohol he became. He could be a messenger sent by Martha and Lucas, part of a Byzantine conspiracy so convoluted she feels herself getting lost.

"He's capable of that, isn't he?" The little jagged moon of white paint at the base of his thumbnail disappears as he runs his fingers through his beard. "I'm going to call him, feel him out."

That had been *her* intention, until the answering machine cut her short.

If she tells Johnny about the anonymous call, he can monitor Lucas's reaction. He can talk about *protecting the children* and listen carefully for a gasp, a choked response, an indignant protest-too-much tone that would indicate he'd rattled Lucas.

Except that Johnny might decide to call the police, and the caller might find out somehow and carry out his threat to harm Joanna.

"You sure you can handle talking to Lucas without becoming that gangly, uncomfortable boy again?" She hears the cruelty of doubt in her own voice.

"I can do it. I know what's important here." His eyes lock onto hers. "I need you to trust me, Val."

"Trust you? Based on one hour of repentance? I don't have time to conduct a character investigation. I have to find Joanna." There's the little matter of Esther's murder attached to the question of what happened to Joanna, but he seems to have forgotten that.

He rises from the bench and heads down the path toward the tulips, which make a splashy pink and white show around the edges of a fountain. His shoulders slump and his hands are shoved deep into his pockets. He looks like a child who just lost a baseball game.

She's curiously detached. She wants only one thing from Johnny Starr. If he can't—or won't—deliver, she'll find another way to get to Martha and Lucas.

When he heads back to her, his eyes are red but his shoulders are straight, his head erect.

"Come on, Val. You're asking me to prove to you in an hour that I want to find Joanna too," he says as he lowers himself to the bench. "I used to think getting sober was the hardest thing I'd ever do."

"You have to tell me now if you're willing to do whatever it takes. Because if you're not, we don't have much to talk about."

This time, she's the one who gets up, walks toward the fountain glittering with the reflections of the pennies that line the bottom, a copper mosaic of wishes. Make a wish, toss a coin. What nonsense. Make a wish and make it happen. That's more like it.

She doesn't hear the footsteps behind her, is only aware of the heat of his body close to hers.

"Anything." Johnny grips her shoulders and she tenses, a signal that he's on dangerous ground if he tries to touch her more intimately. "I'll do anything, Val, and if you're thinking that when it's over I'll try to take Joanna away from you, don't. You don't have to worry about that from me. Martha and Lucas, maybe, but not me. I wish it could have been the way we dreamed, Val, but I messed up, and now I have to try to fix it."

She wants to believe him. "You're willing to call your father? You're ready to come with me to the nearest pay phone and find out what Lucas has to say about Joanna?"

Why should she expect him to be more loyal to a child he's seen only once and an ex-wife who threw him out than he is to his own parents, even though he's aware of their manipulations, their self-serving righteousness? On the other hand, he *has* changed—even his walk is different, looser, as though he's more at ease in his own body. Still, she's been hurt too many times trying to predict what Johnny would do.

When he nods his agreement and reaches for her hand, she's shocked at how easy the fit is, how comforting the contact. "Let's go, then," she says, moving out of his reach and heading toward the heavy gates that lead to the street. "Before either of us changes our mind."

seventeen

"No, Martha, you've got to enter the password to get into the bulletin board. You can't just sign on. It's not magic, you know. A computer is a fool piece of equipment with wires and electricity and it only does what you tell it to."

And she'd better not look at him again with those big eyes asking for forgiveness. She'd done this, what, thirty times for sure, and she knew. Martha was nervous today, still upset by that snooping visit from Riley Hamm, but she had to remember to keep her head.

"There." She swiveled in her chair and looked up, imploring him for approval. Well, she'd earned it this time.

"Good. Now go right to the new posting, the one just below the calendar of events." The blinking cursor skated to the bottom of the screen. "What's the matter with you today, Martha? Go ahead, we need to get to where it says Operation Safe Haven."

Nodding, she hit a key and moved to the listing. "Now we want to open that file, right?"

Well, what did she think they were doing all this for, fun? Before he could answer, the phone rang. "Forget that. You go on and see what it says. Just copy it out exactly like you see it on the—" The noise of the damn phone was like a dentist's drill in his head.

"I know, Lucas. I remember."

He stalked out of the room, ready to pull the contraption out of the kitchen wall and be done with it, but he waited for the answering machine to announce that he couldn't come to the phone right now, waited to see if Miss High-and-Mighty Valerie would try again to get him to call her, the way she did yesterday. Leaving a fool message on his machine—and expecting him to hurry up and call her.

"Dad? It's me. Johnny. If you're there, please pick up. It's Johnny, Dad."

That was fast. Miss Valerie must have figured out a way to get in touch with him. Wouldn't be a big surprise if she'd known all along where John was. Lucas yanked the receiver off the hook. "Where are you?"

"I'm at a phone booth in Brooklyn. How are you? How's Mom?"

Lucas snorted. "If you cared, you'da been in touch before now. Let's not make small talk, son. Why'd you call?"

"I'm trying to find out what happened, Dad. With Joanna. You know anything about that?"

"I'll tell you the same thing I told Riley Hamm. Why doesn't her mother know where she is, that's the real question. Her and that Carrera woman she's staying with, I bet they're at the bottom of this whole thing." Maybe he'd gone too far with that one. He had to be more careful.

John's voice was like a finger pointing across the telephone lines. "You've spoken to Valerie about this?"

Was he slurring his words? If John were standing right in front of him, Lucas knew he'd be able to tell just by looking at his son's eyes whether or not the boy had been drinking. Never mind the smell, the *stink* of his breath, or whether he could put three words together without getting sloppy. It was those eyelids, half closed like he wanted to shut the world out, that gave him away. And gave Lucas the willies, seeing his son near out of his mind with drink. Boy needed to take himself back to church and get some teachings.

He was going to plant whatever seeds the good Lord handed him and make sure this time they grew right.

"I haven't spoken to that woman in months. Where are you? You think you can just call here out of the blue and get what you want without any single word of explanation, you got another think coming." No need to scare the boy off completely. He needed to be firm enough so his message got across, but he had to make John understand his father wasn't some unfeeling monster. "We've been real worried about you. Your mother prays to God every night that you'll call and say you're ready to come back. Where you been, John? What have you been doing?"

"I've been in the city. New York. We can talk about me some other time. I want to know if you know anything about Joanna. About her disappearance."

This was what they'd been warned to expect. No one understanding, everyone accusing, just because they couldn't find the way to God in their own lives. But John was doing exactly right now, asking after his own child, finally showing a little spine, taking some responsibility for his own life. Still, he'd played, so now he'd better be ready to pay.

"Maybe I do and maybe I don't. We can talk about that when you come up here. Maybe I can help you get your daughter back but you have to do something first. You know, you've been in what I'd call a skid, John. You prove yourself to me first. Quit drinking, get a job and keep at it." What should he say? Six months? No, that was too long, too risky. "Three months, say, and you go to church, too. I know you're a good boy at heart. Maybe this is all you need, a shock to your system to break you out of those habits you fell into after you married *her.*"

"This isn't going to work, Dad. It's blackmail. I'm not going to let you do that to me."

Total calm. The boy had total control, didn't even raise his voice. A flicker of anger licked at Lucas's gut. "Then we got nothing to talk about, do we?"

"I'd say we had a lot to talk about. Like what happened at Valerie's on Halloween. Like where my daughter is."

The old John would have been sputtering into the

phone, sounding all indignant, the way he used to when he was ten and Martha would go into his room for Sunday evening inspection. Always had been hard for that boy to accept that God and man had given the world rules to keep things running smooth.

Maybe John knew more than he was saying. But if he thought he could change everything with a single phone call . . .

"You're making a big mistake, lots of them. Besides, that's not the subject here, John. You're really paining your mother, you know that, don't you?" Lucas turned to see Martha, standing with her arms crossed under her breasts and watching him with a confused look on her face. "Now, you think about what I said. I'll call you in a couple of days to get your answer. What's your number?"

Martha handed him a pencil, then reached out for the phone. "Is that John? Oh, Lucas, let me talk to him."

He waved her away. "I didn't catch that. What did you say?"

"I said, you still haven't answered me about Joanna. You know where she is, don't you? Dad, if anything happens to her—"

"You trying to say something, John? Because unless you can come up with a good reason for me to stand here and listen to your accusations, I have better things to do." That ought to be clear enough.

"She's a baby, you know, Dad?" John was still talking in that spooky, quiet voice. "I want you to tell me where she is. She's just a kid. She can't argue her own case and tell anyone what she wants. It's up to the adults in her life to protect her."

Lucas started to break the connection but his hands were trembling. Did John know what he was saying? Couldn't let him think he'd hit his mark, had to say something. He cleared his throat. "You wouldn't know a thing about protecting children, mister. If you cared so much, you would have stuck around to watch over her. Now don't call here again, you hear me? Unless you're ready to stop these accusations and talk civilized."

Now he did slam the receiver back into the cradle.

Lucas Starr was not about to stand around and listen to all that bull piss, and from his own son, too. He had to report in to George Perry in New Jersey. And Martha better not start her snuffling and whining. He was in no mood for that.

eighteen

If only he would stop looking at her, she could manage to finish her meal without feeling like some exotic creature in a glass cage.

"The coffee is particularly strong, darling. Would you like some cream to take the edge off?" Charles Babcock's voice, barely audible above the polite chatter at nearby tables, trembled with adolescent shyness. He held the silver pitcher as though it were an offering, incontrovertible proof of the depth of his devotion.

Kristin shook her head, swallowed the bitter coffee.

He half rose and leaned across the table to brush her cheek with his warm, dry lips. "You seem tired, darling. We can skip the party tonight, if you like. Is your throat bothering you again?"

So solicitous, all that concern flooding his eyes. And he was handsome, even with his forehead wrinkled in worry. What was the matter with her, anyway, that she couldn't simply accept his love and delight in the pampering?

"I feel much better, Charles." She tried on a brighter smile. "No, even if it's just for a little while, it's important we show up at the party. Berger and Rienzi will be there. The last two holdouts on the board. You still want to convince them that the merger is a good idea, right? It struck me last night that they're both heavily involved in the pharmaceutical industry. You can show them how the technology you'll be developing in the new company will benefit them. By providing them with capacity to store the massive amounts of data they need to track during testing protocols, for example."

She'd been mulling over the problem, intrigued by the challenge of selling two smart men on a completely unnecessary change that would consolidate Charles's power on the board of directors. Kristin took a sip of water from the crystal goblet; she had more to say, much more.

"Your throat *is* bothering you," Charles said, frowning. "I promise we'll leave early. I'll have you home by ten."

"I feel fine," she snapped. "I told you that."

She wouldn't explain, for the hundredth time, how much difference it would make if he would truly *listen* to her. Perhaps if he allowed himself to discuss actual ideas with her, the ending of their story might be more to his liking.

He peered at her over his glasses. "I hope you're not still upset over our canceled vacation. Because I'm not, not in the slightest. Aruba is no fun if you can't go to the beach and stay up late in the casinos. Of course it made no sense to go if you weren't feeling well."

God, what accounted for the changes in men like Charles when they fell in love? What sapped their intelligence, drained away their strength of will, the sense of purpose that made them captains of industry and champions of the current ruthless version of democracy?

"Honestly, Charles, I'm much better," she insisted.

He graced her with his aristocratic, thin-lipped smile, equal parts victory and disbelief at his good fortune in being with her. "We have a lifetime of vacations to look forward to, anyway. I hope it's not this thing with Antonia that's bothering you."

Kristin searched his face. "This thing with Antonia?"

"She called me at the office to ask if you'd gone away after all. Said she'd left several messages on your answering machine to thank you for taking care of the errand she'd sent you on." His hand wrapped around hers. "You must set limits, Kristin. You cannot allow her to go on thinking of you as an employee at her beck and call. Now, if you want me to say something to her on your behalf I'll—"

"Ssh, Charles. Don't worry about Antonia. She needed a favor and I was glad to do it. I don't expect she'll get confused about who I am to her. We're both perfectly clear about how much our relationship has changed." Kristin smoothed her skirt. "Charles, you're staring. I'm going to the ladies' room. Be right back."

"I'll miss you," he said, clutching her hand a little too tightly before he released her and sat back against the plush banquette.

Kristin rewarded his restraint with a smile, wriggled away from the table, and threaded her way between the damask-draped tables through the bustling restaurant.

That smile was about all he was going to get from her tonight. The lie was wearing her down. Antonia had been wrong: acting the part hadn't made her sufficiently fond of Charles Babcock. If only she could convince herself to love this man who courted her with expensive presents and trips to lazy, sun-kissed islands . . .

Maybe it had worked that way for all the other women Antonia had managed to marry off. For Kristin, the pretense had never been transformed, by magic or by will, into truth.

The ladies' room attendant smiled listlessly when Kristin walked in. "If you need anything, just let me know," she said, nodding to the array of creams and cosmetics on the marble counter before she resumed staring at her hands.

Kristin yanked a tissue from the plastic holder, blotted the shine on her nose, dusted her cheeks with powder. Beneath all his polish, at least Charles Babcock was a decent man.

Antonia, however, was a different story. That was outrageous, calling Charles at his office. Charles shouldn't be the one to do it, but Antonia had to be set straight. The woman had to understand she couldn't have it both ways. She'd been the one to declare the old agreement void.

For all those years in the brownstone across from Prospect Park, Kristin had thought of herself as a sailor charting a life course that responded to even the slightest change in the elements. Antonia had been the tide and the wind.

But she'd become a raging hurricane when Kristin said she planned to decline Charles's proposal.

You must marry him to ensure your future. You're nearly thirty, you know.

As though thirty were some magic number, and her discomfort with his fawning attention was of no consequence. She did appreciate his decency, his reserve, the tasteful, carefully chosen objects with which he surrounded himself. But she was going to decline, with regret and with the hope that they might continue their friendship, she'd told Antonia, because she didn't love Charles Babcock.

Love. Antonia's voice had turned cold as she described how she fell in love when she was twenty-two with Willard Kinsolving, a poet who had run away from the family farm in Kansas, seeking the spirit of Walt Whitman in Brooklyn, finding Antonia instead in front of one of the used-book stalls outside the Strand.

Ten months later, convinced that her passion for Willard was destined to die a little at a time and leave her impoverished in soul and bank account, Antonia had married Miguel Carrera, whose family owned coffee plantations in three South American countries.

Even that first year, it was clear that, other flaws aside, Miguel Carrera drank imported Russian vodka prodigiously, expansively, as he did everything. Kept drinking for six years. Had been drinking since noon and all through the afternoon of the winter day he ordered his pregnant young wife into the car, drove to the airfield, and declared that they were going to Montreal for dinner. He loved his twin-engine plane, which he flew into a snowy mountain in Vermont, killing himself and their unborn child, and rendering Antonia's eyes useless and her legs paralyzed.

Twenty-six years ago: the year Kristin started nursery school.

She'd learned a lot in those years, some of which Antonia had taught her, none of which made it quite clear what exactly she should be doing to turn this mess around.

nineteen

When Johnny leaves her to return to Manhattan, she slips into character, tries it on to see what fits and what might need alteration. Crossing the park, she practices walking, thinking, reacting the way *she* would. She'll become that schoolteacher making inquiries about DASH, anxious to ally herself with an organization that cares deeply about children. It's only a small step from the truth.

Maybe she won't have to go that far, if Johnny can convince his parents to share their secrets.

She's fumbling in the bottom of her purse for the key when a cat bounds across her path and lands in a profusion of tulips blooming in a small patch of dirt surrounded by a fence of iron fleur-de-lis, the spearlike points protecting the tiny yard next door. Brilliant reds and yellows on bright green stalks, the tulips remind her of tropical birds in a topless cage, and she wishes she could watch them fly away into the sky.

"That's better."

Startled, she turns to see the young man who scolded her the other day for not being cheerful enough to suit him. He's wearing a brown uniform and toting a small carton on one shoulder; a clipboard dangles from his other hand.

"They look like parrots, don't they?" She puts the key in the lock, feeling for the right fit, then turns around, aware that the young man's still standing behind her on the street. "Can I help you with something?"

"This is for Kristin Denby." He taps the label on the carton. "I know she doesn't live here anymore, but I was passing by and I remembered about this package. I mean, it's Sunday and all, but I was right here. Anyway, I wonder if Mrs. Carrera wants to accept the package or what. Maybe she knows where I should forward it. Or should I just send it back to Bloomingdale's?"

"I'll take it." She rests the clipboard against the box and scrawls her signature in the space he indicates with his pen.

"So now I know your name. Nice to meet you, Valerie . . . what does this say?"

She's already written it, line fourteen, just as he requested. There's no harm in saying it aloud, certainly. "Valerie Vincent."

"I'm Cameron Zax. My real name and my stage name. I'm studying what it's like to be a UPS driver for this great role in a new play that's opening on Broadway in—" He frowns and backs away, then offers her his hand. "I'm one of the lucky ones—an actor with a day job. Listen, I'm sorry for ragging you the other day about not smiling. That was really out of line. Anyway, I'll just leave this here. I have miles to go before I sleep."

"And not too many promises to keep, I hope." A normal exchange, amazing. A conversation, however brief, that's not loaded with the possibility of danger or hope. "Apology accepted."

He skips down the steps, half running to his van as though he's excited about whatever adventure the next stop will bring. Nice to know someone still feels that way.

She pushes the door open and sets the package on the table in the hall.

"There you are, Valerie." Antonia whirs into the doorway. "I expected you twenty minutes ago."

"I guess I walked the long way." To give herself time alone, to think without anyone asking questions about her daughter or her past, to be where she might see trees and flowers, even if they're shrouded in the soot the city spews in great clouds over everything. "There's a package in the hall. For Kristin. Maybe I should call her, let her know it's here. It's from Bloomingdale's."

"No need." Her hand drifts to her forehead in a gesture that's the first sign of one of Antonia's headaches. "She phones me often. Prenuptial jitters, although I don't understand why. Charles Babcock is such a lovely man. I'll tell her about the package the next time she calls."

"Any calls for me?" Valerie knows the answer, realizes she doesn't really have to ask.

"Of course not. I would have told you right away, wouldn't I, my dear? Tell me about your walk."

What she's really asking about is her time with Johnny. How close to the mark was the warning that he might know about what happened Friday night, that's what Antonia really wants to know.

"I don't think Johnny has a clue about Joanna's disappearance, Antonia. And I'm pretty sure he hasn't spoken to his parents in a very long time. We called them from a phone booth and Johnny asked right out if they knew anything about Joanna's kidnapping. But they just stonewalled."

"Did you ask him about that awful telephone call?"

"No, I decided . . . That's wrong. I haven't really decided anything. Maybe the call *is* some kind of test, to see whether I can be trusted. I'm still not sure what I should do about it."

The pearls at her throat glimmer with pink lights as Antonia shifts in her chair. "I'd say you've made a decision, and a wise one. To do nothing. To wait for further contact. Tell me, my dear, have the police said whether you can go back to the Klein woman's apartment?"

"Not as long as they consider it a crime scene."

Antonia sighs. "Well, let me know, will you? I'll arrange for Carl to go with you. You'll need a car to collect your things and Joanna's and bring them back here so you can finally settle in. I imagine you have quite a bit of—"

"We won't be staying here, Antonia. I just want to find my daughter and take her back home to Taconic Hills. In fact," she adds gently, "maybe you should start looking for someone else. I could call an agency and you can start interviewing. . . ."

Shallow little breaths lift Antonia's chest. "I've got Nadia for emergencies. You're in no state to make such a decision. I refuse to make plans that involve your leaving. This is your home, Valerie."

Antonia simply won't hear what she's saying.

"And I do hope you've abandoned that foolish idea you told me about this morning, Valerie."

Foolish? Maybe it's *risky*, but DASH still looks like her best hope for finding Joanna. At least it's something to *do*. "No. No, I'm pursuing it. I have to. Can I get you something for your headache, Antonia?"

"Don't dismiss me that way." She says it softly, as though she's asking Nadia for more coffee. After each word, a pause that's long enough to indicate the control is hard-won, or perhaps it's an underscoring of her displeasure. "You're emotionally vulnerable now, and even if you weren't, from everything you've said these people won't be easy to fool. If they discover that you've tricked them . . . You mustn't do this."

"And I can't sit around and do nothing! It's my daughter's life, Antonia. I have to do what I can." She runs out of the room, trembling with anger, ignoring Antonia's voice as it follows her up the stairs calling her name.

By the time she's splashed cold water on her face, she knows what she'll say when she goes downstairs to apologize for her outburst. *I'm just not used to the idea that someone in my life cares so much about what I do, someone whose advice makes me question my actions. I didn't mean to shout at you that way.*

But she'll say it later, when she's sure she won't erupt again. After the jitters are gone and the impulse to slam doors has died. After she's called Kevin Murchison.

He answers on the second ring.

"Mr. Murchison, it's Valerie Vincent."

"Hey, it's Kevin, all right?"

"All right, *Kevin*. Do you have a few minutes? I need a little information. DASH must have meetings here in the city, right?"

She lays out her plan.

She'll be a teacher devoted to saving children. A woman haunted by her encounter with a group of Satan-

worshipers when she was a child. A person the members
of DASH will trust with information about rescued children.

"I'm glad I took your advice and stayed away from
the press," she says finally. "Nobody will connect me to
Joanna, nobody will know who I am. Will you help me
find out when and where these people get together next?"

His long silence is broken by a gust of laughter. "I'm
sorry, Ms. Valerie Vincent, but I'm laughing at myself. I've
been crazy to get into one of their meetings but they know
me, and it's impossible. And you propose to go in there,
when it's the last thing in the world you'd choose to do on
your average weekday evening. But if anyone I've met in
the past eight years has the brains and the *cojones* to pull
this off, I do believe it's you."

"So where do they meet?" she demands.

"You're not up to that yet. First problem is you're
missing a husband. A single woman will trip their alarms.
I can't be your husband because they know me. Mitch
Russo can't do it because he's been in the papers a couple
of times in the past three, four years. You have some guy
in your life you can absolutely, solidly, completely trust?"

Her laugh is bitter. "Is there anyone in the world *you*
feel that way about?" Johnny. How clever of him to show
up just now. How perfect, confronting his parents on the
phone while she was standing beside him. Too clever,
maybe. Too perfect? Her mind races with other possibilities, Peter Hoving, Mike Hammond, Paul Cooper, but it's
not like asking someone to mail a letter for you on their
way to the supermarket. "I'll have to think about it."

"I can't help you out on that one. All I can tell you is
it's critical you have a man with you. Who he is is up to
you."

"Okay, assume I have someone." One thing at a time.
It will come to her, the answer is waiting for her to find it.
"What else?"

"You have to look like you're about to step into a
church in Iowa. No jeans, no Doc Martens, no Cleopatra
eye makeup. Conservative. Totally untrendy. You know
what I mean. I better check the time of their next meeting,
but unless they changed it, it's this Tuesday. Second Tues-

day of the month. You do understand that you could be in real danger if you're discovered, don't you? This is not some game of dress-up you're playing here."

She's already gone over that, had the risks pointed out to her, no, *shouted* at her, by Antonia. "I'll take my chances. I have to find Joanna. So, if I do get myself a husband, does my story work? I can say I found out about DASH from those people in Montana, the Murphy family."

"Tell them you heard about DASH from a friend of the Murphys'. I remember someone, Kitty Stevens. Say she told you about Operation Safe Haven when you were passing through Montana four years ago. And she also told you where to look for notices of New York meetings. Hang on, I have to check something."

Maybe Peter Hoving would be the right choice. Peter's smart, steady, will never tell anyone except Sarah.

And it's not fair to ask him to risk exposing himself to DASH.

"Okay, yeah, they still put their notices on the back page of the *Village Voice*. Ironic, right? All those old-time liberals would crap hammers and sickles if they knew what DASH was. The next meeting is day after tomorrow. There's one in Manhattan and one in Brooklyn. You think you can be ready by then? If you don't get this together— husband, clothes, everything—don't do it, Valerie."

It's the first time he's used her name, and she feels somehow safer. "I'll be ready," she says firmly. "Is there an address in that notice?"

"Here's what's going to happen. You'll call the number in the ad. If no one's there you'll get a message telling you when to call back. They'll ask you a bunch of questions about how you heard about them, what you believe, and they'll tell you where to go. It's a different place each month. They don't encourage drop-ins. You got all that?"

"I guess. And you're sure I can't do this alone?"

"Absolutely. Things might move very quickly, and you don't want to be caught short. Don't even pretend you know anything about DASH except they're concerned about the welfare of children. Play dumb. I know that's a stretch but try anyway."

She laughs as she hangs up.

Her hand is still on the receiver when the phone rings. *Her caller?* She snatches it up, says hello at the same moment Antonia does.

"Valerie? It's me. Johnny."

She hears a soft click as Antonia breaks the connection.

"Do you have a minute?" Johnny Starr asks. "I've been thinking about that phone call. About my father. Maybe he won't try his snort-and-bellow routine if I'm right in his face. I can pick you up in half an hour."

"You want me to go to Taconic Hills with you?" A two-hour drive up, two hours back. Time enough to tell him about DASH, to brief him on the story they'll both have to have down cold, no flaws, no missing pieces. "I'll be ready. Half an hour."

twenty

The only conversation has been about Joanna.

Johnny has asked a few questions, and she's answered him, but mostly they've watched the landscape change. As they've gotten farther from the city, the yards have grown more spacious, the trees denser, and the silence thicker.

The sun is dipping toward the far hills; they want to get to Warren's Rock Road before Martha and Lucas sit down to dinner, which they surely still do at exactly six every evening.

Johnny has borrowed a small truck from a plasterer he knows, an old Ford with enough dings and quirks to look as though it's done its fair share of country work. She's borrowed a little hope from her own shrinking supply.

They're well into Dutchess County, flying up the Taconic State Parkway, only five minutes from the Pine Plains exit that will bring them to the road to Taconic Hills, when Johnny says, "You really think my parents are clever enough to kidnap Joanna and figure out a way to hide her from the police?"

It's time for him to know.

She can't tell him about the phone call, not yet. And she won't mention the meeting until she's sure he can be trusted. Lucas and Martha aren't the only ones whose reaction she'll be watching this evening.

This little jaunt to the country will be a test of another sort, one that experience has taught her Johnny might fail. In which case she'll have to find someone else to stand beside her at the DASH meeting, two days away.

She choses her words carefully, remembering Kevin Murchison's warnings. She tells him about DASH, careful to give him only as much information as she thinks he needs to know.

"I don't get it. These DASH people snatch kids out of their homes? Because they think their parents are going to turn them into some kind of Satanic robots?" He's incredulous—or, at least, he's very convincing.

"I'll show you the articles if you don't believe me. Kevin Murchison's been writing about them for years."

"This Murchison—maybe he's exaggerating, you know, to make a better story. I never read—" And then he stops, mouth agape, and turns to her. "You think my mother and father . . ."

"I don't know, Johnny. Maybe. They could be. But we can't accuse them. We have to be careful. Murchison says when these people smell exposure they're even slicker about keeping kids hidden."

He slows for the exit, his eyes fixed on the road.

She should have told him sooner. He has less than ten miles to absorb the facts about DASH; she's had days, entire nights, to let the idea sink in.

Rolling fields slip by, green streaks splashed against the blur of cloudless sky. When a sprawling white farmhouse winks from behind a stand of tamarack pines, the threat of tears pricks her eyes.

Martha and Lucas Starr took so much away from her, and she's angry at herself for letting it happen.

Johnny glances away from the road to look at her, and she shifts in her seat, her back to him as she peers out the side window. "What?" he says, still watching her when she turns to meet his gaze.

"I miss it here. I couldn't let myself think about it while I was trying to get my paper done, and now . . . well, I haven't thought about anything much except Joanna and Esther. But I do miss it. More than I realized. I feel so stupid. Crying about *scenery,* of all things." The tears are real, her face is damp with them, and she wishes she hadn't done this now.

He reaches across the seat, the way he used to for no reason at all; his hand stops just short of touching her. She wants to comfort him, but she can't let him use this terrible situation to erase the mistakes of his past with a loving gesture.

"You think you'd like to come back here? When this is all settled, I mean." He grasps the steering wheel again; he's been looking at her instead of the road for too long.

"Yes. I don't know if it will be Taconic Hills exactly, but somewhere nearby." If moving back here means having Martha and Lucas for neighbors, she'll find another town. But, yes, her heart is here, where she can let winter coerce her into solitude and summer conspire to keep her in the garden until the sun has disappeared behind the tired old mountains to the west.

No need to ask him if he plans to return to his ancestral home. The answer is obvious. It's right for him to be in a city. Funny, she hasn't recognized until now that his paintings throb with city colors. Even before he went to Manhattan, his basic palette of grays and blacks, shot through with those red or white or yellow slices of pure energy, vibrated with a kinetic power that's missing in Taconic Hills.

When they reach the intersection that marks the center of Pine Plains, she's assailed by doubt.

"Hold on, Johnny. Pull over and let me make a quick phone call, okay?"

The light changes. As he slips the truck into first gear, he looks down at his watch. "It's five-thirty."

"I know. I won't be long. I just want to call Antonia and tell her I won't be back for dinner." *And I want to find out if there's been another call. And I want to postpone what's coming.* She gathers enough change to make the long-distance call as the truck lurches into the parking lot of Peck's Market.

Johnny pulls into a spot near the store entrance, and she hops down to the blacktop, runs to the pay phone, dials and tosses the coins hurriedly down the slot. From the cab of the truck, Johnny watches a young man with

two school-age children as they head into the store, but
she can't tell from his face whether he's feeling longing or
contempt or recognition.

When Antonia answers, she says, "It's Valerie. I'm out
with Johnny. I didn't want you to worry. I'm not exactly
sure when I'll be back but it might be as late as ten."

"I'm not keeping track, my dear. You come and go as
you must. I'll see you in the morning." Then a click, and
Antonia is gone.

She's still angry, that's clear from her voice. There
wasn't even time in that terse exchange to ask whether any
calls have come in, but Antonia surely would have said so,
wouldn't have hung up so quickly if the anonymous caller
had made a second contact.

The truck idles noisily; she climbs into the cab, and
Johnny pulls onto the road behind a station wagon piled
with kids and groceries. "You can't even say the name of
this group to your parents, okay, Johnny?"

He doesn't answer. She almost asks him to turn back,
forget the whole thing. But it's too late. He knows about
DASH, knows the dangers. She told him because she believed he would want to protect his daughter, and now she
has to see this confrontation through. She can't control
Johnny Starr; she can only pray that she was right to trust
him.

She barely notices when they pass the Taconic Hills
General Store and the Historical Society building, doesn't
comment when Ben Yarnell, the editor of the *Taconic
Journal*, squints with open curiosity at the truck as they
drive by.

When they pull into the driveway of the Starrs' white
frame house, she's calm. Like a camera, she's going to
record in her mind everything she sees, everything she
hears them say or not say.

The boxy Cape Cod sits on a hillock of green. The
colonial blue of the shutters has faded a little, but the
leaning oak that shades the living room tilts at the same
funny angle, and the hedge beside the path leading to the
front door has been kept trimmed so that it's still exactly
three feet tall. Even the white sheets and towels on the line

in the back look as though they might have been hanging there the day she left.

Before Johnny's out of the truck, Martha appears in the doorway, her ample body blocking the entrance to her home. Her face registers first confusion, then surprise, then the delight that Valerie has dreamed about in the past two days, the sheer joy of seeing her child again after she thought that might never happen.

"Johnny!" Martha's found her voice, but she can't seem to move. Her hands are thrust into the pockets of the yellow checked apron she's wearing atop a shapeless, colorless dress.

And then Lucas is standing beside his wife, and the twilight turns steely. He elbows Martha out of the way, then spreads his legs wide and plants his hands on his hips.

"What's *she* doing here?"

She's here to uncover secrets. Valerie pushes open the door and hops out onto the gravel, returning his glower with a curt nod. Johnny has come around the truck to stand next to her, his shoulder touching hers.

"Can we come inside?" he asks, his voice controlled, neutral, eerily casual.

"You can come inside if you're ready to reconsider what we talked about this morning." His face an alarming red, Lucas shakes off Martha's hand on his arm. He's rigid with anger.

"Then maybe we better do our business here." Johnny takes one step and then another, gravel crackling under the hard soles of his city shoes.

Martha doesn't seem able to move.

They're not responding to Johnny, but maybe that's because he hasn't said anything provocative. "This is ridiculous. Johnny and I are here to talk about Joanna."

Not yet. She can't say the words until she's close enough to see every twitch of a reaction.

"Nothing to talk about." Lucas holds his position in front of his wife, as though he has to shield her from the horrible menace in the yard.

How do you engage an adversary who refuses to admit there's a war going on? She thinks about flamethrowers or bombs, signals that Lucas and Martha wouldn't be able to ignore. Maybe they'll have to practice a little guerrilla warfare . . .

Johnny advances another step toward the battleground, hands in his pockets. "Yes, we do. We have a lot to talk about, Dad."

She's about to say something when Johnny reaches back for her hand and squeezes it. She understands—he wants to take the lead. That's what Lucas will expect, that's what he'll want, and she'd be foolish to disturb the tension that's strung between her ex-husband and his parents, drawing them closer in painfully small steps.

"You got that one right, mister. But you don't want to do that now, do you? You don't want to talk about coming back to the Lord's path. So, the way I see it, we got squat to talk about."

"I can't let you do that, Dad. You can't turn this into something that's about me. Valerie's right. This is about Joanna. Joanna is missing. A woman's dead. I'm not saying you're responsible, but I get the feeling you know more than you're letting on."

Lucas gives no indication he's heard Johnny's words. He stands there, like the oak tree only straighter, no bend, no tilt, as though his feet have suddenly grown roots that go down so deep he'll never move, even in a gale.

Johnny lets go of her hand. He strides the last couple of steps that separate him from the two people in the doorway. If he can't control the rage that's making his gait so stiff . . . but he passes Lucas and wraps his arms around Martha and presses his face against hers.

Lucas pounces. Both hands on Johnny's shoulders, he yanks his son away. "You stop that! Your tricks aren't going to do you no good!"

Martha is frozen, bewildered.

It's up to Johnny; he's the key. For a moment Valerie's sure he's going to swing his clenched fist at Lucas but his hand drops and he takes a step back.

"I'm sorry, Mom." His voice is soft, and he reaches for Martha again, touches her sleeve. "I'm sorry for the pain I've caused you."

"Oh, Johnny." Martha swipes at her eyes, her cheeks

wet with streaming tears. "Just tell him you're going to go to church. That's all he wants."

Johnny shakes his head. "I can't. I can't lie. That's not what I'm going to do. That's not the only way for me to serve what's right and good. Where's Joanna, Mom? Where is she?"

Lucas bounds down the steps and heads for the truck. Directly for Valerie.

He's not going to provoke her into doing something she'll regret—but she won't allow him to run her down, either.

"What're you doing here?" Circles of white rim his dark pupils, his nostrils flare, his mouth quivers with fury. "I thought you were out of his life for good."

Now. "We're here because it's our burden to protect the children."

Martha's hand drops to her mouth and her eyes widen. She pulls the screen door open and stumbles inside.

"What are you talking about?" Lucas thrusts his face closer. "You think letting your child get taken away is protecting her? You think you protected *my* child by driving him to drink?"

"Tell me where my daughter is." It's a kind of trance, she knows it, and she's glad, because it allows her to stay in the same spot, to speak without shouting Joanna's name or Esther's. She can't tell, she just can't tell what those words and that burning stare mean.

"If you'da done your job right, if you'da paid attention, she wouldn't be gone." Johnny's father whirls around and stalks back to the stairs.

His words are like a knife.

"It's her fault—that dead woman, Joanna, all of it. If only—"

"Don't talk to her like that." Johnny is blocking Lucas's way, keeping him from going back into the house. Martha is only a shadow behind the screen door as the two men face off. Johnny's voice edges into a shout. "You can't bully people into doing what you want. You can't trick them into godliness. It doesn't work that way."

And then he walks away.

Lucas stares after Johnny, openmouthed. "John Starr!

John, you come back here. John Matthew Starr!" His head whips around as Martha pushes open the door and reaches for his arm, but he brushes her away and starts down the stairs. "You ungrateful, unholy sonofabitch. You come back here!"

By the time Lucas stomps to the gravel drive, Johnny has started the truck and Valerie is rolling up the window.

As they pull onto the blacktop road, she can see Martha in the rearview mirror, sagging against the door-frame, her face slick with tears. Alone in the driveway, Lucas raises his fist at the departing truck, his mouth wide and his hair blown into sharp spikes by the soft spring wind.

monday

twenty-one

The voices rise furiously, two women hurling accusations that the other is lying, has always lied, can never be trusted.

A few minutes before nine and Antonia is at it again after a two-day silence, tuned to the hype-and-heartbreak on the television in her bedroom, where Nadia has just deposited a breakfast tray. How can she bear to listen to all that wretchedness so early in the day?

Valerie blocks out the noise, retraces her own thoughts, remembers.

They're going to do it.

Yesterday's telephone call to DASH went well; tomorrow night, she and Johnny will smile and bow and scrape and lull the people at that meeting into telling them about Joanna. Surely one evening with DASH will turn up more than the "hundreds of man-hours" Russo said the police have put in on the case. He'd dragged out that figure to try to placate her this morning when she phoned for an update. Was Russo including Teresa Gallagher's time in that calculation?

". . . still have no suspects in the murder of Esther Klein."

She races down the hall to Antonia's room, listening for Joanna's name, but the volume has been turned down.

"Did they mention Joanna?" Her daughter's name lodges in her throat.

Frowning, Antonia nudges her dark glasses, fusses with the pillow behind her head. "No, not a word. I must say, I find it odd. Doesn't your detective think it will be easier to find your daughter if they make more of it in news broadcasts?"

Relief or disappointment: Valerie isn't sure what she feels about Russo's continued silence to the media. She explains Murchison's theory to Antonia as the bright voice of the weather forecaster promises sunshine. "Part of me still wants to see her face plastered all over the news. Maybe it *would* help."

"They're the experts. You must have faith in that."

Even though Antonia has raised her voice to be heard above the television, the note of sympathy is unmistakable, welcome after that argument the day before.

Impulsively Valerie says, "I'm sorry, Antonia. It was terribly rude of me to blow up at you yesterday morning. I've been so—"

"Shh. Please. Don't do this to me."

So, she's not even going to let her finish, is so upset and insulted that the gap between them can't be closed.

But Antonia points the remote control at the television, clicks it off, and turns toward Valerie. "I'm the one who must apologize. You're under such strain, and then I make it more difficult by arguing with you. I'm so very sorry, my dear. It's just that I can't bear the thought of anything happening to you. I don't know what I'd do if . . . Please forgive me."

A thick lump swells in her throat; Valerie clasps the trembling hand. When she can speak again, she says, "If you're not careful, Antonia, you're going to make me cry. I'm so sorry to burden you with my problems. Maybe I shouldn't talk about—"

"No!"

The sound is like a slap, harsh and startling. Reflexively Valerie withdraws her hand.

Antonia continues. "That would be awful for both of us. When you went off with that man the second time, I was sure you were so angry with me you'd never come back. It was such a relief when you called. If you keep things from me, I'll know something is wrong, and I'd only be able to guess the worst. I'd hear it in your voice, in the way you walk across a room. No, Valerie, that would be cruel, don't you see?"

Oh yes, she understands too well the subtle torture of living with someone who mutters answers to even the simplest questions and shuffles from room to room and pushes food around his plate, or slams doors and taps his foot relentlessly when he's supposed to be reading.

Johnny was a master of body language, and she struggled to translate for years, at first trying to guess and finally asking what was wrong and always getting the same response. Nothing. Nothing. And the rest of it, the why-are-you-asking-such-a-dumb-thing, that reverberates in that one word. She doesn't intend to do that to Antonia, who has been so good to her.

"I'm sorry for snapping at you. There *is* something I want you to know: Johnny's coming with me to a DASH meeting. Kevin Murchison says if Johnny and I present ourselves as a couple who believe that God has sent us to help children, we'll be okay.

"There's only one problem. If the anonymous caller is from DASH, I can't give them your telephone number. How could Valerie Vincent, Joanna's mother, have the same number as some sweet, inquiring schoolteacher from Montana? They'd know right away, don't you see? So if it's okay with you, I'd like to ask Nadia and Carl if I can give DASH *their* number. It will mean changing the message on their machine, at least for a while, but I can't think of any other way to keep DASH from getting suspicious."

Antonia shrugs. "They're out taking care of some errands for me right now. I have no objection, as long as they don't mind. I expect they'll be back in a couple of hours."

"Then that's the last little piece. Johnny and I have some details to go over, but I really believe we'll be ready. I've been thinking a lot about how we have to act at that meeting."

"Fervent." That's all she says, but it's a sign that Antonia has accepted the inevitable.

"Yes, I suppose that's what we have to convey. That we're pious people who—"

"Not pious. You don't want to set up a holiness competition, if you see what I mean. Not pious but fervent and willing to suspend your own judgment in deference to the will of the group." She's nodding, as though she's turned the words over in her mind and found them sound. Antonia is in her element, giving advice about propriety. "Miguel knew so many different people from his business dealings, and I met a lot of them during the few years we had together. You'd be surprised how many people need clearly defined rules and identifiable enemies. That way, if they fail at something, they can find fault outside themselves. I know how those people think. You must be well-mannered and narrow-minded."

Antonia has neatly labeled the ideas she and Johnny discussed; remembering her words will make the act easier to pull off. "Low key, I think. I don't want to say more than I have to because that would appear rude, and besides, I don't want to make a mistake and give myself away."

"Good, excellent. And you mustn't rush around. It's not ladylike to hurry. Be calm and deliberate. You remember Mrs. Dillon, the woman in the blue bedroom in East Hampton? Think about her, become her, and you'll be halfway there." Antonia is enjoying the game.

Mrs. Dillon. The woman who shrank as though she'd been physically assaulted when Antonia told the story of Miguel Carrera standing up at a black-tie banquet to announce that he hadn't yet been served his main course when everyone else was already up to dessert.

"Oh, Lord, if I have to become Mrs. Dillon, I hope it's a very short meeting." Valerie laughs, and the last frozen layer of tension between them melts away.

"I'm sure you've already thought about your appearance. You must wear simple lines and unobtrusive colors." Her cheeks glow and her words tumble out as her excitement mounts. This is Antonia's forgiveness, and it's welcome. "Good fabric, simple styles, no display of skin. A skirt and matching jacket with a high-necked blouse underneath, I think. Shoes with heels no higher than an inch.

No colored hose. And very little makeup, although you must wear lipstick."

Despite herself, Valerie can't help laughing again. "And how shall I wear my hair?"

"Tied back." Antonia's head is cocked, as though she's selecting from a lineup of hairstyles. "Low on your neck, with one of those dreadful fabric-covered elastics everyone's wearing these days. Isn't that what you told me last week? That everyone on the afternoon dramas had the same hairstyle? Well, that's how you should look. That's what they'll expect."

"You're wonderful." She leans down and hugs Antonia gently, gripping the thin shoulders beneath the satin bed jacket.

"I'm just trying to help. Now you go ahead. I'll be all right here until Nadia comes back. Tell MaryBeth you're looking for an ensemble that reeks of quiet elegance. No, that's not right. Not elegance. It should be—"

"Restrained."

Antonia smiles and nods. "Exactly."

Seventh Avenue is thick with young women pushing strollers. She wants to warn each of them to hold on tight to their babies. Instead, she averts her eyes to the shop windows and reads every sign and poster with meticulous attention until she spots the sign for MaryBeth's across the street. The shop is in the middle of the block, its doorway flanked by pots of daffodils and hyacinths.

She starts to cross, looks to her left to check for oncoming traffic. A blue Ford shoots the light, and Valerie does a double take. Is that Kristin Denby driving? She's only met her a few times—in the job interview, and her first week of work at Antonia's—but something about the driver's face makes her think of Kristin. Didn't Antonia say she was away on a vacation, some island, Hawaii, the Caribbean? The car reminds her of Johnny's Mustang, his first convertible, the car they drove to the Great Smoky Mountains on their honeymoon.

She rushes across the street and heads for MaryBeth's before the memories can slow her down.

A bell jingles when she pushes the door open. The

store is like a summer garden, scented with the lilies of the valley that brighten the counter. In the corner, a freshet of water flows over a carved, glinting stone into a catchpool. A perfectly coifed blonde in a flax-colored sheath introduces herself as MaryBeth and asks if she needs help.

The woman who answered the phone when she called about DASH had that kind of voice, a bit of cultivated country club hush in her responses. *Yes, certainly, tomorrow night at six. On Albemarle Road. I look forward to meeting you and your husband.*

"I'm just looking, thank you." Valerie can't quite bring herself to say she wants something quietly restrained.

"Here's an outfit I love." MaryBeth's face is hidden for a moment as she grabs a flowy silk blouse and leggings, both in an oatmeal color, from the rack.

Not exactly what your average Iowa mom would wear to a PTA meeting.

She wanders along the racks of spring clothing, thinking about Joanna. Two and a half days and still no sign of the woman who walked down the subway stairs with Joanna in her arms. The earth has not simply swallowed them whole. They're out there somewhere, *some*where, unless—

No. She won't succumb to her worst thoughts.

MaryBeth is hovering; Valerie can't stand being in this scented, expensive atmosphere much longer.

In the end, she walks out with an A-line skirt and matching blazer, a pair of low-heeled pumps, and two blouses, one white, one to match the wheat-colored suit. Even on sale, they cost as much as she used to spend on food for three months.

Laden with packages, Valerie Vincent walks briskly through the late morning crowd. She has to hurry so she can meet Johnny at one, to go over their stories, work out the details, look for the holes.

She can't stand here on this friendly, crowded street as though she were just a shopper like everyone else, a woman with her life intact.

twenty-two

He had the order sheet right in his hand, but Lucas Starr was sure he'd forgotten something. Tenpenny nails, caulking, ax handles. His regular customers finally understood that he wasn't just after their money when he advised them to replace their ax handles every couple of years. Any fool could see that when an ax handle gets all banged up, it loosens so that splitting large pieces of wood becomes a dangerous proposition.

Was it something Martha reminded him about?

Not this time. She hadn't said more than four words to him since John and that woman left, as though he was too dumb to tell she was angry just from looking at the way her mouth pressed together.

She'd get over it. She knew what was important. You couldn't go around letting people disrespect God, disrespect the rules He'd given to man and beast alike so they could live on this green earth and do right. Maybe she had to work up to the kind of firmness it took, a woman like Martha, always trying to make people feel good by giving them what they wanted instead of what they needed, what was good for their souls. That was part of the problem, he had to admit, with John. They'd always been too easy on him, mostly because of Martha's softness.

Well, that wasn't how it was going to work this time. Lucas turned the corner, passed the housewares——stupid that people expected a hardware store to carry kitchen doodads, not hardware at all but these plastic dish drains and little cutesy containers with flowers on them that cost $3.99. Didn't have the sense to know that a plain old canning jar would do just fine. He looked at his order list again, wandered past the paint section, then headed down another aisle.

That was it. Clothesline. Thick, strong, twenty yards to a package. So many things it was useful for . . . And the price was going up next month. Who ever heard of prices going down these days? So he better order more than he really needed, take advantage of the low price while he could.

Same principle applied to John, didn't it? They had this one last chance with the boy, and Lucas Starr wasn't about to let his wife talk him out of what he knew was right.

Nodding agreement to his silent resolve, Lucas Starr headed for the cash register. John was just going to have to make some changes in his life. That was all there was to it.

Another time, he'd allow himself to get royally, luxuriously pissed. But he wasn't going to let himself brood about his father and he wasn't going to give him what he wanted just to make peace. Those days were over, and besides, he had other things to think about, other things to do.

Like that DASH meeting Valerie had managed to talk her way into. *His* way, too, and he'd said yes.

For Joanna.

Johnny Starr took another bite of his salami and provolone sandwich and licked a spot of mustard from his thumb. The room looked good; whoever was moving in here was getting his money's worth. Or hers. Theirs, probably, in a three-bedroom apartment like this. One kid, two, maybe, each in one of the smaller bedrooms. Family.

In his mind he placed furniture around the room. A queen-size bed with a headboard that had one of those built-in bookcases, light wood for the dressers, maybe a rocking chair in the corner. And in the other two bedrooms, bunk beds for the boy, shelves for displaying model airplanes and Little League trophies, twin beds with ruffled skirts for the girl, dolls on the shelves instead of model planes.

Or maybe she was still only a toddler. Maybe she'd wake in the night in her new room and not know where she was, disoriented and tearful until her father heard her and came in to comfort her, and sang her to sleep with a half-whispered lullaby. Brushed the hair away from her head. Tucked the covers around her little shoulders as her eyes drooped closed and made sure she had her teddy bear. A teddy bear like the one he'd seen in that store window on Second Avenue, a smallish creature all golden tan, his amber eyes inquisitive, serious, as though he knew wonderful stories and was likely to share them with the little girl as soon as her father walked out of the room.

Laughing to himself, Johnny Starr wrapped the half-eaten sandwich in the paper, tossed it in the bag, and patted his back pocket to make sure he had his wallet. That teddy bear couldn't be so very expensive, but there had been only one left and he had to make sure he was the one to get it. It was perfect.

The silk scarf wasn't right, and she wanted to find something more suitable today. Antonia's birthday had come and gone; Kristin Denby couldn't let her believe she'd forgotten.

She knew the scarf wouldn't do two weeks ago, when the salesgirl, snapping her gum noisily, had folded it into the box and done a surprisingly good job with the wrapping paper and bow. She'd taken it anyway. It was always so hard to find exactly the right gift for Antonia, and this was a birthday she seemed to think was a particular milestone.

Kristin glanced at the white plush slippers. Not fine enough, although Antonia would scorn a gift that was chosen just because it was expensive. She fingered the rich, blue piping on a satin robe; Antonia never wore bathrobes, only bed jackets, always insisted they be white. Like her furniture. Like those snow-topped mountains in Vermont. Like the carefully combed mane of Charles Babcock's hair.

Books on tape? No, Antonia wanted the stories to be hers alone, created for no one else, shared only by the storyteller who crafted them.

As she passed the window, she stopped to look at her own reflection. Paolo had done a superb job with her hair; Antonia was sure to approve, would say how pleased she was that Kristin had finally made the change she'd been urging for so long.

A new bowl, filled with gardenias—that might be exactly right. But it would have to be black, and the perfect black bowl might not be so easy to find, might take more time than she had.

Resigned to the search, Kristin started for the door, turned where the glass counter opened onto a wide aisle.

And there it stood, the perfect gift. The largest bottle of that bergamot-scented cologne Antonia adored. Since the company went out of business, the cologne had become a precious commodity in that house. Antonia would cry out in delight, thrilled that someone knew her so well and had been so thoughtful.

Maybe, when she presented her special gift to Antonia Carrera, the woman would understand.

twenty-three

"You were successful, yes?"

The question comes from the study, where the television is tuned to the news. Valerie's in no mood for chitchat about clothing. "I did find an outfit," she says, at once relieved and disappointed that Antonia isn't announcing another phone call that's come in her absence.

"Show me your treasures, will you?" Antonia clicks off the television.

One article at a time, Valerie pulls the garments from the bag and offers them to the scrutiny of Antonia's fingers. As she handles each piece, Antonia keeps up a stream of questions, asking about how Valerie was treated by the shopkeeper, inquiring about the activities on Seventh Avenue, the volume of foot traffic, the presence of new stores or restaurants.

Valerie responds automatically, embellishing on the mundane details of the shopping trip while she goes through a mental checklist of all the things she and Johnny have to talk about when he comes by. But something Antonia says about how hard it is to park near MaryBeth's jogs a memory.

"I thought I saw Kristin Denby today driving down Seventh Avenue. But it couldn't have been her, right? You said she was leaving for a short vacation in the Caribbean, right?"

"Oh, I think that's not until next week. Actually, maybe you did see her. She stopped by while you were gone. To bring me a birthday present, of all things." Antonia seems uncomfortable with the idea; she points to a familiar gold box on the desk. "Can you believe it? She gave me the same thing you did."

Except that the bottle in the gold box is three times the size of the one *she* bought. Tropical Nights Après-Bain. As the weather gets warmer, Antonia splashes it on as though it's a replacement for air conditioning. "Well, then, I applaud her good taste."

Antonia smiles weakly at the joke, then touches her forehead with the back of her hand. "I've just taken some of my headache medicine. I'll be all right in a little while. Will you spend some time with me, my dear? Just a few more minutes, until the medicine starts to work?"

How can she refuse? Antonia wants to be surrounded by words, to help her forget her headache. That's not a lot to ask. "Of course," she says, and she sits at the desk. What can she talk about that won't end up upsetting both of them?

"What's it like near the park now? Is anything happening out there?"

Even with a headache, Antonia has sensed her dilemma. From the bay window, the scene outside is singularly uninteresting. Or maybe she's just too worn out to see the story potential. "There's not much traffic. The sun is just turning the tops of the trees bright gold."

"Tell me about the people. Is anyone walking into the park?"

Uneasy, Valerie looks up the street, down the street, sees no one. There, on the corner—she'll move the young couple closer to the park entrance.

"Only two young people, they're standing with their foreheads touching and their hands on each other's shoulders."

"Ah, good. Tell me more."

There's not much to see, but she continues anyway. "From here, they appear to be no more than seventeen or eighteen. Something's made them both sad. He's got his hand under her chin—"

She watches as the two take off down the street, a vigorous, decisive energy propelling them forward.

"—and she's turning her head away. She's wearing a tan raincoat, comes down almost to her ankles, and she's got a huge purse, maybe it's a book bag, slung over her shoulder."

Specifics. Antonia always wants specifics, as vivid as she can make them. But the young couple is nearly a block away now, the details sketchy at best. Surely Antonia will know she's making up a story and not really describing the scene outside.

"And the boy, what's he wearing?"

"One of those black leather jackets, you know, with epaulets and lots of zippers. He's got the collar turned up and his hands are stuck into the pockets of his jeans. He's wearing pointy-toed boots, too. Oh, and there, when he turns his head, I can see he's got a small gold earring."

The street is deserted now, the couple long gone around the corner.

Valerie continues: "She's started to walk away from him and he's standing there, frozen. With his hands out, but she's not there for him to touch. Now he's going too, in the other direction, kind of shuffling along. He's turning to look at her, but she's still walking at a brisk pace, head up."

"It's not an argument, am I right? What do you suppose has come between them?" Antonia's hands grip the armrests of the chair expectantly.

She wants speculation, too. Not just description but reasons, motivations, history. History: she can do that.

"I'd say she was breaking it off with him. They seem too young to be so serious, but she's the one who's having an easier time of it. But, honestly, neither of them seems to be very happy about parting."

But, honestly, it's all a lie.

"You were that age when you started college the first time, weren't you?"

Antonia might need the distraction, but she just can't do it, can't give away another piece of herself right now.

"I don't want to talk about myself, Antonia. I'm sorry." Not really sorry, but she has to say it. Maybe she could have avoided all this by feigning her own headache. She could have escaped to her room as soon as she came in, a perfectly reasonable reaction to everything that's been happening.

"Nonsense. Again, I'm the one who should apologize. Of course you can't concentrate on stories now. We'll have plenty of time for that when things are resolved. When you and Joanna are all settled in here, and life is calmer."

Quietly, through clenched teeth, Valerie says, "Please, try to understand, Antonia. When Joanna and I are all settled, it's going to be in Taconic Hills. Maybe I should find somewhere else to stay for—"

"I won't hear of it, Valerie. I didn't mean to upset you. Now, you must be exhausted. Why don't you go upstairs and lie down, my dear? I do feel much better."

Reprieved.

All she wants is a door closed behind her and a quiet space. "I'll be down in a while."

Her face still wreathed in light as the sun strikes the window, Antonia waves, and Valerie escapes up the stairs.

She tosses the new clothes on a chair, pushes aside the canopy curtains, and lies down on top of the green quilt. She stares blankly at the picture on the wall, a watercolor of a girl in a yellow dress walking on a leaf-shaded path in a country estate. No wonder Kristin chose that painting—she must have wanted to look at something that reminded her of solitude and languor, after a day of filling Antonia with stories.

In truth, the account of the two young people in the park really did distract her for a time, took her mind away from Joanna for a few seconds, the way the stories she told herself as a child kept her from disappearing.

Not really disappearing. But somehow those tales assured her that the world made emotional sense.

Whenever she walked into a new school, it was the free times she dreaded. Recess, gym class, the lunch periods when she'd sit at a table with a crowd of kids who had known each other all their lives. Sometimes she even wondered if she was really there. In her long-ago stories, no one looked through her as though she didn't exist. People were generous, fascinating, curious, reliable, and their lives were free of conflict and full of adventure. In the stories of her childhood, everyone lived in a universe defined by compassion and shared laughter.

So different from the stories Antonia demands, with their intrigue and their intensity. She's gotten better at creating those dramas, and it's a good thing, too.

The story she and Johnny will tell tomorrow night to a group of strangers will have to be the best one yet.

tuesday

twenty-four

Oh, Lord, it's going to be a long day.

Somehow, the time will pass.

She'll take a walk, find out if Antonia has any errands to keep her occupied until afternoon. She really should try to write at least a page for Kevin Murchison, a paragraph, even, but she won't, she knows, because sitting still will be impossible.

Valerie Vincent tucks the blanket under the corner of the mattress, stands back, pulls it out, and starts again. By the time she's satisfied with the results, only four minutes have passed. It's five minutes after seven. Ten hours to go before she can start to get dressed for the DASH meeting. Ten hours of trying to squash every horrible image that comes up when she thinks too long about what's happening to Joanna.

Ten to eight: Russo's not in his office yet, but the newsstand on Seventh Avenue is open.

She slips on her shoes, looks in the mirror above the curved dresser, stops to shove her hair behind her ears. Alice Monroe would never go out without lipstick and with her hair springing out in five directions. But she's not Alice yet; it's Valerie Vincent who needs to know whether anything's appeared in the papers about Baby Jane Doe, and right now Valerie doesn't care what people think when they pass her on the street.

The carton from Bloomingdale's is still on the table in the entryway when she returns, three newspapers tucked under her arm. Another chore to help pass the time: she'll call and tell Kristin about the package, maybe even offer to bring it by. Didn't Antonia say Kristin's apartment was in the neighborhood? That ought to be good for at least forty minutes.

Twenty minutes to nine. Not too early to ask Antonia for Kristin's phone number; she's already burrowed in her little nest in the study with the television for early morning company.

But when she steps into the room, carton in hand, the television screen is dark. A man with tortoiseshell glasses stands beside the desk, tugging at the cuff of his tan and brown plaid shirt, smoothing the knife crease of his immaculate khakis. What she thought was an early morning talk show was only early morning talk.

"Oh, I'm sorry. I didn't realize you had a guest." She backs away. She's seen him before, she's certain. He's been here recently, one of Antonia's East Hampton friends, perhaps.

"Valerie, there you are. I was just saying good-bye to Mr. Mattucci. You remember Ernest Mattucci, my accountant."

Of course. He's come by several times since she started working for Antonia, but he's out of uniform this morning. Without his usual three-piece suit and starched shirt she hasn't recognized him. She forces a smile.

"Good morning, Mr. Mattucci."

"Ms. Vincent." He nods, gathers up the envelopes from the desk, then fastens the clasp on a leather attaché case, his movements economical and impersonal.

He usually comes closer to the end of the month, midmorning, nearer to noon than to nine, unless her mind is playing tricks. No, that *is* right. He always begs off Antonia's invitation to stay for lunch.

"I'll talk to you in two weeks, then, Ernest. You'll take care of those arrangements?"

"This morning." He clasps Antonia's hand; a gold ring with the letters EM carved into the band glint in the morning light. "I'd better be going."

His voice is deep, but is it distinguished? Senatorial?

She's getting paranoid, losing her composure. She has to get hold of herself. If she doesn't, she'll blow the DASH meeting, and she can't afford that.

"Good-bye, Antonia. Ms. Vincent." And then he's gone, his footsteps crisp against the wood floor.

"Did you want something, my dear?" Antonia's cheeks glow with color, her flawless skin a study in contrasts, all cream and berries this morning.

"I forgot about this package, the one that came the other day."

"Package?" Evidently Antonia has forgotten too.

"It's for Kristin, from Bloomingdale's. I think I'll call her and ask if she wants me to bring it by. Do you have her phone number?"

Antonia tilts her head in thought. "It's 555-0976. I don't know if you'll find her home, though. She has so much to do; what with wedding plans and fittings for her dress and appointments with interior decorators, she's seldom home."

"Thanks. I'll try anyway. Just for something to do."

Valerie reaches for the phone on the desk, dials the number she's written on the small pad. It rings only once, and then a voice announces, "You've reached the Denby residence. Please leave a message."

For days, it seems, she's been talking to machines.

"This is Valerie Vincent. I just wanted to let you know there's a package here for you from Bloomingdale's. If you're going to be around this morning or early afternoon, I'd be happy to bring it over. Just give me a call at Antonia's when you get a chance."

"A machine? You see? Perhaps she *is* on that trip. Would you like breakfast, my dear? Today may be moving too slowly for you, but you can't let yourself get lightheaded. Your blood sugar will drop if you don't eat. Low blood sugar can be a real problem. After one of his nights of hard drinking, Miguel would eat a pint of ice cream and drink three cups of sweet coffee, and then two hours later, when the first rush was over, he'd sink into this terrible stupor." Antonia smiles. "I don't mean you've been drinking, but you should eat something so your mind is clear."

The thought of food makes her feel ill; even coffee would be too much right now. Valerie shifts the newspapers and edges toward the doorway. "Maybe later, Antonia. You go ahead without me. I'll be all right."

"I know you will, Valerie." She reaches out her hand. "I understand. You're nervous and excited. You go ahead and read those newspapers. I'll be here if you want company."

Valerie squeezes the outstretched hand and rushes upstairs.

By eleven o'clock she's gone through the newspapers, heard Detective Russo's obvious discomfort when he told her they'd put six more detectives on the case, decided that the sink and the tub in her little bathroom could use a thorough scrubbing.

She's rummaging in the utility closet for a fresh sponge when the phone rings. Before she can stand, she hears Nadia's voice calling to her from down the hall.

"Miss Valerie, it's for you. Miss Kristin."

Her heart stops racing, and she steps into the bedroom and picks up the phone. "Hi, Kristin. Thanks for returning my call."

"Hello, Valerie. I was out shopping. I've been so busy lately, I practically have to make a list to remember to brush my teeth. And then, when the day's over, I don't even know what I've accomplished." Kristin chuckles softly.

Valerie smiles to herself, recognizing all those feelings, wondering when she'll have the luxury of forgetting about time again. "I'm sorry I missed you when you stopped by yesterday," she says shyly.

"Oh, I was only there for a few minutes, and then I had to rush to an appointment. Seventh Avenue is becoming a madhouse. Park Slope is getting almost as crowded as SoHo. At least there's less attitude here."

If she weren't going back to Taconic Hills with Joanna when this is all over, she might even enjoy getting to know

Kristin better. "And more reasonable prices. Listen, about that package. It came the other day. If you like, I'll walk by with it."

"Thanks. That's nice of you, but it's only a sweater I ordered a month ago. I can't imagine why they sent it there."

"I don't mind, really."

"Don't bother. I'll pick it up when I can. By the way, how's Antonia today? She had one of her headaches yesterday. I'm sure she's allergic to spring grasses or maybe the cherry blossoms. Every year it's the same thing, those headaches start right in the middle of April. I've been trying to get her to see a specialist for six years. But you know how stubborn she can be. And how right she usually is."

Antonia's not right about the DASH meeting. Not right about the risks being too great.

Suddenly impatient, Valerie wants to end the conversation. "Well, as long as you don't need that package, I guess I'll—"

"Have you had any news? About your daughter, I mean?"

How does Kristin know about Joanna? Maybe there's been an article in one of the newspapers or something on the television news, the radio. And then she remembers: Antonia called Kristin that first night, to bring groceries into the house.

"No, nothing yet. Thanks for asking."

"Well, I hope things work out. Tell Antonia I sent my regards, would you?" Without waiting for an answer, Kristin hangs up.

Only six more hours to go.

Fervent and deferential.

The buttons of the silk shirt lie flat behind the placket, the linen skirt grazes her knee, the leather belt from Kristin's closet matches her shoes. The very picture of restraint.

"Valerie, please come into my sitting room when you're dressed." All vigorous authority, that voice from the other end of the hall. No indication that Antonia Carrera has ever in her fifty-five years experienced even a speck of self-doubt.

Valerie gathers her jacket and her purse, flips off the light, and follows the scent of Antonia's floating gardenias down the hall to the alcove beyond the high, curved archway at the far end of the bedroom.

"There you are, my dear. Come here and tell me about the light before you leave."

The scene on the other side of the curtain is so familiar she hardly needs to look to describe it. But Antonia will be listening for the whisper of fabric being moved aside, will wait to feel the sun or its absence on her skin.

"It's one of those wonderful, metallic afternoons. The sky looks silver, light and high, and beneath the clouds the air is golden. The shadows of the trees in the park are longer today. They're reaching like tentacles across—"

"Now tell me about the people. Is the young woman and her friend with the leather jacket there?"

She can do this, but only for a few minutes. The clock on the bedside table ticks off the seconds—what has Joanna been doing in the time since she walked to the window?—as she scours the street for something to present to Antonia. "No, I don't see them. But a florist's delivery van is parked at the curb and a man in coveralls—they're faded but you can tell they were blue—is leaning against the back of a bench. He's the only one on the street right now."

"That's fine, dear. You sounded so tense before, I thought a little conversation would help you relax. Now, you mustn't appear too anxious and you shouldn't be late. You're wearing the silk shirt and linen skirt? Good. You'll be home when, my dear? I'll wait up."

Wait to suck the juices out of her experiences.

Later tonight, Antonia will wheel herself into the living room, allow them each a single glass of brandy, and indulge herself in the only gift Valerie can offer, a neat little package containing details of the evening. Everything she's seen along the way. The people, the décor of the house. Overheard conversations on the street, if necessary, something unexpected, certainly, all for Antonia's amusement.

"I expect I'll be back by nine or ten, but it might be later. No need to wait up. If you're asleep, I'll see you in the morning."

"Remember—use their family names. Mr. Smith. Mrs. Jones. Don't call them Tom or Mary, even if they call you Valerie. Good luck, my dear. Be careful." Antonia tilts her head, offers her cheek, and Valerie leans down and skims the parchment skin with her lips, startled by the touch of Antonia's hand reaching for her throat. The elegant fingers run along the collar of the silk shirt, then float back to her lap. "Very good. You must keep that top button closed. Class, my dear. It shows in the little things. Now go on."

Valerie tucks her purse under her arm. Deliberately. Without haste. *It's not ladylike to hurry.*

twenty-five

"I told you," Johnny says as they wait for the light to change, "the subway was stuck for almost half an hour on the Manhattan Bridge. I even left myself an extra ten minutes but there was nothing I could do about it."

A trio of women in saris threaded with gold, their dark eyes crinkled with some private amusement, are waiting on the corner for the light to change. A gangly black man in oversized pants stands beside them, shoulders rolling in time to music only he can hear. These people aren't from DASH, she's sure of that, and on the busy street she stops, closes her eyes, and sends her fears sailing off into the clouds.

Blaming Johnny for breakdowns in the city's infrastructure isn't going to make it any earlier. And walking into a convocation of judges twitching with annoyance at their tardiness isn't going to help gain their trust. As they scramble across the wide street graced with gabled frame houses and venerable trees in full leaf, she slips her hand in his.

It's just a role; she's only staying in character.

"Try to calm down and I will too. I'll tell them something, I don't know . . . a sick aunt. Kevin Murchison says they're big fans of traditional families, so maybe they'll forgive us for being late. And you remember—we're Mr. and Mrs. Monroe. Martin and Alice."

Martin and Alice Monroe are going to find Joanna.

Unless the members of DASH have been warned about the interlopers. Unless the people in that house are donning somber robes and fortifying themselves with Scripture readings before they accuse her of making a pact with the devil and flying through the air to attend a Black Mass.

The house looks much like its neighbors, broad porch wrapped around two sides, hydrangeas blooming in a neat border along the walk that leads to the front steps.

"You okay?"

Johnny nods but he seems coiled inside himself, his hand locked tight around hers.

She presses the buzzer beside the carved oak door, steps back, as she's been instructed in the phone call, and waits. Her calm astonishes her. Curtains are lifted aside, but she continues to examine the brass doorknob, the gleaming knocker in the shape of a lion's head, the dry, crinkled leaf beside the welcome mat.

The door is pulled open by a woman about her age, surely under thirty, dressed in a slim blue skirt, matching jacket, and white blouse, the uniform of a mid-level paper-pusher. She's scowling, as though everything is a little too tight. "Can I help you?" she asks.

"I called the other day. My name is"—not Valerie, not Vincent or Starr—"Alice Monroe. This is my husband Martin."

The prim woman peers behind Valerie, as though she suspects someone else might be lurking in the bushes. "We thought you were coming at six. It's almost half past."

"I'm so sorry. We tried to call and we got a busy signal. My husband's aunt, the one we're living with until our apartment is ready, she's blind and in a wheelchair, and her usual attendant called in sick. Martin and I had to wait for the agency to send someone else. It seemed better for us to come late rather than miss the meeting altogether."

The scowl widens into a smile. "Come in, Alice. I'm Pamela Cleary. We're just about to begin."

The house smells of cinnamon and coffee, as though Danish pastries have just been pulled from the oven by a round-cheeked grandma in an apron. A grandma like Martha perhaps, the very picture of a matriarch whose sole pleasure is serving her family.

Even with the lamps turned on, the living room is deep in shadow; from the doorway, she memorizes faces she can barely see. Pamela Cleary bends over a man in a business suit, whispering her report about Martin Monroe and his old auntie, probably. Two other couples, older by at least a decade, sit on the twin upholstered sofas. They look like large bookends dressed in bland expressions and sensible shoes.

The young woman makes introductions, each person rising in turn to shake Valerie's hand, each hand a new test. She won't pull away, even though she recoils inside. She smiles and repeats their names to fix them in her mind: Jack Cleary, Colleen and Patrick Barnes, Helen and Arnold Lewiston. Such good, solid, Anglo-Irish names. Fine, upstanding citizens. Murmurs of welcome and forced smiles follow them around the room to the two cane-seated chairs near a brick fireplace.

Too far from the door, she thinks, smoothing her skirt over her knees and glancing at Johnny. *No way out except past the troops.* Valerie swallows hard and folds her hands on her lap.

Jack Cleary rises and straightens his tie, and suddenly she remembers where she's heard his name. In one of the articles Murchison gave her.

"Would you mind telling us what you told my wife on the phone, Mrs. Monroe? I want everyone to hear it in your own words." He brushes at his already perfect hair, a strange, horizontal smile on his face.

The same smile he wore when he wrote letters to the editor of the Des Moines paper to denounce his brother? She has to push that image out of her mind or she won't be able to do this.

"Four years ago, I guess it was, we were traveling through the Northwest on vacation and we met the Stevens family."

It's going to be okay. They aren't scowling, aren't poised on the brink of their seats ready to pounce on her.

"Kitty Stevens told us that her friends the Murphys

joined a group that does a lot of good things on behalf of children. We care very much about children, my husband and I, and so naturally we were interested in the work DASH does."

Stares and silence. *What do you know about my baby?* Valerie banishes the question; she'll get all tangled up if she lets her mind wander.

"I mean, I don't really know all that much about your activities, except that, when Mrs. Stevens talked about it, it sounded like something Martin and I would find satisfying."

Helen Lewiston smiles. "And how is Freddy?"

Freddy? The Murphy children—Murchison has told her about them. There is no Freddy. Smiling, she says, "You must mean Philip, their son. I never really knew the Murphys, except for what Kitty Stevens told me about them."

Sinking back into her chair, Helen Lewiston nods. "You're right. Philip. That's his name. I'd forgotten. Now, you do understand about confidentiality. We don't talk to outsiders about our work, only to people we're sure share our values and our goals. It would be so easy for the public to misunderstand what we're about, so we ask that you tell no one what happens at these meetings. That way, everyone is protected."

The way you protect the children? Valerie nods, hears the rustle of Johnny's movements, wills herself not to look at him.

"Pamela told her all that when she phoned, Helen." Jack Cleary stands with his back pressed to the fireplace mantel, hands clasped behind him as though he's about to step onto a balcony and deliver a papal blessing. It's his rhythm that makes this group move from one thing to the next, and he fixes a piercing gaze on Valerie. "And she told her about our no-tolerance policy for people who lie to us."

Everyone wriggles forward, empty vessels yearning to be filled. They're inclined toward Jack Cleary as though he's their direct link to salvation.

What a waste. He could be using all that power to send them out into the world to solve the problems of homelessness or bigotry . . . but that would be a different world and she wouldn't be sitting here wondering where her daughter is, who is feeding her, washing her face, tying her shoelaces.

"Please tell us why you want to join DASH. Why you want to work with us. Beyond the obvious, I mean, your *personal* reasons, if you have any."

Now they shift toward her like a flock of expectant pigeons. She's done enough preparation to have a response, and enough worrying to wonder how they'll react to the crumbs she'll toss them.

"I didn't tell your wife about this on the phone, Mr. Cleary, but I do have personal reasons for wanting to be involved in your work." Pause. Show them how difficult it is to dredge up her painful past. "I'm not a hundred percent certain about the details—I was only six years old and I still wake up with nightmares, so I'm not sure what part of it is bad dreams and what part I really saw. But I know something happened. In my neighbor's living room. I was sleeping over at a friend's house. It's funny, I don't even remember her name anymore because we moved away a few months after this night.

"All I know is there was a baby and lots of candles and people dressed in black robes. Everyone had these large medallions hanging from long chains around their necks, five-pointed stars in a circle. Gold, I think."

The narrative is beginning to flow, and she has her audience's attention. Everyone's gaze is riveted to her face, except for Jack Cleary, who stares at the chair beside her, at Johnny.

"They kept putting drops of some red stuff, now I think it must have been wine because the baby didn't make a sound the whole time, into the baby's mouth, passing her from hand to hand. Funny, I'm not even sure why I thought it was a girl. It just never occurred to me to think anything else. There I was, halfway down the stairs, unable to move. I'd gotten up thirsty and couldn't find a glass in the upstairs bathroom. Anyway, I couldn't make out what they were saying, except I remember hearing a strange singsongy chant, kind of like a constant hum. And then one of them picked up something shiny, it gleamed in the candlelight the way my father's fishing knife glittered in the sun. That's when I got too scared to stay there.

"I was terrified they'd discover me so I crept back to the bedroom. After a while I heard cars driving away and then my friend's parents came up the stairs and looked into her room. I pretended to be asleep. But I couldn't stop thinking about that baby and those stars around their necks. And the knife. I lay on the bed until the sun came up. Then I tiptoed down the stairs and ran across the wet grass to my own house. I never told anyone except my husband. Not until tonight. I always had this feeling that maybe I'd imagined it all and that people would laugh at me."

Stop. Murchison has warned about too much embellishment. This is the right place to sit silently, to watch for signs of how they've taken the story.

"Nobody here thinks it's a joke, what you saw." Jack Cleary is the first to speak. The others haven't even looked at him, but she knows they'll take a stand only after Cleary's given them their cue.

"You poor thing, carrying such an awful memory around all these years." Bright tears splash from Colleen Barnes's eyes. "You've come to the right place, dear. We've all had similar experiences, or friends of ours have, or . . ." Her voice breaks. "Some of us have children who have been forced to take part in those disgusting rituals. We know how far these people can go, how much of a shield has been put up to keep the public in the dark about their activities. Teachers, judges, social workers, cops—all bought off in bargains, literally, with the devil. They cover up for each other and they just keep on doing these—"

The woman's face crumples, not with a look of outrage, but with the sagging, fearful expression of someone who knows she's about to be chastised. By Jack Cleary?

"Grandparents too," Patrick Barnes adds into the silence.

"And day care workers and priests. Can you imagine? *Priests.* You can't believe how far, how deep their network goes." Arnold Lewiston's eyes bulge with excitement.

"All right, everyone. I can see Mr. and Mrs. Monroe understand the urgency of our mission. Now, we have an important piece of business before we go on to matters that we must discuss in private."

Valerie waits, not eagerly but with the acquiescence she knows he expects. Johnny is balanced on the edge of his chair, concentrating on Jack Cleary.

"It has come to our attention that a child must be protected."

This is not a dream, not some high school drama production in which she has a bit part. This mild-looking man really is talking about protecting children.

He's referring to her daughter. He must be talking about Joanna.

"We need to find a placement for the child. A safe haven. And we must do this within the next two weeks. She's been removed from immediate danger, but we have indications that it won't be secure, this haven, not for much longer. I'll open the discussion by asking for recommendations."

Valerie keeps her eyes on her folded hands, not daring to look at any of the people in the room. Good-girl training—she's absorbed enough of that to know it isn't her turn to speak. She can't, anyway; her throat is tight with fear and anger.

"I assume you're talking about something that requires local action." This from Patrick Barnes, whose voice is thin, watery, not at all *senatorial*. His wife reaches for his hand, but Barnes pulls away. "We need to do it differently this time. Too many people know us."

That's why it's been so easy to gain access to this group.

This whole show has been for her sake, hers and Johnny's. If not exactly street theater, then a bit of living-room dramatics so she and Johnny will agree to be the front-line troops for DASH, its public face.

They all watch Jack Cleary intently, except for an occasional glance tossed in her direction to see if she's properly impressed, sufficiently motivated, can read between the lines.

Colleen Barnes pats her husband gently on the knee. "That's a good thought, honey."

"Maybe," Valerie says, having no trouble making her

voice sound hesitant, "it's a sign that my husband and I are here today. A sign that we should be involved in this mission."

The smiles are unanimous.

"I don't know if we can let you do that, Mrs. Monroe." This from Jack Cleary, delivered with paternal solicitude. "If you don't have personal experience working with a group like ours, you have no idea what you might be up against. Before we ask you to participate in one of our missions, we need to hear what your husband has to say. You do understand? We must ensure that children remain within intact families."

Johnny is sitting beside her like an alabaster statue. Maybe it would have been better if she'd found someone else, a cop with undercover experience or a friend from Taconic Hills. They've gone over and over the story, until he swore he was ready, but he's so stiff. If he blows this . . .

"Look, Mr. Cleary," Johnny says firmly, "I can appreciate your concern for your group's interests, but I want you to know that I'm one hundred percent with my wife on this. She wakes up in the middle of the night with nightmares. I don't want other kids to have to go through that. We are definitely in complete agreement about this."

No one moves until Jack Cleary rises and extends his hand. "Good, that's very good. We'll see how things work out. There's another meeting you should both attend on Friday night. Someone will call you before then to tell you where to go. We'll see you then, Mr. Monroe, Mrs. Monroe. God bless you for coming."

twenty-six

They should run for their lives.

When she hears the click of the lock behind them, she wants to vault over the porch railing and fly down the street until she can't see the rambling old house or that fellowship of self-appointed judges. Instead, she and Johnny slowly make their way down the steps to the street, hand in hand. A slab of pavement juts up in the middle of the street, a gnarled tree root forces its way through two spikes of a rusted fence, supermarket flyers litter the sidewalk. Funny—did she see any of these things before?

On the corner, Johnny has an attack of the shakes.

"You did fine," Valerie assures him. "Thank God it didn't go on any longer. I don't think either of us could have lasted *another* thirty minutes."

"I have to get out of here, Val. Will you be all right if I leave you here and catch a subway home?" His mouth twitches, and a tic she knows too well dances in the corner of his eye.

Better alone than trying to control his anxiety too. "Go ahead. I need to walk off some of my own nerves anyway. I'll talk to you later. After I hear from them."

"Or if you hear anything else, right? You'll phone me?"

Yet when Johnny Starr leaves her, she almost calls to

him. She wants to ask if he feels deflated too, if some part of him expected to walk out of that house with Joanna chattering between them.

Prospect Park lies just ahead, and she heads for one of the dark paths carved into the green, undulating meadows that resemble alfalfa fields after first haying. Taconic Hills—she belongs there, in her small, sunny house, writing about her poor, benighted Salem women, with Joanna sitting beside her, piling wooden blocks into a teetering mountain. And Esther should be puttering in her tidy kitchen, playing bridge on Thursday nights with her cronies. Was Lucas Starr right? Has she lost two people she loves because she didn't do her job right?

The old boathouse, rising at the end of the path like a columned Greek temple, is the backdrop for a group of people who glide into Tai Chi positions, knees bent, elbows crooked, faces stern with concentration in the twilight. When she slows to watch them, the footsteps behind her slow too.

She slips the strap of her purse across her chest, picks up her pace, but the footsteps keep a steady counterpoint to her quickening gait. She kneels, pretending to shake a pebble from her shoe.

"Alice? I didn't mean to frighten you." Pamela Cleary looks down through dark lashes. Her smile is apologetic. "You seemed a little upset. I didn't want you to go off that way. Where's your husband?"

Was she watching from down the street when Johnny escaped in the direction of the subway station? Surely this young woman hasn't followed her just to offer a few comforting words. She has to stay sharp so she can—no, she won't use that word. *Protect* herself. She has to watch her back, that's all.

"He, uh, he was concerned about his aunt so he took the train. I wanted to be alone for a while."

Pamela Cleary lays a hand on her arm. "Oh, of course. I'm sorry. I'll go back to the house. Unless you want to sit for a minute and talk."

That Tai Chi class—they're practicing movements that turn their opponents' attacks to their own advantage. Away from her overbearing husband and his sycophants, this woman might be led into a discussion of things she couldn't talk about in the house on Albemarle Road.

"That's very kind. But just for a minute. If I'm late, my husband will worry. Besides, I don't want to take too much of your time." They walk to a bench that offers a lovely view of a thick-trunked willow whose new leaves are already trailing like languid fingers in the lake. In the distance, a radio throbs.

"You know, I've always thought it's a little unfair, the way new people get put on the spot. We all went through it, of course, but that doesn't mean it's fair. You have to tell total strangers these terribly personal things about yourself and we tell you nothing except group business."

Like so many of the closed societies she's read about—the Rosicrucians, medieval clerics, the underground railroad of the Civil War days, the Salem conspirators—the lines of communication in DASH are controlled by a strict set of rules. It's good to be able to put it in this perspective.

"I'm sure there's a reason. I expect that if you do accept me and my husband, we'll hear more about all of you as time goes on."

"Oh, I'm sure we will accept you, Alice. You'll get a chance to help the children." Pamela Cleary toys with the clasp of her handbag, and Valerie waits her out. "I didn't believe my husband at first," she says finally, her face reddening. "I have to admit Jack's stories were so terrible I thought he must be making them up because I couldn't conceive of people being that . . . I guess the only word is *bestial*. He told me about them but I still didn't understand. We were eighteen when we met, twenty-three when we got married. On our wedding night, when I saw the cigarette burns on his buttocks and his groin, I thought I'd pass out. It was terrifying to think his own grandparents could do that to their own flesh and blood in their demented ceremonies. Can you imagine?"

"That's awful." She can*not* imagine. She won't let herself think that such awful things might be happening to Joanna. Will not lose her focus to consider that Jack Cleary may have been a victim of unspeakable horrors. "It's hard to believe his parents didn't know what was

going on. This little girl your husband was talking about,
s it like that for her?"

"Little girl?" Pamela's frown deepens. "I don't think
ack ever said the child was a girl."

Yes, he did, he had to, she has to dig back and find
some reference to a little girl. "Didn't he say *she's* got to
be protected?"

"No, I'm sure he didn't say that. He said 'the children.' He always says that. We all do."

And then Valerie remembers: it wasn't just because
she was thinking about Joanna, she really *was* listening to
him. "He did say she's out of harm's way, actually his
words were, 'She's been removed from immediate danger.'
I felt so hopeful when he said it, wishing I could help."

Pamela Cleary's frown evaporates. "You're right. You
are. Usually he's very careful about not revealing anything
that would accidentally put a child in greater danger. I
didn't catch his slip, but now that you say it, I remember."

"I'm so relieved I finally told someone else about what
happened that night. It's like a weight has been lifted."
Valerie mustn't let herself dwell on the subject of the child,
can't give this woman the chance to see into her secret
heart, where she keeps Joanna hidden away. "Did all the
others really have similar experiences?"

"A lot of us," Pamela says, but she's retreated inside
herself again. The welcoming smile is gone and she won't
make eye contact. "You know, there's something I don't
think my husband told you."

This is the real reason she's been followed. Whatever
the Cleary woman has said until this moment, it's been
preparation for what's coming next. Valerie's heart bangs
wildly against her ribs.

"There's this journalist—that's what he calls himself—with some very twisted ideas about what we're doing, a man named Murchison."

Valerie doesn't flinch.

"He's done some really awful things, bribing a postal
worker to intercept our mail, harassing us with phone calls
in the middle of the night. He's tampered with people's
cars and left things in their mailboxes. He thinks someone

connected to us is responsible for killing his sister so he'
doing whatever he can to stop us."

Murchison hasn't said a word about any of this.

"He sounds like a lunatic," Valerie says finally.

"He is, and he's a dangerous one. He once even sent a
spy, someone who came around to one of our meetings
pretending to be interested in our organization. Luckily
my husband did a little checking around and found out
before it was too late."

Such a gentle voice, such a simple statement. But it's a
warning, and Valerie feels a chill. "This person, this spy
never had the chance to do any real harm to DASH?"

"Oh no. Jack made sure of that."

This isn't the time to find out what Jack Cleary did to
Kevin Murchison's spy. "I promised my husband I'd be
back by dark. I better get going. I'm glad we had the
chance to talk, Pamela. I do feel much better."

Pamela Cleary hugs her, breaks away as though she's
overcome by emotion, and starts down the path that will
lead her across the park, back to that awful house. After
only a few steps, however, she turns. "If this Murchison
character should try to contact you, Alice, the best thing
would be to get in touch with Jack. Jack will know what
to do."

twenty-seven

A bell is blaring.

The room is dark, except for the illuminated numbers on the clock radio beside the bed. Ten twenty-eight. She must have fallen asleep after she gave Antonia a quick report on the DASH meeting, so tired by the time she got upstairs that she dropped onto the bed fully dressed.

The bell sounds again—Nadia and Carl must be out, and Antonia's room is dark and silent. She bounds down the stairs to the foyer, nearly knocking Kristin's package off the hall table. When she looks out through the etched glass, she finds herself staring at Mitch Russo.

The lock seems to have a mind of its own, but finally she manages to open the door.

"Detective Russo." His expression, harsh and forbidding, terrifies her.

His eyes narrow as he closes the door and steps past her. "You mind telling me why you and your ex-husband went to that meeting tonight? What exactly did you think you were doing, Ms. Vincent? You put yourself in danger and maybe even screw up our investigation and what do you have to show for it? These people are deranged. I don't want another death on my hands."

Another death—surely he's referring to Esther, not Joanna. He shouldn't have frightened her that way, and he certainly has no right to reprimand her like an angry parent. Detective Mitch Russo has made his fair share of mistakes, and one of them may have cost her Joanna. "Did you come here to yell at me?"

He scowls and runs a hand over his hair. "Damn right that's one of the reasons I'm here. Look, Murchison's a good guy and all that, but maybe he's got a real blind spot when it comes to DASH, you know what I mean? They're not like the PTA, you understand? It's too damn dangerous."

Antonia used nearly the same words, and they're no less condescending coming from this harried man. "Did Mrs. Carrera tell you that I went out tonight? Or was it Murchison? Who's keeping tabs on me for you?"

"I'm just doing my job," he says, turning away from her gaze and looking out the window, "or trying to, anyway. Only I feel like your little game is making it harder."

"Well, here's how *I* feel, Detective Russo. My daughter has been missing for four days. You're only looking for Joanna because you think she'll lead you to the person who murdered Esther. Which means that I'm going to keep putting one foot in front of the other until I find her, even if you happen to think I'm walking into a minefield."

"Even if it means putting Joanna at risk? And don't tell me what my priorities are, okay?" Russo glares at her. "Let me tell you something, lady. Right this minute, two New York City undercover cops are putting themselves on the line by infiltrating a DASH meeting. We *are* doing our job, the one we're trained for, the one we have the resources for. Will you promise to stay away from DASH? For your daughter's sake and for the safety of my cops?"

Damn Russo and his tight-lipped silence and his undercover cops showing up at a DASH meeting. He never said a word. *No news. Nothing to report.* So she made sure Alice and Martin Monroe filled the gap. They'd gotten so close so fast. "Why didn't you tell me what you were doing?"

"Tell you? If we went around talking about everything we do, three quarters of our cases would be ruined. Tell you? No, Ms. Vincent. I did say we were doing everything we could." Russo's face burns red. "Now, will you back off?"

She can try to convince him that the contact she and Johnny already made with those people in DASH is valuable. She can tell him whatever he wants to hear so he'll stop this harangue. Or she can ignore him. "I don't know," she says firmly. "I have to think about it."

Again Russo runs his hand over the bristly hair on his crown. "Your choice, lady. Your daughter and your decision. Anyway, that's only one of the things I need to talk to you about. You haven't gotten any ransom demands, have you?"

Joanna's all right now but if you contact the police . . .

The phone call Antonia intercepted doesn't qualify. Nobody's asked for anything. She can't chance it now, can't risk the caller—whoever it may be—finding out she's betrayed him. Joanna's life could depend on it. "No. No ransom demands."

"You'll tell us if you do, right? You won't try to play that game alone?"

That *would* be foolish, he's right about that. "I'll tell you if I get any demands for ransom. Are we through here, Detective Russo?"

"Not quite. We had a call from a neighbor of Mrs. Klein's. Brought up some interesting questions. This might take a while. You mind if we sit down?"

She ushers him into the living room, lowers herself to the sofa. Russo chooses the white leather armchair near the fireplace, his dark eyes flicking over the brass lamp, the glass coffee table, the marble mantel. Whatever he thinks about Antonia's spare, geometric grandeur or Valerie's peculiar dishevelment, it doesn't show on his face.

"We get these people all the time who call with wacko theories. I mean, they sit around with nothing to do all day but mind other people's business. But this guy, this Mr. Sadowski, doesn't seem the type. He phoned the TV station that ran the story the night of Esther Klein's murder and they sent him to us. Mr. Sadowski told Teresa he remembered seeing someone about two weeks ago in a store on Flatbush Avenue. This woman was wearing a pin like the one your daughter was playing with the night she was kidnapped."

"Pin?" She runs through the news story in her mind. Joanna's tears, the yellow dump truck—that's all she remembers.

"When we brought her in, she was holding onto this dump truck for dear life. Wouldn't let go of it, so we figured we'd let her keep it. You know, this kid had been through so much and it seemed to make her feel better to play with the stuff in the truck. Two shells, the kind my kids made into ashtrays at summer camp. A thimble, with all these painted roses around the edge."

"That was Esther's. I remember she was afraid Joanna would pick it up and put it in her mouth and swallow it. I told her not to worry, that she stopped doing that when she was eleven months old."

"And a pewter pin. You didn't see it that night? On the news?"

"A brooch?" Not hers. And unless she kept it hidden away, Esther didn't have anything like that, nothing pewter. The only jewelry Esther ever wore was a simple silver bracelet and the Star of David that hung around her neck on a gold chain.

"We got a copy of the tape from the news producer so we could show it to Mr. Sadowski. Teresa and I watched it with him maybe fifteen times. I want you to look at it and tell me if you recognize the pin."

That would mean seeing Joanna, those tears, her quiet, blank stare again. And her hair, Lord, so many tangles in that baby hair . . . "Of course. Come into the study. We can watch it there."

She's out of her chair, crossing the hall, turning on lights, flipping on the television, pushing the power button on the VCR. When she holds out her hand for the tape, he slips it into the machine and steps away.

Jagged lines dance across the screen. As soon as the announcer's voice introduces the Brooklyn reporter, she feels the damp sea air and smells the spilled gin again, as she did that night in East Hampton.

Then Joanna's face fills the screen and everything else disappears.

In the bright lights, her hair shimmers, fine and glinted

with sparks of auburn, not as snarled as she's remembered. And the tears aren't nearly as copious, just a trickle that finally leaks down onto her cheeks. But the smile and her sweet mouth, the way she looks directly into the camera with those green eyes—Joanna. Perfectly Joanna.

When the screen goes blank, Valerie says, "Wait." But the moment is over, and Joanna has been stolen from her again.

"Well? That's a pretty unique piece of jewelry. You recognize it from anywhere, Ms. Vincent?" Russo leans back against the desk, thick legs crossed at the ankles. A scrap of paper is stuck to the sole of one of his shoes.

"I'm sorry. I didn't even see it. I was looking at my daughter." And feeling the fresh pain of loss, and a surge of anger at the woman who had stolen Joanna and at Russo, who had been her unwitting accomplice.

"I'll rewind it and run it again. I'm going to freeze it on the truck. It's not a real good shot but we're having one of our techs making a still of it."

She won't watch Joanna's face this time, will only look at the bright yellow toy, at the thimble and the shells. And at the pin.

"There." Russo presses the pause button.

She steps right up to the screen, but she's wavering, her eyes drifting back to her daughter's face. The pin is lovely.

"I don't recognize it. I'd remember it. It's definitely not the kind of thing Esther would own or wear."

She's never seen it before, this faceless crescent, its curve a swing for a creature who appears to be a dragon-fly-woman with delicate wings, her long dress flowing behind her as she rides the moon.

Where did it come from?

"You didn't keep it?" Of course he doesn't have it. If it's been stored in an evidence room somewhere, she'd be examining the real thing.

Russo shakes his head. As the tape rewinds again, he says, "Joanna was still holding it when they left. That woman came into the interview room, she picked the baby up, truck and all, and started crying and kissing her face and talking to her in this teary, husky whisper. Damn good actress, if you ask me."

Damn uncritical audience, she wants to say, but doesn't.

"The other reason I'm here is to tell you the medical examiner's ready to release Mrs. Klein's body. Have you made any arrangements yet?"

"I phoned . . . yesterday, I think it was. Parkview, on Coney Island Avenue. I'm supposed to call them as soon as I hear from you. To tell them where they should go to pick up the body."

Body. The word is awful. It's not really Esther she's talking about.

What happens to people who die without relatives, with no one around who can afford to bury them, or at least borrow the money from a kind employer? Are they dumped in some deep hole in the ground or thrown on a mass pyre, does someone say the proper prayer? Who cries for them?

"Here's the address." He hands her a card.

She slips it in her pocket, out of sight, but the talk of Esther has raised new questions. There's the matter of rent on the apartment, the need to dispose of Esther's belongings, to retrieve her own. Joanna's toys, their clothes, the notes for her Salem paper . . . "Does this mean I can go back to her place and get my things?"

"Sure, we've gone over everything and taken pictures and picked through the place. We've found whatever we're going to by now. But listen . . . you probably should get one of these services to come in and, well, scrub it out real good first. They know how to take care of these things."

Then there was that much blood, enough to make Mitch Russo think to tell her to get the apartment cleaned. Oh, God, *Esther's* blood. The thought makes her stomach churn. How did she think someone was murdered, anyway, all clean and sanitary and confined in a small space, neatly, considerately, so that you could just roll up the mess in a paper towel and toss it in the trash?

All these days of focusing on Joanna, she hasn't even allowed herself to think about how Esther died, couldn't bear to imagine her enduring a long, painful death. Now it's imperative to know everything.

"Detective Russo, how was Esther murdered?"

His eyes narrow again and he looks away from her. "She was hit over the head with a cane. Hard enough to crack the cane. Cracked her skull when she fell."

Polished wood, a plain rubber tip—Esther kept the cane in the umbrella stand near the coat closet to remind herself to take her time on icy streets so she wouldn't slip again and twist her knee, as she had two years earlier. "So there must be fingerprints on the cane."

"Sure, yeah, and—surprise, surprise—they match the prints of the woman who walked away with your daughter. Which means we still know zilch about who she is. The other set is Mrs. Klein's." He replaces the videotape in its cardboard sleeve. "She was one spunky lady."

"Spunky?" How would he know?

"The M.E. found a clump of hair. Darker than yours. Twisted around Mrs. Klein's fingers."

He doesn't say the rest. That Esther fought to save Joanna. That she died in the struggle.

"Listen, if you want, I can pick you up and take you to the funeral home tomorrow. Just leave a message at my office and I'll come by half an hour before. I should be there anyway. You never know with a murder who's going to turn up to check out the body. I mean, here's a perfect example. What if someone from DASH shows up and sees you there? I don't think that's going to happen, you understand, but I still wish you'd stay away from DASH."

She's not going to promise him anything, but she won't argue with the man, either. Esther's bloodstained image keeps her silent.

Russo stands in the doorway, the videotape stuck under his arm. "Just because you haven't answered me, Ms. Vincent, don't think I'm dropping this. I want you to tell me you won't go to any more of those meetings."

Maybe he's right. Maybe she should leave it alone. The cops have been trained, have the support of backup waiting to break down the doors, pull guns if things go bad, the way all those television cops do.

Television cops . . . On one of Antonia's shows,

they'd reenacted an undercover operation in which a county road worker, an ordinary guy who'd worked his way into a motorcycle gang, went to some meeting in the woods and helped the police find out who murdered his brother. Why not? Why couldn't she do it the same way?

"Look, I've already been to one meeting. As far as I can tell, they bought my story and they trust me. And they told me about a child they're getting ready to pass on to some new set of parents. To protect her from Satan, they told me. I want to go to the next meeting with Johnny, just like they said we should. And I want to wear a wire." Said aloud, the words sound like a line from one of Antonia's television dramas. "I'm safe, you get information, and I get my daughter back."

Russo frowns. "No. I told you, it's too dangerous and we've already got our people working that angle."

"Then I'll go without you. It's not illegal, and I can't see how it would make it harder to find Joanna, just the opposite."

Mitch Russo looks as though he's going to explode. Veins bulge on the side of his neck; he holds his clenched fists tight against his sides. "You're blackmailing me, right? I'm going back to my office now so I don't say something I'll regret. Sure, you're not breaking any laws if you go to the meeting, but it's not a real smart thing, you understand. Call me when you know about the funeral. Meanwhile, don't mention this wire idea to anyone, not your ex-husband, not Mrs. Carrera, not even Kevin Murchison."

He's going to go along with her plan. Maybe he won't let himself say yes right now, but he's going to see the wisdom of using her as a way in to DASH.

"Okay, I won't tell anyone. But I need to know in a day or two."

"You want to think about what would happen if one of them decides to show you a real welcome or something and they hug you and then start to wonder about the hard square attached to your ribs. You want to consider that, Ms. Vincent."

"You're right. I have to think about it so I'll be prepared. But that's why it's better if we do this together. You let me know what you decide, Detective Russo."

He wheels around and stalks down the hall without saying anything. The door closes behind him, a polite click in the quiet night, and she pictures him walking along the park, shaking his head, and finally realizing she's right.

wednesday

twenty-eight

"I'll come with you." Antonia reaches across her dressing table and dips three fingers into the jar of face cream, then slathers it onto her face until she looks like an actor in a Japanese play. "I'll have Carl bring the car around and we'll go together. Funeral homes are difficult enough if you're with someone, but they're truly awful without company. You shouldn't be alone."

How many times has Antonia said that in the past week? But being alone is exactly what she needs now, the chance to be quiet when she says good-bye to her friend. At least Russo won't follow her into the chapel and eavesdrop on her sorrow.

"That's kind of you, Antonia, but Detective Russo is coming by to pick me up."

Antonia's concerned frown changes to a smile. "Of course, my dear. I only thought . . . Never mind. I'm glad you've got someone to drive you there. You can't get a cab anymore in Brooklyn and those car services, well, frankly, the vehicles smell of smoke and sweat and God knows—"

The telephone cuts off Antonia's words. This has to be the phone call. About Joanna. Trembling, Valerie reaches for the receiver. "Yes, this is Valerie."

"This is Sally from Paragon Travel. Is there a Mrs. Carrera at this number?"

She can't catch her breath, can barely see through the haze of her frustration. "Antonia, it's a travel agent, for you."

Antonia wipes the cream from her fingers, then smiles and holds out her hand for the phone. "Ah, Kristin's honeymoon arrangements—it will be my gift to the newlyweds. Here, take these tissues with you, Valerie. I expect you'll need them."

"You mind the window open?"

Russo's voice startles her. He's hunched over the steering wheel, shoulders tensed and the back of his neck pleated against the collar of his shirt.

"No, it feels good. I can smell flowers in the air, almost like springtime in Taconic Hills."

"You mean you don't appreciate car exhaust and rotting garbage and that steam or whatever it is that comes out of those manhole covers?" For the first time since Friday, Russo seems so uncomfortable that he's actually chattering. "When I was a kid, my mother told me it was hell down there. I kept waiting to see a devil dressed in red pajamas like my uncle Mario's union suit, dancing in the fires and poking people in the fanny with a pitchfork."

If only it was so easy to identify the true devils . . .

"I'm still not sure what makes that steam. I should find out, I guess. Someday."

All the things she planned to do someday. She can't start feeling sorry for herself now.

"You gonna be okay for this? I mean, you tell me what you want him to do and I'll tell the funeral director." The car rocks as they wait for the light to change, as though it's straining to race away. Russo keeps his eyes on a sign across the intersection.

"No. I'm fine. I already explained everything to him last night on the phone. I'll be fine." The hush, the feeling that she left her real self behind and sent a shell that looks like her—she knows how it's going to go, remembers from her mother's funeral, when Esther was with her every minute, through the planning and then the ride along the road so glazed with ice the limousine crept for miles to the cemetery.

And now, with Esther dead, there's no one. The last person, except for Joanna, she thinks of as family, even though she shares none of Esther's blood. She's an orphan.

She wonders about the word, what it will mean, until they've parked in the lot behind the square gray building with the PARKVIEW sign in block letters above the door. Two men hover outside, yarmulkes fixed to the backs of their heads with bobby pins, the fringe of their talliths hanging below their belts like the tails of stray animals that have wandered under their shirts. The professional mourners. She shivers as she pushes past them through the heavy doors.

The carpet is deep gray. A worn path leads to the chapel, but she turns in the other direction toward the door marked OFFICE and knocks twice. Russo follows her inside.

How did gladiolas become the flowers of the dead?

The funeral director has the bland, disinterested face of a newscaster; he beckons them to seats and offers stale crumbs of condolence. Then, as she knew he would, he gets right down to business.

"With a body that's been subjected to an autopsy, as I told you last night, Mrs. Vincent, we strongly urge a closed casket. You did say you elected cremation. Mrs. Klein wasn't Orthodox?" When she shakes her head, he goes on. "We can do it this afternoon and you can come back later, any time, really, to select an urn."

"I do want to be alone in the room with her for a few minutes."

If Esther had a daughter, if she were that daughter, she'd be granted that much. The ruined body, organs removed and slits running the length of the abdomen, is no longer the woman she loved, but she still needs to tell her, whatever bit of Esther's soul is within hearing, that she's sorry. That she loves her, and is grateful for being loved. She has to do that.

She follows the director out of the nondescript office through the waiting area empty of people, its chairs ready to receive mourners. He opens the chapel door and points to a closed casket lying atop a carpeted platform, then disappears as the door swings shut.

The fine grain of the wood, polished to a sheen, is the same lovely, burnished golden oak as her hat forms. She's letting her mind wander, not saying any of the things she's planned. Perhaps Esther has some way of knowing. Maybe her spirit really can find its way into the deepest, most private places in her heart, to feel the love, the grieving, the wish that Valerie could somehow turn back time to a week ago.

What would you tell me if you could speak?

She'll never know, not if she stands here for a year, but she's not ready to go yet.

This is the woman who made enough noise to scare off her attacker, even as she was being murdered, did it to protect Joanna, and she paid with her life for the ferocity of her struggle. Esther fought back, the police said, and the fingerprints on the cane and the strands of hair tangled in her fingers will help them convict someone. But first the person has to be caught. Fingerprints, hair strands, pewter pins, what does any of it matter now?

Dear God, where is Joanna?

The chill air raises goose bumps on her arms and she shivers. Wear a wire—that was such a dramatic offer, but it will work. Before she and Johnny go back to the house on Albemarle Road on Friday she must convince Russo to let her go through with it.

Both hands on the casket, the words she wants to say to her friend finally come. "I know you don't believe in revenge, Esther, but I promise you, I'm going to do everything in my power to make sure you're not forgotten. Justice, Esther, not revenge. I love you."

Now she can go.

Russo is waiting in the reception area in a chair near the door, his legs crossed and his jaw slack with inattention because there's nothing to do, no one to watch. She hadn't realized how exhausted he looks. When he sees her, he rises.

"You okay?"

She nods, dry-eyed and composed, but she knows he's

not convinced. "I've been better. Have you thought about it? The wire, I mean."

"Sure. I've thought about it. And the answer is still the same."

Bright daylight assaults her as he shoves the door open. All right, then, she'll have to do it without him. "I want to walk back. It's only about a mile. I'll talk to you later."

If he'd given her a different answer, she might have been able to sit beside him in his car and make small talk, but now she can't bear the thought. She heads off down the street toward the park, a green blur in the distance.

Halfway down the block, a horn beeps. It's Russo, motioning to the car. She scowls and shakes her head, and he pulls away behind a city bus spewing exhaust.

The house feels almost like home, sun striking the uneven surfaces of the brownstone at an angle that makes it glitter with tiny lights. Not quite *her* home, but familiar. Except for the cottage she and Joanna shared until the Starrs invaded her life, she's always lived in *their* homes, her mother's, Johnny's, Esther's, and now Antonia's, who has been so good to her through all this.

It's cool inside, and silent. Antonia must be napping; just as well, since she has things to do. She takes her shoes off so Antonia won't be disturbed and then heads for the second floor. The risers are so solid that nothing creaks as she makes her way upstairs. When she reaches the top step, a voice calls to her from the bedroom at the end of the hall.

"Valerie, I'm so glad you're home. Please come in here."

And she knows. These are the same words, and it's with the same tremulous insistence that Antonia says them. Something is wrong.

Antonia is propped against the pillows, the remote control in her hand; a black and white Ginger Rogers twirls across the television screen to the strains of a gentle soft-shoe.

"What happened, Antonia?"

The blind woman reaches out as though she's searching for Valerie's hand. "There's been another phone call, Valerie. The same man, the same voice. Oh, my dear, I'm so hopeful."

twenty-nine

"He said it was very wise of you to take his advice about not contacting the police. And he said Joanna was doing fine. He made a point of that. I asked who he was, but he refused to tell me. He said, again, that he wanted to talk to you personally, and that he'd call another time."

Valerie's caught in a repeating loop of tape, reliving the hope and fear of that first phone call with each word Antonia says, mesmerized by the spinning in her own head.

Her anonymous caller might be the person who will bring Joanna to the DASH meeting Friday night. Maybe he's called just to let her know her daughter is unharmed, that she doesn't have to worry about Joanna's health and safety. But why would he do that?

"I think we both need coffee after all this, my dear. I'll have Nadia bring some up." Antonia reaches for the brass bell on the bedside table. Nadia appears, nods when Antonia tells her what she wants, and then goes off to fill the request.

Antonia lies back against the pillows. She's thrown aside the light afghan. The soft fabric of her trousers drapes against her withered legs, and she reaches down and pulls the afghan back up. "Was it very difficult?"

It takes a minute for Valerie to realize she's talking about the trip to the funeral home. "About what I'd expected. It's almost a relief to be done with it. It feels a little like losing my mother all over again, in a funny way."

What made her say that? She doesn't want to unburden herself to Antonia. But now that she's said it aloud, the hard shell of pain has a tiny chink, a promise that it may someday crack a little more. It's true, she does know about the rest of this, how she'll turn around expecting Esther to be there to hear her musings or to tell her about her day.

"You must have been quite young when your mother died. You're *still* young. I imagine you must have had a hard time of it." Antonia's head is canted toward her. With her finger she flicks off the remote, silencing the musical entertainment.

"She got sick the summer after I graduated from high school. I used to think my mother was trying to torture me by moving around so much and she was sure I was trying to make her life miserable by acting out in every adolescent way I possibly could. I'm glad we cleared things up before she died."

Her mother would have adored Joanna. It's hard to think about that now without feeling a wrenching sense of loss.

Nadia's footsteps click along the wood floor. Coffee . . . Suddenly she knows she can't get through the rest of the day without a jolt of caffeine to keep her from sinking into the abyss of waiting.

"Would you pour for me, please?" Antonia holds her thumb and forefinger half an inch apart. "Just a bit of cream, please. Then, she never knew Joanna. That's too bad."

What an eerie feeling, as though the woman has been listening in on her private thoughts. "She told me the day before she died that she knew I'd have a daughter someday. She said I should remember all the things she'd done wrong as a parent so I wouldn't make the same mistakes. I tried to make her laugh, told her I was insulted that she considered me a mistake. And then I said I planned to remember all the things she'd done right, so I could pass them along to my daughter. Really, we were both apologizing for hurting each other."

"I can hardly believe you ever did anything to hurt her, not by design. You're such a joy to me, I can't see you doing anything malicious."

In the shadowy room, Valerie understands she's been invited to explain.

"It wasn't malice, but I can see now I was pushing her deliberately. I wanted her to either throw me out—which would prove that I was truly as bad as I was trying to be—or put up with my antics until I wore myself out, ran out of ideas, and settled into adulthood."

"But that's not the way it went, is it? You reached some sort of understanding before either of those things could happen."

She can see her mother, arms folded, waiting in the doorway, and she shivers, remembering how close they came to going their separate ways that day.

"I'd been out with my friend Gene. Eugenia. Except she'd never let anyone call her that, insisted we call her Gene even if she got teased about its being a man's name. We were poking around the back roads, stopping every once in a while to pick berries or talk to one of the boys driving tractor in a field we'd pass. We had a six-pack in the car and we decided to go sit with our feet in the stream out behind an old apple orchard where our friend Larry showed us morel mushrooms the month before.

"We polished off the beer. It got cold, and I had to get back to study for my chemistry final. So Gene dropped me at home and there she was, my mother, standing in the doorway and looking like one of the original Furies.

"She never got mad, you understand. It was always more like whenever I did anything wrong, she'd get sad, kind of close herself up and give me one of these looks loaded with messages. About her disappointment. About my failure to help her get through her difficult life."

The coffee cup clinks against the saucer, and Antonia slides a finger along the inner rim until she's found the right spot. "No wonder you felt you had to misbehave. It was the only way to break her out of that stupor."

Amazing how she seems to know certain things with such clarity.

"That *was* what I was doing, only I didn't know it at

the time. Anyway, I tried walking past her to go to my room, but she grabbed my arm. 'We may be poor,' she said, 'but you don't have to steal.' I was indignant. I might have gotten into all kinds of trouble, but I'd never stolen a thing in my life. I had no idea what she was talking about and I told her so.

"She started screaming that I knew what she meant, that I'd been breaking into people's houses and taking their jewelry and silverware. She demanded to know where I kept all the loot, yelled that I was doing this to her just to make her life hell. I was really bewildered until she said something about Corrine, where did I meet this thief, she was going to call her parents and tell them to keep their daughter away from me."

Alarm and confusion make Antonia's voice shrill. "You stole things from people? Their jewelry? With this Corrine person? She was the instigator, I presume."

"Corrine Malfemme. Gene and I took forever to come up with the right name. My face turned a very bright shade of purple, I'm sure. I told my mother she had no right to go into my room and read things I'd written in my notebooks. I was seventeen and I was entitled to privacy and what was she doing snooping around reading things that didn't have anything to do with her. When I finished, she told me that I'd left the notebook open on my dresser and she was putting my laundry away and saw it and couldn't help reading it.

"She didn't believe me at first so I told her again. What she thought was my diary was really just a story Gene and I were making up, an adventure we'd started to write after the incident I told you about the other day, when we cooked breakfast at the reporter's house on Copake Lake."

They'd labored for hours, when they were supposed to be doing English homework and when they baby-sat for neighbors' kids, adding a silver tea service here, a home alarm system there, trying to make the story sound as bad and real as they could.

Antonia laughs, a staccato burst of sound that ends in a sigh of relief. "I couldn't imagine that I'd misread you so completely."

"My mother said something just like that. We talked and talked about it, and finally she just got up and hugged me. That's all, just a hug, but it was the first time she'd done that in such a long time that I began to cry, and we just held on to each other until we started laughing."

"Surely incidents like that prepare you to be a better parent. You must have given a lot of thought to how you can keep the lines of communication open. With your daughter, I mean. So you don't have to repeat the same difficulties with her as you did with your—"

From another room, a telephone sounds. It's Nadia's phone, the number Valerie gave to Jack Cleary. Before she's halfway down the hall, the ringing stops.

A loud, cheerful stream of Polish and Nadia's husky laughter roll out into the hall from the bedroom she shares with Carl.

The call isn't for her.

Isn't an instruction from a honeyed voice telling her to be on a street corner to get her daughter.

Isn't Russo or Gallagher, saying that Joanna is waiting for her at the precinct, that this time they'll make sure the child is released only to her mother.

Mommy.

When she returns to the master bedroom, Antonia has finished her coffee. Valerie gathers the empty cups and loads them onto the tray.

"I'll just take these downstairs and put them in the dishwasher. Can I get you anything before I go?"

Antonia's smile is touched with sadness. "No, I don't need anything right now. You go ahead. We can talk about what you planned for your daughter another time. I know you're restless. When you want some company, my dear, I'll be here. You didn't really tell me very much about what it was like at the funeral home, either. Maybe later . . ."

And maybe not.

Some things won't ever become stories.

thirty

It was the first good break they'd had.

Ramon Feliciano and his girlfriend had been seen on the street with a toddler.

As soon as he heard the beat cop, what was his name, Sawyer, tell the story this morning, he'd had a good feeling about it. Sawyer was bragging how he busted Feliciano two days ago for carrying a pebble of crack. Boasting about how he fought off an attack by Feliciano's girlfriend, a hellcat of a woman with long dark hair who nearly scratched his face to ribbons while a kid in a stroller hollered like crazy.

He'd turned it over in his mind, talked it over with Gallagher, until it made some sense.

Ramon Feliciano needed money to support his crack habit. His sheet was a long list of breaking and entering charges, ten years' worth, plus the occasional late night flip of an old woman who should have known better than to be out on Fourth Avenue alone after dark.

So maybe Esther Klein had been marked as an easy target by Feliciano and his girlfriend and they followed her home.

Maybe the girlfriend noticed Valerie Vincent's ID, thought the credit cards would be useful, only the Klein woman tried to chase them away, got noisy, which attracted the attention of the downstairs neighbor. Maybe she put up a struggle when they grabbed Vincent's papers and one of them reached for the cane and smashed the old woman in the head again and again. Then, realizing what they'd done, they'd fled.

Then they saw the kid and that piece of jewelry on the television news and really got scared because the pin was the girlfriend's and could tie her to the murder.

She came down to the station, claimed to be the kid's mother, had all the papers, and off they went.

It could have been like that. If they could find her, they'd know. If she was the woman who came down to collect the kid, he'd recognize her right away, he was sure of that.

Mitch Russo walked to the corner again, but he didn't expect to see anything on the fifteenth pass that he might have missed the first fourteen times.

"Okay, Mitch, let's get this figured out." Teresa Gallagher passed him a folded paper plate and some napkins.

He peeled the plate back and pulled the sticky mozzarella back onto the slice of pizza. "You first," he said, his stomach doing a somersault as he watched the oil gather into a pool on top of the thick cheese.

"Where's Feliciano and his girlfriend and the baby Sawyer saw with them? They're not home, they're not at the garage where he hangs out, and nobody on the street's saying a word."

Russo tossed the uneaten slice into a trash can, then wiped each finger carefully with a wad of napkins. "First thing comes to mind is they're hiding. We have to put out the word we're ready to cut him a deal on the crack bust if he comes up with the right information. Feliciano's ripe for being hit hard, if the judge is in the mood. So maybe he'll listen."

Gallagher shook her head. "Okay, macho man, who do we tell? You have any good contacts in this neighborhood, or do we have to get someone who's closer to the streets, Sawyer, maybe, to do our talking for us? 'Cause I think my people aren't going to give Feliciano up if there's a murder charge involved. And I want to have something to show for this time besides a case of heartburn and a receipt for ten gallons of gas." She bit into her pizza and chewed thoughtfully.

Russo looked away. She was probably right; it wouldn't be so easy to break community solidarity, if it meant turning in one of their own to a murder rap. "What about that guy at the bakery down near Atlantic Avenue? You think he might get the word out to the neighborhood?"

Instead of answering his question, Gallagher pointed to a white Honda pulling up to the curb on the other side of the street. Two people in the front seat. A man and a woman? Maybe two women, it was hard to tell from here. Might have been hard to tell even right up close, the way people all looked alike these days.

A trickle of oil ran down Gallagher's hand; she blotted it with a napkin, crumpled the greasy paper plate, and stuffed the mess into the trash can. She lifted a pair of binoculars from the glove compartment of the car, sighted on the vehicle across the street. "Holy shit. That's Feliciano. See that tattoo on the side of his neck? The Chinese dragon? It's them."

He grabbed the binoculars and did a quick scan. A man with a scrawny ponytail and a woman with long dark curls. And a child on the woman's lap. He could see part of the child's arm, the top of a head, not enough to be sure.

"Let's do this easy." He laid the binoculars on the seat. "You stay on this side of the street and walk slow, like you're out for a stroll, so you end up on the passenger side. I'll cross over and come up behind the car and take the driver's side. Let me get there first."

"Aw, gee, Mitch, you went first the last time." But Gallagher was teasing, smiling at him, and they started walking at the same time.

He stuck his hand in his pocket and curled his fingers around his revolver, the windbreaker suddenly too warm for the bright day. The couple in the Honda were arguing, shouting in Spanish. Feliciano's hands smashed against the steering wheel. That little quarrel would keep Feliciano and his passenger occupied, would keep them from noticing two pedestrians closing in on their car.

He was almost behind the car now; his mouth was dry but he looked straight ahead. Not yet. Another couple of steps.

A Boar's Head Provisions truck rattled by, and when it passed the driver glanced at the car. Russo wiped the sweat from his forehead and approached the Honda. Gallagher was about fifteen paces behind, walking as though she were out for a Sunday stroll. Her hand, too, was stuck in the pocket of her blazer.

Now.

He leaned into the car. "Hey, can you tell me how to get to Prospect Park?"

Feliciano's head whipped around, his eyes glittering with anger. "Get the fuck outta my face, man. Who are you? Get outta here."

Feliciano turned his angry glare on Russo long enough to give him a good look. Gallagher came around from behind to the passenger side of the car and bent toward the car, her face not two feet from the child squirming on the startled woman's lap.

It wasn't them.

Wasn't the woman who'd come to the precinct. Wasn't Joanna Vincent.

"You have a hearing problem or what?" Feliciano snarled. "You better get away from my car and keep walking, buster."

Buhstuh. Definitely a mean sonofabitch. But definitely not hooked up with the woman who carried Joanna Vincent out of the building Friday night. And certainly not sitting in this car with the child he was desperate to find.

"Hey, man, take it easy. No problem." Russo held his hands up and backed away, waited for Gallagher to come around beside him. They strode down the block in silence.

"Shit," he hissed when they turned the corner. "I was sure we were gonna wrap this whole package up, neat and easy."

"If you're really bored we could bust them." Gallagher grinned up at him. "Threatening an officer. Disorderly conduct. If we wait long enough, maybe we catch him being really abusive to her. Crime of the nineties, you know. Spousal abuse."

"I'm not that bored. And don't joke about that. You ever see what these guys—"

"Come on, Russo." She stopped walking, and stood, head bent, in the middle of the sidewalk. Her red hair blew across her face, and she reached up and brushed it away. "I was just blowing off, you know, so I don't have to be thinking every ten seconds about where that baby might be. A little black humor. That's what they call it, right?"

"No, they call it cynical bullshit. And it doesn't sound so hot coming from you." They had to stop this bickering. It wasn't going to get them anywhere.

But Gallagher's face got all tight. "Because I'm a woman? Guys are the only ones with a license to be sarcastic? You sound like my father."

If he were her father, he'd be even sadder to see his daughter turning harder by the minute on this job. "I'm sorry, okay? We're both disappointed. I'm running out of ideas here."

"That's why you need me." Her grin was a sign that the sniping was over. "I think we should talk to her. Valerie, I mean. Tell her what happened and find out if there's anything she might have remembered about kids in the neighborhood bothering Esther Klein. Because even if it's not Feliciano, the theory still makes sense."

"Sounds pointless to me. She already gave us everything she could think of. If she had any more ideas, she would have called me."

"Yes, I guess Valerie wouldn't keep something like that to herself. Funny how I think of her that way. *Valerie.* Doesn't it seem like Valerie Vincent could be your sister or your neighbor or something?"

Or yourself. He could see how hard it was for Teresa Gallagher to keep her distance, but he understood. He'd felt that way so many times through the years, especially when he first made detective. He nearly blew a case because he'd felt sorry for the guy whose furniture store was hit three times by thieves. When he found out the guy was running an insurance scam, he vowed never to put himself in that position again. They weren't his friends, they weren't his cousins. They were perps or victims. But Valerie Vincent had definitely gotten to him. To both of them.

"So, how would you tell your sister we came up empty again? She's gonna look at us with those eyes all full of disappointment, and finally she'll let us know she expected nothing else from us anyway." He wasn't exactly thrilled at the prospect of going back there, but maybe Gallagher was right about asking one more time about Esther Klein and neighborhood kids. "Let's get out of here."

They walked to the car, past the spot where the white Honda had been parked minutes before. When Gallagher clicked the seat belt in place, she said, "You know, I've been thinking about her offer to go into DASH with a wire. Valerie Vincent can be a tough customer. She has to be, or she'd have fallen apart by now. That scheme of hers actually might work. She's already gotten pretty far with these nut cases."

"And you'd want your sister to go in there with a wire? Your *civilian* sister?" He turned the key and the engine kicked over. "Maybe it's worth a shot. I hate the idea, you know, but maybe . . . I don't know. She's smart, but she's also too close to this case, too emotional, to be reliable."

"Too emotional? Look at it this way, Mitch. She's the most motivated person around." Gallagher swigged from her diet cola and nodded. "And she's already met those people. They told her to come back on Friday, right? So that proves she knows how to handle herself."

He felt his resistance sliding away in the face of Gallagher's argument. They sure as hell hadn't made any progress. And if the media found out about Joanna's disappearance, the NYPD was in for a shredding. How much worse could it get?

"I'll drop you off," he said as though the matter was settled, "and then go over there and talk to her."

He couldn't do it.

He kept seeing her face, those eyes, and he couldn't bear knowing that, before he spoke to her about going in wired to the DASH meeting, he'd have to tell Valerie Vincent he hadn't found her daughter yet.

At least it's not worse news. He tried to take courage from that thought, but he drove right past the brownstone and kept going, all the way down Prospect Park West to the traffic circle at Fifteenth Street, hooking a right at the south border of the park and driving on until he realized what he was doing.

The parking spot in front of the insurance office was empty, as though someone knew he was coming and had cleared a place for him. He locked up, headed for the door, but Cissie must have seen him pull up. She ran to him, her face white.

"What happened? Is it David? It's that motorcycle, isn't it? Tell me, Mitch."

"No, babe, David's all right. He's twenty-one. You have to stop thinking about him like he's still your little three-year-old. Nothing happened. I just needed to see you for a minute." He'd never done this before. And now he felt stupid, totally dumb to be standing on the street in the middle of the afternoon, in the middle of the messiest case of his life. Frightening Cissie like that. "I'm sorry if I scared you, Ciss. I drove over here, I didn't even know why or where I was going. I just needed to see you."

The color was returning to her cheeks, and she stepped back and frowned at him. "It's that missing baby, isn't it? Tell me. She's not . . . It can't be. I told you this morning. I woke up with this feeling, it was so strong. Like God was telling me that little baby was going to be okay. I'm never wrong when I get that feeling. You didn't—"

"No. That's not it. Nothing like that." He told her about the confrontation on the street, about his frustration and his anger and his embarrassment. Finally he understood why he'd come to see Cissie before he spoke to Valerie Vincent. He could see it in his wife's eyes, and he wanted to say it first. "I have to go talk to her about an idea that Teresa and I kicked around, but I needed to work this out before I saw her. It's not about me feeling like a failure. It's about a dead woman. And a missing kid and her mother."

Cissie wrapped her arms around him, and he buried his face in her hair. "You better go talk to that mother

bout your idea," she said firmly. "And make sure you
ell her about my feeling. You're a good man, Mitch
Russo."

Maybe he was, but he'd rather be hearing someone
ell him he was a good cop right now.

thirty-one

Just as she steps out of the shower, the telephone rings. She can't tell which phone it is, Antonia's or Nadia's. DASH or her anonymous caller?

She's dripping water all over the floor, can't stop to towel off. She wraps Kristin's robe around her wet body and opens the door in time to hear Nadia say, "Yes, just a minute. I'll have to get her."

DASH.

"I'll be right there, Nadia." Her wet feet slap on the wood floor as she runs to the bedroom, pushing clumps of dripping hair out of her eyes. "Thanks."

Nadia hands her the phone and pads away down the hall.

"Yes?" She's a little out of breath, but she manages to get the single word out.

"Is this Alice?"

A familiar voice. A woman, someone she's talked to recently. Pamela Cleary.

"Oh, hi, Pamela. Yes, this is Alice." She's not Valerie. Not Joanna's mother. She's a teacher. She's Alice Monroe, and she wants to join DASH.

"Now don't be disappointed. We all know how much you and your husband want to help. Don't take it personally. It's not all decided yet, but I have to tell you the truth: we may use another family on this mission. Some members of the group believe it wouldn't be fair to ask you to do this so soon, not until you know a little more about what's involved. You know what I'm saying?"

What Pamela Cleary's saying is they want to know more about her. And if what they find doesn't meet with their approval, they'll send Joanna away with someone else.

She forces the panic from her voice. She must play the role—tell the story—of Alice Monroe.

"That's a shame. My husband and I went out and got a youth bed and some toys, new clothes, you know, little girl things. We thought you told us we'd be able to help. Can I ask who it is, this other family?"

"I'm sorry, I can't tell you that." Pamela sounds truly regretful. "Please, don't worry about it, Alice. You can still come to our regular meetings. Even if it doesn't work out this time, there will be other opportunities. Jack says this is for the best."

Pamela's heart isn't in it. She's parroting his words, but the tone is all wrong, too apologetic, much too compassionate. "But the decision is still going to be made by Friday?"

"That's my understanding. Jack never tells us the details until the last minute except we do know it's going to be soon. We make plans and we wait to be told who, where, when. But not before tomorrow, I know that."

"Listen, Pamela, I'd really like to talk to Jack. Can I stop by tonight, this afternoon, whenever it's convenient?" She'll spin a tale for Jack Cleary to convince him that this child's best chance for a positive, productive, yes, even *pious* future lies with Alice Monroe and her husband Martin.

"Hold on a minute, all right?"

Pamela is going to plead her case.

She's taking a chance, pushing like this; she's not showing the proper respect for the authority of the group leader. She should have gone along with Jack Cleary's plan, a good soldier.

Oh, God, what's she done? They're going to give Joanna away again to the wrong—

"Alice? Jack says you and your husband should come to the house tomorrow night at seven. Both of you. Can you be there at seven o'clock?"

It's going to be all right. She can do this.

"We'll be there," Valerie says, hoping that Pamela Cleary can't hear the note of triumph in her assurance. "Thanks."

She sets the phone back in the cradle and follows her damp footprints back to the small bedroom at the end of the hall.

Every time she passes a window she pauses to look out. Traffic rolls by, people stroll or scurry along, and then disappear from the framed scene, and Valerie Vincent goes on with the business of waiting. This time, however, a dark car draws her attention. She watches with interest as it glides to the curb and parks near the fire hydrant two doors down.

Detective Russo gets out and heads toward the brownstone. He turns left into the walk leading to the front door, and with each step he takes, she knows.

The shoulders, the purposeful gait as he approaches the house, that look of anticipation on his face all give it away and she knows.

Joanna has been taken to a hospital so they can do tests to make sure she's really as fine and healthy as she looks.

Or they're holding her at the police station, asking her questions, showing her pictures of suspects in Esther's murder.

Or Detective Gallagher is going to drive up in another car soon and Joanna will clamber out of the back seat and race to the steps.

Unless Russo's found her, and she's not with him because he's discovered something terrible, some unspeakable, unthinkable horror, and he—

She flies to the door. Russo's standing with his hand on the buzzer, startled, mouth open.

"I don't have any news, Ms. Vincent. I'm sorry, I really wish I had something to tell you, but I don't."

He's talking but she can't hear his words. She's re-

reated again to the place inside herself where she goes to
ecover from disappointment. She's become so good at
his in the past few days, it doesn't take very long for her
o motion him inside. He heads for the study, and she
ollows behind.

"If you don't have any news, why are you here?" She
owers herself to the desk chair and waits for his answer as
e sits across from her.

"I talked it over with Teresa—Detective Gallagher—
nd she convinced me we should let you do it. Go to that
meeting on Friday with a mike and a recording device
aped to you. I'm not completely okay with the idea, you
understand—we must be nuts to let an amateur take this
n—but we're going to do it. If you still think you can."

She could kiss him.

She could lift his lumpy body from the chair and twirl
im around the room in celebration. "Yes! Of course I can
o it."

"Look, besides the risk, there's something else we
didn't discuss. You gotta understand: going to that meet-
ng—with or without a wire—is no guarantee of anything.
Maybe nothing will happen. I mean, maybe they'll all just
it around and talk about the weather. You can't get your-
elf worked up thinking this is the end of it."

He can try to add his sober little note of warning, but
Mitch Russo isn't going to steal this moment of victory
rom her. That meeting Friday night will be the key to
inding Joanna.

Better than that, she's still holding out for the possibil-
ty that her daughter is going to be there, waiting to be
aken to what they all think is a new home.

Waiting to be folded into the loving arms of the
woman who will feed her, bathe her, care for her with a
mother's love.

"I have plenty of time to think about all the ways I
might be disappointed later. Right now, I just want to be a
ittle excited, okay?"

Russo shrugs, his face impassive. "Fine. Now listen.
Detective Gallagher will come by on Friday afternoon and
et you up. We want you to have a little time to get used to

how the wire works. We have to test the equipment and make sure the damn thing isn't going to jam up at the wrong second or something like that."

It won't jam. It can't happen like that.

"Sure, good. I'll be here."

"They called you, right?"

A pulse hammers inside her head. Russo couldn't possibly know about the phone calls. Unless someone else told him. "Called me?"

"About the meeting Friday. You told me they were going to call you back to let you know where the meeting was."

She almost laughs with relief. "I spoke to Pamela Cleary about an hour ago. The Friday meeting is at the same place. We're supposed to go talk to them tomorrow, too. A second interview. I think they just want to know a little more about us. And then we're to come to the house again on Friday. Do you think we can get everything set up for tomorrow? I can do both meetings with the tape and—"

"Let's leave it the way we planned it, okay?" Russo pushes himself out of the leather chair. "I'd rather you didn't go to that meeting tomorrow at all, but if you do go, you go without the wire. We'll do it on Friday. Meanwhile, I want you to think again about any neighborhood kids Mrs. Klein might have told you about. A delivery boy. Someone who followed her on the street, a kid who tried to snatch her purse, maybe. Like I said yesterday, we can't just give up on the other stuff. So you think about it. And call me later."

If she thinks about purse snatchers from now until Christmas, it won't help them find Esther's killer. She knows that with a certainty she's rarely felt since the moment in East Hampton when she saw Joanna's wide eyes looking up at her from the television screen.

"I'll try, I really will. It's probably a futile exercise, but I really will try to remember if I've heard her say something about problems in the neighborhood."

Russo hesitates, then says, "My wife says we're going to find her. Cissie always has these feelings—it's kind of weird to be saying this—but she made me promise to tell you."

"Thank her for me, would you?" She closes the door quickly, so he won't see her tears and change his mind.

thursday

thirty-two

The second one tasted even better than the first. Johnny Starr wrapped his fingers around the handle of the squat, thick mug and licked at the foam that lingered on his lips.

Everyone was always trying to tell him what to do.

Francine, Valerie, his boss, those peculiar, uptight people sitting around that house in Brooklyn, Martha and Lucas, especially Martha and Lucas, all his life, never trusting him to make the right choices. Even when he was fifteen, sixteen years old and buying jeans, *jeans,* for Chrissake, they hovered and criticized and second-guessed and never let him exercise his own judgment.

Now Lucas was trying to force him into church and make him over so that he wore their brand of propriety. Well, maybe that was fine for him, a man living out of time, in a past that didn't exist for most of the world anymore, but Johnny Starr was never again going to be held hostage to his parents' demands.

And ramrod Jack Cleary and his prissy little wife, jerking them around, trying to get them to see conspiracies everywhere. Sitting around in their gray suits and ties, with their wives in that Stepford stupor, doing exactly what they were supposed to, all of them worried sick about Satanic cabals, so committed to sanitizing the world. Kevin Murchison's magazine articles were right on:

those people didn't realize the filthy little corners of the
own souls could use a good scrubbing.

He lifted the glass to his lips, hesitated, then gulpe
down half the remaining beer. Warmth coursed throug
his arms; he felt a little lightheaded and a lot more powe
ful, but this was enough. Just this second one, he'd finish
and stop.

He could do this. Two beers, that's all, and then he'
walk away and feel better for it. He was the one decidin
just how far to go. If he'd learned nothing else in the yea
of counseling, it was that he was in control of his ow
behavior, not any of the people on that long list. And nc
the alcohol, that was for sure.

Johnny Starr looked at his watch, glad for the twent
minutes before he had to leave to meet Valerie. He neede
this time to get himself calm, to find that place where h
could meet the person he'd told them he was, God, wha
was the name? He laughed. Anyway, if he couldn't re
member when he got there, they'd only think it was hi
excitement and not that he'd actually forgotten his ow
name.

Michael Monroe, that was it. And his wife was Alice
A my name is Alice and I come from Alabama.

When she was a girl, did Valerie play that game
Seemed like that's all they did in second grade, those girl
with their little pink balls on the blacktop of the schoc
driveway as they waited for the bright yellow buses t
carry them home.

J my name is Joanna and I come from . . . where
Where would she say? Brooklyn, Taconic Hills, where?

"Get you another?" The bartender offered her college
girl smile and nodded at his glass.

"No, thanks." He slid a ten across the damp surfac
and watched as she picked it up and set it beside the cas
register while she counted out his change. He didn't wan
another one, didn't need it, wasn't going to fall into thos
old patterns. Proof, wasn't it, that he was stronger tha
any of them gave him credit for?

If nothing else, maybe Francine would finally agre
when this was over that they should get married. She'
been feeling so safe. Until that detective knocked on th

door and forced Franny to hide in the bedroom and sent her running down the rickety, rusty steps of the fire escape. Maybe now she'd finally see the wisdom of what he'd been saying for months—if they got married she wouldn't have to worry about being shipped back, would be able to live like a normal person, without looking over her shoulder all the time.

Just the two of them, making a life on their own terms. The two of them and Joanna. They'd get Valerie to agree to a regular schedule of weekends, so that Joanna became a real part of their lives.

The last of the beer cooled his throat as the half glassful slid down. Johnny Starr scooped up the change, slid a dollar bill to the edge of the bar, and looked at the door. Outside, the sun was so dazzling, people wore sunglasses to shield themselves from the glare but in here a cool, comforting darkness allowed him to think, really think clearly without the distractions of all that brightness and noise.

He was ready for whatever they planned to throw at him, prepared to convince those Clearys and their gang of four, the puppets, that he was Michael Monroe, husband of what's her name, Alice, that's it, and that they were fine, concerned citizens who wanted to help kids, that he was a good provider who believed that children needed to be shielded from the devil-worshiping idolaters, and that he polished his shoes and combed his hair and made his bed and cared about all those tiny details, that superficial minutiae they seemed to think mattered so damn much.

What a bunch of lunatics.

But that wasn't his problem. And at least he'd prove to Valerie that he was ready to be his daughter's father. Going to these dumb meetings would accomplish that, if it did nothing else.

When this was over, he'd have plenty to do to settle into his new life. The move to the new apartment, setting up the business, starting to paint again so that the images he'd been wrestling with in his mind might finally come alive on canvas. Settling in for all the world to see with Francine and with Joanna.

But first they had to get through the next couple o days.

He was ready now.

Johnny Starr grabbed a handful of mints, popped on into his mouth as he stepped out of the shadows. Fiv minutes left, just enough time to walk from the corner o Seventh Avenue and President Street to the Carrera hous on Prospect Park West, where he was meeting Valerie. H made sure his shirt was tucked in all around as he heade down the street.

thirty-three

Something's going to go wrong.

The persistent refrain is driving her mad. They may have a plan, but that doesn't mean it's going to work. The only thing she can do is stay alert and prepare thoroughly.

First, the costume. A small-town teacher with her white blouse buttoned to the neck, no-color panty hose, and sensible, low-heeled, unscuffed shoes. She looks as though she could stand in front of thirty-five restless ten-year-olds for hours. The small gold hoops in her ears finish the picture.

The image in the mirror is positively dripping with propriety. But it's not only how she looks; she has to play to her audience without hitting any false notes. So many ways she and Johnny can be unmasked. Too many possibilities for blowing the scene.

He'll be here in five minutes, an hour too early for the meeting on Albemarle Road, but he doesn't know that, isn't aware of her little precaution to ensure that they'll ring the bell precisely at seven. Even if they have to walk around the park until their feet ache, they will definitely be on time for this meeting.

They'll tell their story sincerely, emphatically, irresistibly, and she'll have her daughter back.

And then what's to stop them from coming after her when she's settled in yet another small town? What's to keep them from following Joanna, grabbing her up off the street on her way home from school one day?

She'll just have to find a way to keep them both safe, even if it means moving to another state and taking another name and never seeing the rolling hills of the Hudson Valley again.

She tosses two twenties into the zipper section of her purse and lays the snapshot of Joanna in a dresser drawer, runs her finger along the curve of her daughter's cheek before she slides the drawer shut. *Soon, baby. Only a day.* A breeze blows the curtains aside, and she reaches over to shut the window.

Johnny Starr is across the street, leaning nonchalantly against a car as he looks up at her with a strange, sly smile lifting his mouth. His dark trousers and blazer look crisp, his white shirt dances with reflected light. He waves, then crosses the street, and Valerie Vincent runs down the stairs.

How nice that one of them is relaxed and at ease. God's in His heaven, Johnny's ready for anything, and all's right with the world.

"Val, you look like the *Saturday Evening Post.*" He ambles up the walk, grinning broadly as he leans forward to kiss her.

She swivels out of the way of his lips, and he misses her mouth and grazes the corner of her nose. Her shock is instantly replaced by an outrage so fierce she trembles.

"You've been drinking." A sharp pain stabs at her temples as she shoves him away.

He stumbles backward, reaching out for the post of the gas lamp. Just in time, he steadies himself against the flowerpot to break his fall.

Okay, so this is what I was dreading, this is what had to go wrong. She should be furious, wild with anger, but oddly she feels relief.

She doesn't like it, hates it, in fact, but this she can deal with. She can explain this away to Jack Cleary—an accident, Martin's poor aunt suddenly ill, a dead relative in Michigan, something. Because he's not going with her to that house, not with all those eyes watching him. She won't take the chance that Johnny will make a deadly mistake—an inconsistency in their story, an inability to stand without swaying. And they'll smell the alcohol as easily as she has. Even if he doesn't do something utterly stupid, his drinking will be a deadly strike against them.

She's going alone.

"What, Val? What did you do that for?" The linden tree casts dappled shadows that hood his eyes in darkness.

"You've been drinking, Johnny."

"Only one, Val. Only a beer." He moves toward her, his hands in his pockets, diffident, boyish.

Dangerous.

He plants himself in front of her, tears in his eyes, the king of bad judgment transformed into the master of regret.

"Get out of my way. And don't follow me or I'll call the cops and have them ask you a few hundred more questions." Russo would do that for her, or Gallagher, if she can reach them. "You told me you were sober for nearly a year. Great time you picked to break your dry spell, Johnny. I don't care if it was just this once, you're a liar and you're not ready to accept responsibility for yourself, never mind an eighteen-month-old child. I won't risk losing Joanna to save your ego, or whatever it is that made you think you could get away with it. You're not coming with me, Johnny. Now, get out of my way."

To her amazement, Johnny Starr backs down the sidewalk and lets her pass. "I'm going to that house," he says under his breath, "and I'm going to be part of Joanna's life."

The curtain parts in the living-room window, and Nadia's face appears from behind the thick floral drapes. The housekeeper looks like one of those coins cut in half so that two lovers each get a matching piece. The half face turns back to the room, reporting to Antonia, no doubt, and then the curtain falls shut.

"No, Johnny, you're not going. What's your name? Where do you come from? What's wrong with your aunt?" If she had her hands on her hips, if she were shaking her head and wagging her finger in his face, she'd look just like the kindergarten teacher she sounds like.

Have they always chosen these roles: bad boy, reproving grownup?

"Monroe. Michael Monroe. And I'm from—" His face is bright with consternation and he looks away. "It was just two beers, Val. I'm all right now and I'll be perfect by the time we get there."

Now it's *two* beers. Whatever the real number, it doesn't matter. He's not going. No way. *Martin* Monroe is about to be unavoidably detained.

"You remember the time I left your father's binoculars on top of the car and then drove away?" he asks. "And you said you believed in forgiveness? That everyone is entitled to their mistakes?"

"And do you remember the night you told me I could have my heart's desire, that you'd do anything I requested, no questions asked? The game of Anything. If you're going to bring up the past, Johnny, I'd like to remind you that I never collected."

As soon as the words are out, she wishes she could snatch them back. That was another life, one they no longer share.

The game of Anything—she hasn't thought about it in years. She had suggested they play the local version of Truth or Dare, and Johnny agreed, as long as she was It first.

"I want to know the saddest thing that ever happened to you," he'd demanded, and after she pulled on her socks and shoes because her feet were cold in the damp evening grass, she'd told him. About the afternoon when she was seven years old, Wildflowers coloring book and all her crayons spread out on the kitchen table, not really paying attention to the strange man at the back door until she realized what he was saying to her mother.

Her father was dead.

He'd been taken from the speedway to the hospital, but he was dead before they put him in the ambulance. Seething with anger at her father's desertion and at her mother, who just slumped into a chair and sat there for an eternity after the man left, she'd kept her head down and stabbed at the coloring book with the red crayon until her arm ached. Then she'd turned to a new page and colored the petals and the leaves and the butterfly's patterned wings, colored them black with meticulous precision.

When it was her turn to ask Johnny for Anything, she'd been too exhausted to collect.

"That's not fair, Val." His cheeks are flushed, as though he's been stung by embarrassment. "I'm not going with you to that house, but it's not because you want me to stay away. I can see you're right, that I might mess up. I don't . . . I can't . . ."

"I'll walk you to the subway, Johnny. I'll wait with you for your train." *And make sure you get on it going in the right direction. Back where you came from.* Rage swells inside her, a glass bubble in her chest that's about to shatter and cut her with slivers of regret and fear.

"Don't. Give me that, at least. I am going back. Let me go alone." His face is gray now, defeated, and she resists the impulse to hurt him with more words.

"Go home, Johnny."

He walks toward the Plaza in a dispirited shuffle, crossing one corner, then another, until finally he's lost behind a covey of bicycle-riding children in the distance.

When she can no longer see him, she turns and heads down Prospect Park West behind a silver-haired woman struggling with a Jack Russell terrier who seems determined to pull her into the middle of the street.

"You just remember *you're* the dog and I'm the master," the woman mutters as Valerie passes them.

It's all a matter of control.

At Ninth Street, Valerie stops at the monument guarding the entrance to the park. A squirrel, its tail a forlorn imitation of the brushy curl she expects, watches her from the crotch of a tree limb bright with green leaves. In a blink, it scurries around to the other side of the trunk and winds its way into higher branches, as though it won't be visible if it doesn't take a direct route.

By the time she's reached Albemarle Road her story is fixed firmly in her mind. She's become Alice Monroe again. She's ready for whatever is going to happen in the big white house.

thirty-four

Jack Cleary's face is perfectly neutral, the set of his mouth neither smiling in approval nor downturned with dismay. He must have practiced that uninflected expression in front of a mirror thousands of times before he got it right. It's meant to keep her guessing, she's certain, and it would be wasted effort to try to figure out what it means. Alice Monroe wouldn't notice, would simply accept what she sees. Alice Monroe's a good girl, distracted by thoughts of her injured husband.

"Well, I do hope he'll be all right. Methodist Hospital, is that what you said? They've got fine doctors, especially in the emergency room. He'll be fine." For the first time since her arrival, Cleary smiles.

"I think he will. It was awful, though, a pretty bad cut." Valerie maintains the worried frown, concern for her poor husband who was rushed to the hospital after suffering a deep gash on his shin from a chain saw that ran away from him while he was cutting down a dead tree in his invalid aunt's yard.

Pamela Cleary wraps a comforting arm around her shoulder and guides her into the next room. Helen and Arnold Lewiston and Colleen and Patrick Barnes stand two by two beside the fireplace as she's led to the sofa.

This was supposed to be a private interview, just the Clearys and the Monroes. What are the others doing here?

The edge of a glossy photograph peeks out from the top of the manila folder in the center of the coffee table. Valerie twines her fingers together to keep from reaching over and snatching it up.

"As you can imagine," she says, her voice quavery with emotion, "Martin really wanted to be here. We're both so anxious to hear your decision."

Jack Cleary stiffens. She's pushing it again, changing the tempo, stealing control from the maestro. But it's done, and she can't take the words back. A car blasting reggae rolls by outside; the vibrations rise up through the floor, up the legs of the chair, thrumming insistently into her nerve endings.

"With your husband injured, don't you think your place is by his side?" Cleary's standing now, not quite looming over her, but she has to look up to follow him as he moves toward her. He stops at the edge of the rug.

"Martin made me leave," Valerie improvises, grateful for the hours of practice spinning tales for Antonia. "I went with him to the hospital. The doctor told me he needed ten stitches and a tetanus shot and the cut had to be cleaned up. He won't be discharged from the emergency room for another few hours, the doctor said. I couldn't do anything but hang around in the waiting room until then anyway. Martin was really upset that both of us might miss the meeting. He made me promise to come here. To represent us."

"Well, I can understand that. Now, let's get to the business of the evening." Jack Cleary signals his wife with a nod of his head, and Pamela shepherds the other women out of the room.

Patrick Barnes rises. The fearless leader hasn't spoken to him directly or even looked his way, but it's clear he's been given some silent, prearranged cue. Barnes takes up his position in the doorway, hands clasped in front of him, a mannequin at attention.

"You came to us because those people in Montana sent you here, isn't that right, Mrs. Monroe? The Stevens family, friends of the Murphys. That's what you told us?"

As Jack Cleary speaks, Arnold Lewiston joins Patrick

Barnes. Now they look like soldiers guarding the entrance to Fort Knox or something.

This is a new script. She'll have to hit her marks by feel.

"Yes, that's how I knew to look in the back page of the *Village Voice* to find out about DASH meetings."

Just answer his questions. Be a good girl.

She reaches into her purse for a tissue, coughs discreetly behind it, and manages to blot the dampness on her upper lip.

"And you're here because you have a heartfelt interest in children. In making sure they don't have the same terrible experiences you did as a child. You want to protect the children. You and your husband do." Cleary's pacing now, marching back and forth in front of her, staring down at the carpet.

"Yes, that's right. I—"

He whirls around and holds his hand out. "You do understand that there's a reason this organization exists. Evil is being courted by certain people who seek power over the good. These people live to satisfy their own dirty, shameful impulses by enlisting the help of Satan, by becoming his agents and thereby giving up their right to live among the decent, God-fearing Christians of this country."

Jack Cleary speaks so softly she has to strain to hear him, yet he's on fire. His voice burns; his eyes radiate a passion she's only imagined in the expressions of the Salem magistrates she's studied, the men who held the power of life and death in their hands.

"Do you know what happens to people who think they can fool God's agents? We cannot allow that to happen. Divine justice will make sure the liars and hypocrites are given their due in the eternal suffering that will be their lot, but we must see that earthly justice is meted out first."

"Mr. Cleary, I don't know what you're—"

"We must be sure!" His voice thunders across the room and his face twists into a grotesque mask. "We cannot send a child into greater peril. It's hushed up, taken care of by the social workers. They're all in on it. The judges, the judges especially. They sit there in their robes and make sure we look like fools because they can't wait to get home to their own disgusting rituals." Panting, his eyes wild, he crosses the room. "How do we know you're not one of them, Mrs. Monroe? One of the breeders who turn over their babies to be killed on the altar of the devil. A self-ordained priestess with the power to decide that a poor little five-year-old boy who can't protect himself should be forced to wring a chicken's neck until the warm blood spurts all over. Into his eyes and up his nose, so he can't breathe, and then to cleanse him, oh yes, that's what they call it, *cleansing,* they burn the sin away with cigarettes and whip him with green branches until the blood runs down his buttocks. How do we know, Mrs. Monroe?"

His anguish is real, an awful, raw wound that has turned gangrenous.

Murmurs of agreement fill the room, small snuffling sounds from Arnold Lewiston, but Valerie holds herself apart from the sympathy. Whatever his experiences, however he was scarred as a young child, whether by some lunatic devil-worshipers or some unbalanced relative, Cleary has committed himself to fighting a conspiracy of darkness—and Joanna has become one of his casualties.

"You have to believe me, Mr. Cleary. I can't stand to think of what happened to . . . those children. Please, *please,* just let me take care of this child who's in danger."

He shakes his head. "Not good enough," he says, and her heart turns to ice.

The other men disappear from the doorway, and a trio appears in their place, specters draped in long white robes, heavy crucifixes dangling from braided silk cords around their necks. They hold small carved boxes of different shapes in their hands. One of them steps behind Jack Cleary and pulls the curtains closed.

She must go through with this overheated drama they've prepared for her. It's a test, and she's going to pass it. And her reward will be Joanna.

In the semidarkness the white robes flutter silently toward her, spirits drifting without weight across the thick carpet.

All right, she's going to be fine. Pamela Cleary—she's

the tallest of the three, those are her black leather pumps beneath the robe—approaches her chair while the other two hold hands and stand at attention in front of the drawn drapes.

"Lord, we commend ourselves to You for Your blessing and purification, so that we may find the way to serve You this evening and discover the truths You allow us to see. We ask that You give us the strength to perform Your work with love in our hearts and wisdom as our guide. We do this so that we may help the children."

As the figures glide toward her, she pictures Joanna in Helen Lewiston's arms. Her breath aches in her chest. One of the three robed women strikes a long wooden match against a fireplace brick. It flares in the darkness, throwing undulating shadows against the wall and filling the room with a sulfurous stink. The woman touches the flame to the three candles on the mantel—why hasn't she noticed them until now?—and an eerily festive light brightens the room.

The shortest one—Colleen Barnes, that's who it is—motions to Valerie, her arms outstretched and rising, as though she intends to levitate the sofa. The hood falls away from Colleen's face as she lifts her arms higher. In the candlelight, her eyes glow red. Whether those eyes are glazed with drugs or holy awe, the woman's in a state of ecstasy; it trembles in her voice as she commands Valerie to rise.

This is an initiation, some weird pledge night in this sorority of the converted.

That's better—thinking about it that way helps. Those high school girls used to spend hours coming up with stupid, demeaning tests for all the silly, eager applicants. This test is no different, except she's no giggling schoolgirl and there's more at stake than the right to wear some cheap piece of jewelry.

Alice Monroe will get through this just fine.

"Kneel in front of the candles."

This from Colleen Barnes. Surprising to hear such a direct command from that mousy little person who wouldn't even look at her the first time they met. Funny, what courage people get from anonymity.

The sound of children's voices laughing and shouting at their twilight games startles her. They're out on the street, unaware of what's happening just a few feet away. Who's protecting them? She hopes they've learned how to do that for themselves.

"Kneel." This time the command is sharper.

She walks to the spot designated by the pointing finger and sinks to her knees. Instead of letting her mind go blank with fear, she commands herself to stay alert, to think not only like Alice Monroe but also like Valerie Vincent, the woman determined to get her daughter back.

Three pairs of shoes—she can tell which is which. Helen Lewiston's high-shined brown loafers approach until Valerie can almost see her face reflected in the gleaming leather surface.

"First we offer a prayer to the goodness of God to direct us to the truth." Pamela Cleary is still standing in front of the fireplace. The guttering candles spin glinting lights from the metal box in her hand. Another match is struck, and the heavy perfume of incense drifts down on a cloud of smoke.

Aren't these women even a little embarrassed to be playing dress-up? Surely they can see that all this ceremonial nonsense is just a device to whip them into the proper frenzy, to give them the courage to perform someone else's dirty little secret rituals.

She turns when she hears footsteps behind her, but a hand splays out on her head and forces her to face front. The brown loafers straddle her kneeling form. Two hands appear, a piece of black cloth suspended between them. Before Valerie can protest, a blindfold is slipped over her eyes and fastened at the back of her head by deft fingers.

Antonia can't see but she listens better than most people.

Despite her physical limitations, Antonia manages to carry off an air of mastery. It's not just her money and the worldly knowledge she's acquired. The woman exudes authority, and everyone around her knows she's no fool just because she can't see.

Feet shuffle on the floor behind her; a slight breeze stirs the air beside her face. Crepe-soled pumps: Colleen.

Valerie's spirits are buoyed; she can do this, she's certain of it now.

"Rise." Behind her, Pamela Cleary touches her shoulder and then lifts her hand away.

Valerie stands up, spine straight, head high, shoulders pushed back. Joanna's image shimmers in the void before her, and Valerie resists the impulse to rub her throbbing knees, which ache from playing supplicant.

"You must understand," Pamela says firmly, "that we are doing this only because we must. We cannot allow an emissary of the darkness to come into our midst. For our own protection and to protect the children."

There it is again; the phrase makes Valerie's teeth clench.

"Remove your clothes. I pray God clear you if you be innocent, and if you be guilty, discover you."

Valerie Vincent recognizes those centuries-old words. John Hathorn, Salem magistrate, to Rebecca Nurse. A month ago she copied the passage into her notebook from the trial transcripts.

She's about to undergo an examination.

thirty-five

"I don't understand what you said. You want me to . . ."
She must delay them while she remembers the procedures.
They'll look for devil's marks, witches' tits, places on her
body where the devil would suckle. Nothing as ordinary as
a breast. A mole or a discoloration of the skin. Everyone
has moles; she has several on her arms, a small one on her
upper lip, but they'll be looking for hidden places.

On her abdomen, to the right of her navel and an inch
or so lower. It was how she decided whether or not to buy
a bikini—if the mole showed, she'd feel too exposed. And
on her back, below her shoulder blade, a place that
Johnny used to kiss after they'd made love and were drifting off to sleep.

How many more? Because as many as they find,
they'll do the same thing. And she'll stand here and bear it,
for Joanna.

"Don't be alarmed. We've all been through this," another voice explains—Colleen—although it's hard to be
sure because the sound is muffled as it comes through the
woman's hood. "We have to make sure you don't have
any devils' markings. It won't take long; then we can go
on to the real reason we're all here."

Thank God, Mitch Russo didn't let her wear the wire
to this meeting.

She reaches for her top button, fingers trembling, girding herself against what she knows is coming. Martha Starr had looked at those hatpins on her desk so lovingly. In the Salem courtroom, girls shrieked about a witch causing apparitions to fly through the air and splash milk from oaken buckets onto the walls of a cottage kitchen, then watched gleefully as the jury of goodwives examined the accused for marks of the devil.

And then there's the recitation. A witch is forbidden to speak the words every schoolchild has been taught.

> *Our Father which art in heaven,*
> *Hallowed be Thy name,*
> *Thy kingdom come, Thy will be done,*
> *On earth as it is in heaven.*

What's the rest? She tries humming the tune to herself, gets to the same point and stops. Her blouse is open now and she's shivering with cold.

> *Give us this day our daily bread*
> *And forgive us our debts*

. . . or is it our sins or our trespasses?

What version will they want to hear? What comes after that? *Lead us not into temptation* . . . She'll never get through it. Maybe they won't ask.

And deliver us from evil. This is the evil she needs to be saved from. If God or Kevin Murchison or Antonia Carrera or even Johnny Starr could help her now, she'd accept it gratefully.

But she's going to have to do this on her own. She reaches back to unzip her skirt, lets it fall to the floor, kicks it gently aside. Light seeps in from the bottom of the blindfold; at least she can get a bearing on her examiners. Cleary in front of her, Lewiston to her left. That means Colleen Barnes, slight and timid, is behind her.

"I don't really have to take off my bra or my panties." Defiant. Her voice has that ring to it, she can hear it, and it might make them bolder. Beneath the blindfold, she opens her eyes wide. They'll expect her to cry, that's one of the proofs, witches can't cry. Her detachment won't serve her well. She has to give them at least a couple of tears.

Without warning, she feels the first jab.

She jumps back, clutching her arm, feeling the dampness on her skin. She's bleeding on cue, proof of her innocence—witches' tits never bleed. "What's going on?" she demands, as though she doesn't know the answer.

"Good. This is the worst of it, Alice. Just a few more minutes." And then she's stuck again from behind, right under the shoulder blade.

This time her yelp of pain and outrage is louder and she dances away, only to be shoved forward by hands against her back. Another poke, then another, and now she's in the same fury she felt when she was nine and a group of sixth-grade boys snatched her sweater and played Monkey-in-the-Middle until she realized the only way to make them leave her alone was to stop trying to get her sweater, stop attempting to kick them or hit them. They wanted her to cry, that was all, and she wouldn't. But she will now, because she needs to prove she's human, not an instrument of evil, not a dark visitation on this bright earth. Because Joanna needs her tears.

"Please," she whispers, "please stop."

She blinks her eyes hard beneath the black rag that's tied too tightly around her head. Her face is warmed by the flickering light. Someone's holding a candle so close she's afraid it will burn her, and she thinks of Esther, all ashes and memories now, and the tears start down her cheeks.

Before she can reach up to wipe her face, someone covers her bare shoulders with soft fabric, her own blouse, probably. It's almost over, she's passed this part of the test, there's only a little more she'll have to do.

And then they'll tell her how to get her daughter back. They don't know it, but that's exactly what they'll do.

"All right, you can get dressed now."

She reaches up to remove the blindfold, but a gentle hand on her arm warns her away. "Not yet. One more thing, Alice, and then we'll be done."

Articles of clothing are placed in her hands, and she's helped into her blouse and then her skirt. What else can they possibly do? She's adjusting the waistband of her skirt when she hears an insistent rap on the door.

No one in the room moves. Then she hears footsteps, low voices, a sharp exchange.

Something's gone wrong.

She reaches out in front of her, groping for a wall, the fireplace, a person. Her hand brushes something cylindrical, cold metal, scored vertically. The floor lamp—she's been turned around so completely she's in the opposite corner of the room.

No one has stopped her, no one seems to be paying attention to her. She reaches for the blindfold and pulls it down.

Jack Cleary and the trio of robed women huddle together in the doorway. His eyes meet hers and he stops talking, his whispered tirade interrupted. The women turn, puppets moving in unison, and she yanks off the black cloth.

Where did she leave her purse? It doesn't matter. She has to get out of here. Her mind races in a hundred directions, slams into obstacles at every turn.

This is not how Antonia would handle things.

"What happened?" she asks quietly. "Is something wrong?"

"There's been no Martin Monroe at the emergency room. In fact, no one's been admitted to the Methodist Hospital ER with a chain-saw wound in two months." Jack Cleary advances toward her, his face a chiaroscuro study where the candlelight catches on his chin or slides off into darkness. "You lied to us, Mrs. Monroe. Why did you do that?"

"Mr. Cleary, I don't know who you talked to, but I resent you saying I'm lying. Maybe no one's told the switchboard operator, maybe the doctor listed my husband's injury as something else—" *And if she can say that aloud, she'd better react to the possibility.* Her hand flies to her mouth and she shakes her head. "I'm sorry, but this is very upsetting. His aunt might have heard from him. Do you mind if I call to check?"

Jack Cleary looks as though he's wavering.

Good. All she needs is fifteen seconds, and then she's out of here.

"Fine. You can use this phone." He flips on the ceiling light and points to an old Princess phone, pink and cuffed, on the end table near the sofa.

She dials Antonia's number, struggling to stay alert when everything in her wants to sink into the oblivion of terror. A faint click: someone else is on the line.

A fresh tremor of fear runs through her. Jack Cleary isn't in the room. He's monitoring the call from an extension.

"Yes?"

It's Antonia, and suddenly she knows what she's going to do. "I hope I'm not waking you, Auntie A. I was worried about . . ." *She's got to remember his name.* "Did Martin come home from the hospital already? Did they stitch up that cut so quickly? I—we called there but they said he wasn't there."

In the silence that's fallen over the room, she closes her eyes and prays that Antonia will play along and not react as if she's lost her mind. And then:

"He's sleeping," Antonia replies in her level, husky voice. "He's fine now. They gave him something to help him sleep."

The loud exhale isn't her own, isn't Antonia's. She wants to reach through the phone and hug her. "Oh, that's such good news. I'll be home in a little while, Auntie A. You go back to your television show."

"Martin will be glad to see you. He should be waking up in about an hour. Good-bye, my dear."

Antonia hangs up at the same time the extension clicks off, and Valerie sets the receiver down slowly, deliberately, as Jack Cleary comes back to stand in the doorway.

"He's home, sleeping off a painkiller they gave him at the hospital." She's almost convinced herself, almost believes her husband has been injured, stitched up at the hospital, and now expects her at home. "I'm sorry, I do have to get back to my husband. The last thing he said to me before I left was that I should tell you all he's still very committed to having"—*not Joanna, you can't say Joanna*—"the child be part of our lives."

She can see that Jack Cleary has crossed his arms and planted his legs wide apart, but she can't make out his face. She hears someone breathing behind her, feels the damp exhalation on the back of her neck.

Cleary steps aside, signals her to leave the dark room and follow him to the front door. His disciples maintain a disturbing silence. The light, when she passes the dining room, hurts her eyes, and she squints away the brightness.

Except for the white robes, they look like a harmless little coffee klatsch gathered in an ordinary house in Brooklyn.

"You go on back to your injured husband now. Your place is by his side." Cleary looks like anyone's uncle, a little concerned, slightly disapproving, but willing to extend the benefit of any doubts he might be harboring to a favored niece.

"Can I tell him anything about the child?" She searches his eyes, imploring, but he looks away.

"We'll let you know about the child, Mrs. Monroe. Tomorrow. Someone will call you in the afternoon to tell you where to come for our meeting."

thirty-six

The examination has been conducted, the evidence assembled and presented. And somehow, in the park, trees still line the winding paths and surround the lake, empty benches wait for tired strollers, birds return to their nests as darkness settles. As she passes a streetlight, she notices the thick, dark spot that stains her palm. She bled for them, didn't she, but that may not be enough.

Soon her judges will decide what her sentence will be.

Giles Corey: pressed to death beneath a pile of rocks in 1692, the day after he was excommunicated from his Salem church. At the end, when his tongue stuck out of his mouth, a witness pushed the offending organ back in with a stick. Tituba: imprisoned for eighteen months earlier that same year, until the charges against her were dismissed. When the Reverend Samuel Parris refused to pay prison fees, she became the property of a Virginia slave trader.

Too exotic. DASH doesn't want to call that much attention to itself.

Mehitabel Downing, Elizabeth Paine, Dorcas Hoar: imprisoned in dank, malodorous cells and eventually released.

Not likely, now that she knows so many of their secrets.

John Proctor, Sarah Good, Sarah Wildes, Elizabeth

Howe, Bridget Bishop, Susannah Martin, all hanged in public spectacles. Rebecca Nurse, first acquitted, then found guilty by a jury fulfilling the judge's directions, hanged as a witch.

If he discovers her deception, Jack Cleary may declare her a witch in order to exact revenge, but they'll have to find her first.

Mary and Philip English, Mary Bradbury, Edward and Sarah Bishop: escaped from prison.

How did she get here, only half a block from Antonia's house? She's walked through Prospect Park in a daze, pushing away her rage at their arrogance and those horrible, invasive tests. Only the outcome matters—only Joanna matters—but it's impossible to guess what they'll decide or even whether they'll allow her to return for the Friday night meeting.

She takes out the house key, turns the lock, tugs at the door.

Tense and watchful, Antonia sits in a halo of light that spills from the living room into the hall.

The trial hasn't been adjourned.

"Another call?"

"The same man." Antonia rolls toward her, skirting the long-legged table in the hall and the potted ficus near the study entrance. "The first thing he said was that Joanna was all right, just exactly the way he did last time. Then he told me to deliver a message. He made me repeat the words twice. 'You must follow the rules. I'll be in touch soon.' And he warned again that if you contact the police Joanna might be harmed."

You must follow the rules. What rules? Dear God, whose rules? Even if she manages to figure it out, what will happen to Joanna? And if she fails . . .

"You're sure that's all he said? That I must follow the rules and he'd be in touch soon? Nothing else? Those were his exact words?"

Offended, Antonia lifts her chin and squares her shoulders. "My dear, it's not such a complicated message. Yes, he made me repeat it word for word. Two times. He said you must follow the rules."

DASH's rules or the caller's? The rules of common decency? The law of the land? Gravity?

Maybe, with Antonia's help, she can make sense of the cryptic messages. Unless there's nothing to figure out, unless her secret caller is toying with her. There's only one person she can think of who might take such sadistic pleasure from bringing this special torment into her life.

Lucas Starr. The sentiments are right, but the voice is all wrong.

"Maybe I should call him." She's surprised to discover that she's still in the hall, her legs wobbly and her arms leaden. "Let's go into the living room, Antonia. I need to sit down."

"How can you call him? You don't have this man's number. You don't even know who he is." Antonia allows her chair to be pushed to her usual spot in front of the fireplace. "And if you mean Detective Russo, you'll be taking a terrible chance, Valerie. This man sounded so menacing. If you call the police, something awful might happen to your little girl."

"Johnny. I was thinking of calling Johnny. Maybe he knows someone, a friend of his father's, someone who speaks like a distinguished gentleman."

"What makes you think your ex-husband will answer you honestly? A man like that—a man who turns to alcohol to give him courage—I don't trust him. He'll want to know why you're asking, and if you tell him, he might go to the police. I don't like the way that young man moves, I don't like how he talks to you, I simply cannot trust him." Antonia folds her arms under her breasts and shakes her head.

"Maybe he can help me figure out who's making those calls." From the minute Johnny showed up, Antonia's quivering antennae have been picking up signals that made her suspicious, and Johnny has proven her right. "I don't have to trust him to ask if he knows any distinguished gentlemen, and I don't have to tell him why I'm asking."

"You must do what you think is right, my dear, of course. I offer my opinion, that's all."

Is it never going to stop? Now she has to figure out what Antonia's peevish tone of dismissal means.

If she's not careful, she'll lose whatever control she still has, and with it the hope of seeing Joanna any time soon. Ever, maybe. Unless she can find out who the anonymous caller is.

There *is* a way.

Antonia would have to agree to not answer the phone for a while. If he calls again, the answering machine will record his message and . . .

Of course he won't do that, leave a taped message. Still, she can turn his own weapon against him.

"Whoever's making these calls can only get away with it because we don't know who he is, right? But we can find out, I'm sure of it. Or at least figure out where he's calling from. It's amazing, all this stuff they can do now. The telephone company has been advertising a device . . . They attach some kind of box to your phone line, and it shows you the number of the incoming call."

Antonia's face is washed of color in the glaring living room light. "What do you mean? What kind of box?"

It doesn't matter whether she understands the fine points of how it works. It *does* work, and that little black box, or whatever color it is, will become her partner in the search for Joanna.

"I can't explain the technology, Antonia. All I know is they install this box and it displays the number of the person who's calling. Once I have that, I can find out where the phone is. I'd like to order the service, Antonia. First thing in the morning."

"Of course." Her smile radiates excitement, anticipation. "You're a very clever young lady. You see? You've worked this out on your own, and soon you'll be a step closer to your daughter. You're right. It doesn't matter how it works. The important thing is that it does. Very good, yes, very good indeed. Now, my dear, you must try to relax. I can hear in your voice how agitated you are. Tell me about your meeting."

She will not relive the DASH meeting in a civilized little chat with Antonia. "It was . . . difficult."

"When you called, I knew right away you were in trouble. I hope my answers helped. Someone was listening

n an extension, were they not? What you said—did it
nean that Johnny didn't go to the meeting with you?"

"Johnny and I had an argument and he went back to
Manhattan. I went to the meeting alone. He's not handling
ll this very well."

Antonia is suddenly eager, as though she's about to
eceive a special gift. Her face is flushed; she's breathing
ard, her chest rising and falling with each shallow breath.
'He's behaved this way in the past, hasn't he? Just when
ou need him to be strong, he's proven himself to be weak,
nable to weather the storms. He's left you to ride them
ut on your own. He deserted you when he found out you
vere pregnant, didn't he?"

Valerie's seen her like this before. Every day. Every
ifternoon, in the high-ceilinged living room of the well-
maintained brownstone on Prospect Park West. *And after
very anonymous phone call.*

Surely Antonia's questions are no more than they
eem, conversation to pass the time and take her mind off
he very real, and very distressing, events. It's absurd to
hink that Antonia's doing this consciously.

"No. No, actually, at first it seemed like the idea of
peing a father would make him grow up. It was funny. We
vent together to tell Martha and Lucas the news, and the
irst thing Lucas said was, 'That doesn't mean you're planning to live with us, does it?' "

Thin eyebrows rise above Antonia's dark glasses.
'What an incredible reaction. Did they have a big house?
Why would he ask such a thing?"

She's greedy. She wants more.

It has to be her own exhaustion that's making her
pelieve she's being manipulated. She's tired, becoming
paranoid. If she talks to Antonia a little longer, surely
she'll see how wrong she is.

"I never did understand. No one was using Johnny's
old room, of course, but the house itself is really too small
for four adults and a child, even four adults who like each
other. And no one was even pretending anymore by then.
Maybe Lucas thought we wouldn't be able to afford a
place of our own after the baby came. Anyway, we told
them no, we weren't planning to live with them."

"So Johnny supported you that time. An exception, I'm sure. From what you've told me, it sounds like he had difficulty standing up to his parents. Did he go along with your wishes or *theirs* when you were planning your wedding?"

It's true. The moment is being orchestrated, and Valerie has a part to play. Antonia is prompting her for a diversion, expecting to be transported out of her limited life with a story.

"Actually, that was one time Martha and Lucas didn't raise a fuss. Johnny and I wanted a simple outdoor wedding, and since we'd met at Ruth Hoving's house, we thought it would be wonderful to be married on her lawn."

"And Johnny's parents didn't insist on a church?"

Another question. A prompt to keep talking, to spin another tale. Now that the thought has presented itself she can't shake it. She's supposed to offer a story from her own experiences, the way a penitent would give confession, freely, with the knowledge that she's doing good and will be rewarded.

The only reward she wants, the only thing that will compensate for this terrible, bitter ache is Joanna.

"They tried to talk us into it. They stopped arguing finally, when we agreed to have a minister perform the ceremony. Ruth had let other people use her house before. Her son Peter was married there. And three young people from Taconic Hills she had a special fondness for, and a friend of hers from the city, who remarried after being widowed for ten years."

When she went to see Murchison, she left Antonia alone with only Nadia and the television for company. And when she came back, Antonia told her about the first phone call, and then, to help fill the awful time of waiting, had encouraged her to talk about the past, about Joanna.

"That's quite generous of this Ruth. She must have had a special place in her heart for you."

The second call came after she declined Antonia's company at the funeral home. Again, she spent the hours afterward telling Antonia stories.

"It was almost a Taconic Hills institution by then, so

we weren't reluctant to ask her. Ruth walked us around
he grounds, showed us where the caterer put up the tables, spoke about the other weddings and how much pleasure they gave her, and by the time we left, it was agreed."

"So, Johnny never even tried to convince you to have
a church wedding, to listen to his parents' wishes?"

The pattern is so clear Valerie can't believe she missed
t until now. She's trembling with rage. Self-centered, cold-
blooded, Antonia is taking advantage of her vulnerability
to get what she needs. Except that it's going to stop, and
stop right now.

She doesn't have to keep herself tied to this woman
just because she's lent her money and given her a place to
stay. Lynn will help her, Rosie and Paul will help, Catherine Delaney, Sarah and Peter Hoving, they'll all pitch in so
she can escape the grasp of Antonia Carrera.

"Antonia, I'm sorry. I'm suddenly so tired and so upset I don't know if I'm making sense anymore. I'm going
upstairs."

"Are you sure it's a good idea to be alone right now?"
Antonia smiles in her direction. "I'm worried about you,
dear, about your state of mind."

Worried that a bit of solitude might reveal the truth of
what's going on, perhaps.

"I'll be all right. I'm just so very tired, I think I'd
better lie down."

"You go ahead, my dear. I'm almost ready for bed
myself. I'll have Nadia look in on you later. Will you help
me upstairs?"

Somehow, until now, Antonia's managed on her own
to get the wheelchair to the elevator at the back of the
house, to press the button for the second floor, to maneu-
ver the chair the few feet to the bedroom herself. But it's
impossible to refuse.

"Of course. Are you ready to go?" She stands behind
the wheelchair, her hands on the grips, waiting for a signal
from Antonia.

I'm the movie of the week. The idea is stunning. The
words careen in her head as she rolls the chair into the
elevator, leans forward in the tight space to press the button, feels her stomach drop as the car comes to rest.

"Do you want me to help you into bed?" She's neve done that before, has always left it to Nadia, who know just where to hold her, how to lift Antonia's inert weig out of the chair and onto the bed.

"No, I'll call Nadia. You get some rest now. I'll se you in the morning. You mustn't worry too much, Valeri I know how hard it is to believe it, but something in me absolutely certain that your daughter is all right. Go o now. You can't afford to wear yourself out with anxiety. She reaches back and pats the hand she knows is still o the wheelchair.

Valerie almost jerks away, but she manages to sa good night civilly. What she wants to do is fly away, out the room, out of the house. Instead, she closes the door Kristin's bedroom and sinks onto the bed.

Kristin Denby.

Before she gets any deeper into this story she's spir ning for herself, she should talk to someone who migh know whether Antonia Carrera is capable of such col ness, such calculated exploitation. Kristin lived here fo five years, long enough to learn Antonia's habits, her idio syncrasies, her greedy need for entertainment and contro If anyone can provide an answer, it has to be Kristin.

If the answer is yes, she'll leave this house right away She's got enough money in her small savings account t buy a couple of days. She'll be able to borrow more if sh has to. And if the answer is no, Antonia Carrera is simpl interested, cares a lot, then Valerie will chalk up this epi sode to her own fragile state.

Still trembling with anger, she rummages through th papers on the desk, finds Kristin's number, dials. Th phone rings only once, and Kristin's recorded voice ask her to leave a message.

"This is Valerie Vincent." She hesitates. She's not pre pared, can't say why she's calling in twenty-five words o less to an answering machine. "Please, call me at Antonia' as soon as you can. It's urgent that I speak to you." Sh almost hangs up, but adds, "It doesn't matter how late i is. Please call me as soon as you get this message."

friday

thirty-seven

Even in her sleep, deep in a dream of lifting Joanna in her arms so she can reach an apple hanging from a gnarled tree, Valerie has been struggling to frame her questions so Kristin won't take offense on her former employer's behalf. If she's not careful, she'll sound like a hysterical madwoman who's lost touch with reality.

Reality—which one? And why hasn't the phone rung?

All right, so Kristin came home late and was reluctant to return her call in the middle of the night and wake Antonia. When she finally does phone, Valerie will know whether she's become an unwitting participant in Antonia Carrera's experimental living theater.

Maybe Kristin's not home, not picking up messages regularly. Antonia's talked about the May wedding—Kristin and her fiancé may be living together already.

What's his name? The fiancé, the man Kristin is marrying. *Charles Babcock*. That's it. Still a few little gray cells working.

She dials information, spells out Babcock's name for the operator.

"Just a minute. Hold for the number." The eerie singsong of a computer-generated voice recites Charles Babcock's telephone number.

This is as far as she can go for a while. It's too early to call Charles Babcock's home, and the telephone company business office probably doesn't open until nine. This afternoon, Detective Gallagher will come by with the wire. And then, at the DASH meeting, Jack Cleary will deliver his final verdict, and she'll record every damning word. But for the moment there's nothing to do.

She's got to keep busy. Valerie strips the sheets from the bed as an argument from down the hall shatters the quiet. Nadia and Carl, shouting in Polish and slamming doors. Fine—the whole house seems to be losing its grip, why not them? They've been the stable ones this past week, keeping the household running with their customary efficiency. Why shouldn't they join the insanity too?

Her arms filled with sheets, Valerie heads for the laundry room as Nadia stumbles out the door. The collision startles them both.

"Oh! I'm sorry, Miss Valerie. I don't know anyone's in the hall." The housekeeper's eyes are red, the pouches of skin at the side of her mouth sagging. A coil of hair pinned to the top of her head droops sadly.

"That's all right, Nadia. I was just—"

"Oh, Miss Valerie, I'm sorry." Nadia's voice quavers, and she covers her eyes with chapped hands.

"No harm done. It's all right, really." Valerie shifts the linens, wraps her free arm around the woman's shoulders. "You didn't see me, that's all."

Nadia's mouth opens; before she can utter another word, Carl steps into the hall and says his wife's name softly. Still speechless, Nadia shrugs away, then follows him into the bedroom.

This really is becoming a madhouse. Doing the laundry feels like the sanest way in the world to spend the next hour.

Coffee—that's what she needs. On her way downstairs, a shuddering revulsion sweeps over her. Seeing that face, being in the same room and maintaining her composure in Antonia's presence, is going to take all her will.

You're letting your imagination run away with you.

The thought that Antonia is taking advantage of Joanna's disappearance and those threatening phone calls to satisfy her hunger for tasty little true-life vignettes may be nothing more than another story, one she's telling herself. But the idea has grown overnight like a rampant kudzu vine, and it won't stop curling its tendrils into the corners of her mind.

"Did you want something, my dear?"

Antonia's in the hall, on her way to the study. Her face glows, but it's a mask without feelings, all flawless skin, gloss-slicked mouth, and dark glasses. And no emotions. Not a twitch, not a grimace, not a smile.

"Just some coffee. I—"

Nadia appears in the doorway, pale, her gaze darting nervously from desk to window to floorboard, her usually placid face jittering with agitation. "Can I talk to you, Miss Antonia? Alone?" She tugs her shapeless sweater around her body, won't look at Valerie.

That's a cue if she ever heard one. "I'll just take my coffee upstairs. I'll be down later."

"That's fine, my dear. Now, what is it, Nadia?"

Antonia is welcome to Nadia's problem, whatever it is. At least Nadia's private conference will distract Antonia for a while. Valerie splashes coffee into a cup and races back upstairs to Kristin's old bedroom, dials Charles Babcock's number.

"Hello?"

She's struck speechless. This is the first voice she's heard in a week with the qualities Antonia described: dignified, deep, refined. Senatorial.

The children must be protected.

Joanna is doing fine.

You must follow the rules.

"Mr. Babcock?"

"Yes, can I help you?"

A volley of shouting erupts downstairs, and she reaches over to swing the door shut before she says, "Mr. Babcock, my name is Valerie Vincent. I'm trying to get in touch with Kristin Denby. I left a message at her apartment, but she hasn't called me back."

"I don't believe I've met you, Miss Vincent. Kristin never mentioned your name. How do you know her?"

A note of irritation has raised the pitch of his voice; Charles Babcock doesn't sound quite so refined now. And then she realizes: Charles Babcock has known Antonia for years, had met Kristin at one of Antonia's dinners. Surely Antonia would have known right away if those calls were made by Kristin Denby's fiancé.

"I work for Antonia Carrera, and Mrs. Carrera wants—"

"Mrs. Carrera has got to understand that she's no longer in control of Kristin's life. Antonia Carrera may have insisted Kristin have her scars removed and she may even have paid for the surgery. She probably wanted to finish the job of turning Kristin into the perfect young woman. But all she accomplished was to make Kristin miserable, uncomfortable with my attentions." The scorn in his voice is softened by sadness. "Nobody answers the phone at Kristin's apartment."

"You don't have another number for her?"

"How about zero? All I have to show for my love is a well-written Dear John letter and a pretty velvet box containing every bit of jewelry I ever bought her. So you see, Ms. Vincent, even if I did know where she was, I might not be any more cooperative. But I do not. I do not know where Kristin is. Antonia may have done everything she could to—" His voice catches. "This is ridiculous. What am I doing, going on this way to a total stranger?"

Heartbreak everywhere. Charles Babcock is a decent man who doesn't seem to deserve his pain, but she can't stop now.

"I had no idea . . . If you hear from her, please ask her to call me."

Downstairs, the front door slams so hard the glass rattles in the windows.

"I already told you I don't know how to reach her. I already told you she turned my life into a shambles." He's breathing heavily into the phone.

"I'm sorry. I'll—"

"You'll do nothing with regard to me. I can't bear the thought of prolonging my relationship with anyone connected to that house. Good-bye, Ms. Vincent." Abruptly, Charles Babcock breaks the connection.

"Valerie!" It's Antonia, and she's annoyed.

The curtain hasn't come down on this Grand Guignol yet.

"Valerie!"

The second summons sounds more like a plea, and she races down the stairs. In the study, only the top of Antonia's head is visible above the back of her wheelchair. She's turned toward the window, as though she's listening for the sound of someone coming up the walk, or leaving.

"What's wrong, Antonia?" The street is deserted, except for a maroon and gray station wagon idling at the corner, two people in the front, a man she can barely see and a woman with broad shoulders and pinned-up hair like Nadia's.

Head bowed, Antonia says, "They left. Treachery, that's all it is. Nadia has announced that she and Carl are leaving me for a few days."

Incredible. Nadia and Carl are so attached to Antonia, so steady and practical. They wouldn't just walk away and leave her. "That's all she said? Just that they were going away for a few days?"

"Something about a family crisis, I didn't really understand, a sister of Nadia's who's broken . . . a leg, I think she said, and needs their help. Nadia hopes they might be back by Tuesday or Wednesday."

The DASH meeting tonight—she must go, must be there to take Joanna home. But Antonia can't be left alone for hours, hasn't ever had to manage on her own, isn't prepared for emergencies. Which leaves only one person to be with her. And that one person will not, cannot be tied to this house. "I'll call the service and get a replacement."

"Is that really necessary?" Antonia lifts her head. "We'll be all right, just the two of us, for a couple of days. I do so dislike strangers *touching* me."

"I have to go out tonight, and I don't think you should be alone. What if there's a fire? I can't just walk out the door and leave you. I'll take care of it, Antonia. I'll find someone right away."

"Of course you will. I'm so pleased you're with me, Valerie. I *do* wish you'd reconsider my offer. We'd make a fine family, you and Joanna and me, in this big house." She reaches for the wheelchair controls and the chair whirs away from the window. "This has been such a trying morning. I need to take my mind off all this disruption."

Yes, I'm sure you do want a little diversion. But I'm not going to chop up my life into digestible bits just to feed you tasty little stories for your personal pleasure.

"Why don't you let me help you get comfortable upstairs? I'll set you up with the television and then I'll call the service."

"You'll ask for someone reliable and even-tempered? A young person with a little life to her. That's what I need. Someone like you. Yes, I would like to go upstairs. All this chaos is so unnerving."

Antonia, unnerved, can still articulate exactly what she wants without the slightest problem.

thirty-eight

"I know, I know. So we both blew it. We can't wallow in regret, Johnny. We've got to pick up and go on." Francine brushed her hair out of her eyes and tucked her feet under her. "You feel bad, sure. But you can't use your guilt as an excuse to go all to pot again."

"Pot's not my problem. Sorry," he said, sinking deeper into the lumpy sofa, "bad joke. It's just I can't believe I did that. Walked into that bar as though the past ten months never even happened. Some part of me went to sleep and didn't wake up until I was looking into Valerie's face. She had every right to be furious. But how do I live with it, Franny? What if that was the one chance for Joanna?"

Suddenly she was on her feet, prowling the dingy room. "You have to go forward. That's all I know. That's the best I can tell you. Can't you see, Johnny? You're using your mistake as an excuse not to do the hard stuff. Maybe your mother is going to help you recover that chance. Maybe that's why she's coming to see you. I can't tell you what the next step is. That's up to you."

She was saying all the right things. He could tell because, more than anything, he wanted to clap his hands over his ears and shut out the sound of her words.

He'd already taken the next step—calling his sponsor, being reminded that he needed to go back to the *first* step again, admitting that he recognized the hold alcohol had over him. And then?

"It's totally crazy to think about my mother in this neighborhood. All the graffiti, the broken windows, the garbage on the street—I tried to warn her but she wouldn't let me meet her someplace. You're right, this could be it, Franny, my chance to find out about Joanna. Martha Starr, the redeemer. Whatever she's going to tell me, it's important. She's really scared my dad will find out about her little trip. I should have gone up there instead of letting her come to the city."

"Don't get too protective of her, Johnny. You have to let her do what she needs to. Sure, a mother has to know her child is all right, even if he's a grown man. But maybe even more than that, she has to know *she's* all right. It's good she's thinking for herself."

He pulled her into his arms; his lips grazed her hair, the tender skin stretched over her cheekbone. "What are you going to tell the immigration lawyer?"

"I'm going to find out what all my options are." She pulled away and fussed with the yellowing scrap of lace under the milk bottle, picking tiny lilac petals from the table and gathering them in a heap in her hand. "I don't want to put any more pressure on you now, Johnny. But it matters to me what you do, how you handle this. I'm going to ask him about green cards and renewing my student visa and going back to Belfast—"

"And getting married?" He had to know, whatever her answer.

"Yes. And getting married. But I told you—I don't want to talk about that. Not now. I have to go or I'll miss my appointment." She hugged him hard, then unhooked her corduroy jacket from the chair back.

"You go ahead, Franny. My mother should be here soon. I better get myself ready." From the doorway, he watched as she slipped her arms through her jacket and headed into the dark stairwell. No one had changed that bulb yet. Martha Starr was going to get an authentic introduction to his life.

One thing at a time. That was all he could do.

First his mother's visit. Then he'd go to work. That was as far as he could see right now.

Sometimes, standing there with the roller in his hand, enjoying the patterns the new colors made on the walls, or dipping a wooden stick into the can and watching the thick, creamy swirls, he fell into a kind of trance, and when it was over, when the foreman yelled his name or the roller made anemic little streaks on the wall, he realized he'd solved a problem that hours of concentration hadn't even touched. Maybe that would happen today.

He splashed cold water on his face, patted himself dry without glancing in the mirror, and then slid the change and subway tokens he'd deposited on the small table near the door into his hand and dumped them in his pocket. A little hope, that's all he needed. Just a little—

A timid knock on the door. Unlike the pounding when Detective Gallagher stood on the other side of the door, this was so gentle he wasn't certain he'd heard it. Then again, a rap, and then another. And then his name.

"Johnny, are you there?"

He pulled the door open, and she crossed the worn threshold, her arms outstretched, waiting for him to step into her embrace, the one that was interrupted at the front door of his father's house.

"The train ride was all right? And you didn't have any trouble getting a cab?" He kept his arm around Martha's shoulder as he walked her to the sofa.

"It was fine. The cab driver was a very nice young black man with an accent I couldn't understand, but he was very polite. Johnny, oh, Johnny, I—" She squeezed his hand and studied his face. "I've missed you, son."

He swallowed hard and tried to look away, but her eyes held his gaze. "I'm sorry, Mom," he whispered. "I thought about you so many times, but I couldn't call until I'd gotten myself straightened out."

"That's all we really wanted, your father and me. Just to hear from you. Just to know you were all right. But we'll talk about all that later, if we have time. I have to be on the twelve-twenty train back. Lucas thinks I'm in Albany, seeing some doctor about female problems. I can't live with this anymore, Johnny. I have so many things to tell you."

Martha reached into her purse and pulled out a handkerchief, but there were no tears for her to wipe away.

"I don't know where to start, Johnny. This group your father belongs to . . ." She shook her head. "That's not right. We both belong to it. I went along with him, acted like I didn't have a mind of my own. Oh, Lord, I'm letting myself get all muddled here."

Valerie was right.

They were members of DASH. His mother and father had sat on someone's chintz-covered sofa and made plans for saving children. Had set in motion the plan to rescue Joanna, and he was about to hear the details. The sour taste in his mouth wouldn't go away.

"You want some tea? A glass of water?"

Martha waved away his offers. "I'm all right. It's about this group. It's called Deliverance And Safe Haven. DASH."

He nodded, leaned back and waited for her to go on.

"They think there's some giant conspiracy to cover up Satanic cult activities involving children. They've gone out on these missions, taking children out of homes where someone thinks they're being tortured. They have these photographs, Johnny, they're terrible. Little babies. Your father saw things in Valerie's house that made him think she was . . ." She patted her eyes with the handkerchief and shook her head. "I don't know what he thought. I feel so bad, Johnny. I got caught up in it for a while. And then, when I realized how crazy it was, I wasn't strong enough to speak my mind."

"But you're doing it, Mom. You're doing it now. That's why you're here." His throat was so dry he could barely swallow. She was teetering on the narrow ledge of a decision and he had to be careful to let her proceed at her own pace.

"I thought your father was going to have a stroke when he found out Joanna was missing. You know how he gets." Her deep, shuddering breath trailed into a sigh. "Lucas blamed Valerie for leaving the child with a stranger."

Then Lucas Starr wasn't the avenging angel responsible for Joanna's disappearance.

"Lucas called George Perry the day after Riley Hamm came around to ask a bunch of questions."

"George Perry? Who's that?"

"The East Coast headquarters for DASH is in New Jersey. Toms River. That's where George Perry lives. The other director is a woman, a Mrs. Carmody in Sacramento. Out in California. They have separate territories, but they make decisions together. At least, that's what he told us when he came to what they call a motivational meeting last week. Anyway, this George Perry called Valerie—it must have been Saturday."

Valerie didn't mention a phone call, not when they were in the Botanic Garden, not in the truck when they were driving between Brooklyn and Taconic Hills. Not even on the way to the DASH meeting. "Why did Perry call Val? To get her to give up custody of Joanna? Was he after money or what?"

Martha shook her head. "He had this idea Valerie was making it all up about Joanna being missing. Said she was probably just claiming she didn't know where the child was so Lucas couldn't find her. As far as I know, Perry never even spoke to her, just left a message with someone, a woman."

Why hadn't Valerie told him about the call?

"He didn't get it about Esther Klein's murder? Didn't he have the sense to know Valerie couldn't have anything to do with that?"

"Like I said, George Perry never talked to Valerie. Never did call but that once, because things started happening real fast after that and he got all caught up in planning. That's why I'm here." His mother reached into her purse and pulled out an envelope. "I wrote it down on the train. So you'd have all of it. They can't keep doing things like this. It isn't right. God didn't mean for His message to be delivered by force and trickery. Now, the important thing is that you have to do something by tonight. They're planning to turn a young child over to another family. Operation Safe Haven, that's what they call it."

"Joanna? Is it Joanna, Mom?"

She shook her head. "I don't know who the child i It's going to be tonight, and it's going to be somewhere i New York City, and the child is a girl. That's all I coul find out. It's the way they work it, Johnny. They kee secrets. Only a few people know the important things— the identity of the child, who's going to get her. They say keeps everyone safe. Safe from being caught for doin wrong is what."

Just a little more. He needed to ask the right question and hope his mother had at least some of the answers Martha Starr's life would be different after this, and if h was lucky and somehow strong enough, they'd be able t help each other get through the changes.

"Okay, good. Where's the little girl now? What hap pens to the children until DASH finds a new home fo them?"

"They keep them in safe houses. I don't know if I'r right about this but—oh, Johnny, this is all so strange. Th way a lot of DASH business gets done is on these com puter bulletin boards. Can you imagine me learning hov to use a computer? Well, I did, just so your father coul hook up with these people. I got to thinking about it an figured maybe it wasn't Joanna, but that didn't mean shouldn't help these other children. Help their parents fin them.

"I came across these two messages. It looked like the were about the safe houses so I copied out the addresses You see, it's in code. Well, not code, really, but if you rea every fourth word in the sentence, that's an address. Th sentences that start with the name Robert, they're the one you need to look for. See? Your father left one of thes printouts around, all marked up with red pencil, and figured it out. He'd never tell me, not Lucas Starr."

She was going to do just fine with the changes in he life. Johnny said: "We have to let the police know, Mom It's the only way we can help that little girl."

Martha huddled in the corner of the sofa, her face ghostly, a crumpled, sorrowful darkness in her eyes. "I they ever find out . . . oh, son, I'm so afraid of them They'll do anything to protect themselves from the law They've made examples of people who tried to turn them

n. Don't make me talk to the police, Johnny. Please, not
he police."

He couldn't just sit on this, but he wouldn't call
Detective Gallagher, not if it meant endangering his
mother. He'd find a way to protect the child *and* his
mother from DASH.

"I won't call the police, Mom. I'll figure out something. But, I promise, I won't say anything that would
point back to you. Okay?"

Martha reached into her purse, shuffling things
around until she came up with an Amtrak ticket. "You tell
whoever you talk to there's a young child in one of those
houses and she's going to be moved tonight. You have to
make sure something's done right away. I've got to go
back to Taconic Hills now, so Lucas doesn't get any ideas.
But I'm not going to stay long, a week or two, less if I can
manage it. I think it's time I saw my sister in Delaware.
Maybe I'll stay a month, maybe forever. I know one thing:
I can't stay married to your father, not after all this. This is
not the way God meant for people to treat each other."

With Martha Starr gone, who would save his father?

Johnny held his mother's hand, plump, warm, the
nails cut short the way they'd always been. "You were
very brave to come here, Mom. It must have been very
hard to do this."

She looked away from him and stared at the ticket in
her hand. "It would have been harder not to."

thirty-nine

She has to call the agency.

The Agency—isn't that what they call the CIA? Bu
Nadia and Carl haven't been skulking around Antonia'
brownstone collecting government secrets. It's a domesti
help agency she needs, and Antonia can't tell her who t
call because she's dozing upstairs in the bedroom, the tele
vision droning quietly for company.

Surely the housekeeping agency will be listed on
card in Antonia's file. Apfel, Boldrick, Crowder. Kristi
Denby's number, the one Antonia rattled off so effort
lessly. Diggs, Hassan, Masters, Radwin, Sandler, Valen:
Nothing that looks like an agency.

She'll have to find a pay stub, then.

When he came for his regular appointment at the en
of the month, Ernest Mattucci sat in this study with th
green leather ledger and the big checkbook spread out i
the center of the desk blotter. When he was done, he sli
the checkbook back in place in the top drawer of the desk
Three weeks ago—a lifetime, if you were Joanna Vincent'
mother, Esther Klein's friend.

The checkbook is right where it should be; the nam
of a domestic help agency should be easy to spot. Her ey
skips to the balance column: there's more money in Anto
nia's checking account than she and Joanna lived on all o
last year.

She's the spy, sitting here poring over the details of someone else's intimate financial life.

She runs her finger down the columns. Entries for doctors and pharmacies, Valerie Vincent, Ernest Mattucci, the mortgage payment to the bank, foundations and charities, checks made out to Merry Maids, Ormandy Heating, Con Ed, the cable company, health insurance. Something called NHP. An entry to Paragon.

What's Paragon? She's heard that name sometime in the past few days, but she can't remember where. It sounds like one of the big sporting goods stores in Manhattan, but surely Antonia Carrera hasn't bought nearly four thousand dollars' worth of catchers' mitts and tennis rackets. Maybe she's donating equipment instead of cash to one of her charities.

Valerie flips back to the March entries, marvels at Mattucci's printing, so like an architect's letters, all the same size, symmetrical and precise, as though they'd been stenciled onto the page. The bank, utilities, medical insurance, NHP again, for the same amount. That must be it, the agency Nadia and Carl work for.

Just to be sure, she'll go back one more month. There it is, February, the listing for NHP. Same amount, same day of the month. Gold star to the girl in the white cotton blouse.

If she's lucky, NHP will be listed in the domestic help section of the yellow pages. Valerie drags out the telephone book, runs her finger down the small print. National Home Professionals, on Court Street in Brooklyn.

A woman with an Eastern European accent answers.

Businesslike, Valerie explains that she needs a fill-in to help with Mrs. Carrera. "Just for four or five days," she says. "They're supposed to be back by Wednesday."

"Nadia said . . . Never mind. I can—"

"Just a minute. Nadia told you she was leaving?" Maybe the housekeeper called the agency from the airport with some tale about Antonia not needing anyone for the weekend. Maybe she even phoned on her way out the door.

And maybe Antonia told Nadia not to bother asking

for a replacement. "Valerie will be here," she might have
said. "You go ahead."

"Of course. But I thought Mrs. Carrera didn't want
anyone else. It's fine, though, if she changed her mind. I
can send someone over at eight this evening. That's the
absolute earliest I can manage."

The DASH meeting is scheduled for seven-thirty. Antonia will just have to take her chances alone for an hour.
"I guess eight will have to do. If anything changes, if you
can have someone come by earlier, I'd appreciate it."

She sets the phone down, wondering. Can Nadia's
hurried departure possibly have anything to do with
Joanna? Is that what the woman was really apologizing
for in the upstairs hallway?

Before she can get her thoughts in order, the doorbell
chimes.

A strange stillness greets her when she steps into the
foyer. Dust motes swirl in the sun, and the fragrance of
gardenias drifts down the stairs. The shadow on the other
side of the door backs away and then steps forward again.
It's Kevin Murchison, his lanky figure silhouetted against
the etched-glass panes.

She pulls open the door and sees it at once, a sadness
that darkens his eyes. "Mr. Murchison."

"Last time I spoke to you it was Kevin. You have a
minute? You have time for coffee or a walk or something?
This isn't about your daughter—not directly, but I have to
talk to you."

She can breathe again. He doesn't know anything new
about Joanna. "Can we sit out here? Mrs. Carrera's
housekeeper and her husband—he's the handyman and
the chauffeur—went away unexpectedly. I can't leave her
alone unless it's absolutely necessary."

"Sure. No problem. You okay?"

She hardly knows the man, yet she's filled with an
urge to spill out everything—the anonymous phone calls,
Johnny's behavior, the DASH inquisition, the disorienting
events of the morning. Later. Some other time, some other
place where there's no chance that Antonia might over-
hear them.

Now she's even granting the woman superpowers.

"I'm fine. Actually, it feels good to be outside." She pats her pocket, feels the outline of the lone key through the fabric of her skirt. "I'll leave the door open so I can hear her if she calls, but there's this breeze and if it blows shut and I can't get back in, she'll be stuck alone in there and—"

"Sure, I understand." Murchison hoists himself up to the concrete ledge beside the walk, his long legs dangling in front of him. He smiles with amused perplexity, as though her chatter surprises and charms him.

Everybody's got a problem—that one is all his.

The morning is clear, the sunshine a promise that by afternoon everyone will shed even their light sweaters and jackets. Down the street, two teenaged girls roar with laughter, then repress giggles as they approach the house.

"I got a call from someone a couple of hours ago," he says after the girls pass. "The guy said—"

"A guy with perfect enunciation? A deep voice? Refined?" Her heart pounds with hope. Maybe Murchison's going to answer at least one of the questions that plague her.

"No, just a regular-sounding guy, nothing remarkable about his voice at all. This fellow wouldn't tell me who he was, but he claimed to know where the DASH safe houses are. He also said he'd found out that a little girl was being kept in one of them, he didn't know which one, and that they were going to do a transfer tonight. Anyway, I called Mitch Russo right away, and he contacted the authorities in those jurisdictions. One of the houses was empty, but they found a little girl in the other one. Around Joanna's age. She's been missing from her parents' home in Elmira for two weeks. DASH was planning to place her with a couple in the city tonight."

Joanna's age—he didn't say Joanna, he said she was around her age.

"I'm sorry, Valerie. The parents are on their way from Elmira to pick up the baby. I made Russo swear he'd handle this quietly and not do anything that might set off alarms about Joanna, or any other child in the Operation Safe Haven pipeline."

There's no such thing as a safe haven. Maybe for another little girl, someone else's daughter from Elmira, but not for Joanna.

"Was there a child in that other house?" She has to cling to the last shred of hope. "Maybe the person who phoned you didn't really know what he was talking about. Maybe he was lying about the other safe house."

"Maybe, but he sounded pretty sure that there was only one child being moved tonight, and I believed him. He said something about having to make up for his mistakes. That he was starting over for the second time in ten months, but this time he was determined to do it right."

Johnny Starr. Johnny had somehow gotten Martha or Lucas to tell him about DASH.

"There was something about the way he delivered the information . . . I made some calls, but I'm pretty sure Joanna wasn't in that other house. As sure as I can be, anyway. Which doesn't mean I'm not wrong." His mouth twists sardonically. "It's been known to happen. I'm sorry."

His voice, rough with emotion, tips her over the edge, and she laughs sharply. "I'm glad for those parents in Elmira, I really am. Maybe when this is all over we can form one of those support groups, all of your subjects. Maybe we can take our stories to Oprah or Geraldo. They're always looking for guests who want to tell their stories to millions of people at once."

"Whoa. Enough." Murchison examines her face. "It's not necessarily bad news. But it *is* news and I thought you had a right to know. What's going on with you, anyway? You're extra wired and jumpy. And why did you want to know if the guy who called me had a distinctive voice? Someone you suspect? You're not real good at keeping secrets, Valerie."

"Someone's called here a couple of times when I was out." Saying the words aloud is like ripping off a Band-Aid. The pain is keen yet fleeting, and the relief is astonishing. "Antonia described his voice that way. Senatorial, she said he sounded."

The tiny muscles near Murchison's mouth twitch. "But these weren't friendly calls, right? Did he ask for money or anything?"

"No. He just leaves messages. Something about protecting the children and a warning that I have to follow the rules. And each time he says that Joanna's all right and that I shouldn't contact the police. And then he says he'll call back. But each time he does, I'm out."

"Listen, the guy who called me this morning sounded like your average nervous man-on-the-street type. Nothing special about his voice, but he did say he knew someone from DASH had tried to phone you at Antonia Carrera's. *Once.* The day after your daughter disappeared. I asked him who called, why. He said he wasn't sure, that his information was secondhand, but he thought it was this George Perry from New Jersey. Apparently Perry called to confirm his crackpot theory. He thought you were maybe hiding Joanna from her grandparents by claiming she'd been kidnapped. I've heard Perry speak. He sounds like Ronald Reagan with a head cold. Maybe someone would call that distinguished, I don't know."

"But there have been three calls. Antonia said—"

"You think it's possible this Antonia Carrera hasn't been straight with you? My information is she spoke to the regional honcho of DASH one time. Would she maybe gain something from inventing those other calls?"

Suddenly he's cast a whole new light on Antonia's duplicity.

"Be my reality check, Kevin. What if she reports to me about this sinister-sounding guy and sees my reaction, knows that it upsets me? Knows that I wait for the promised call kind of nailed to the ground by both feet. And while I'm waiting, she gets me to tell her stories. Calls it a way to take my mind off the waiting but it's really her way to devour my life. She wants more, more stories, more pieces of me, so she tells me about other calls. Only she's making them up."

Murchison shrugs. "In my business, you learn that people are capable of every weird thing. Look, the only way to know for sure about any incoming calls is to get Russo to put a tap on the phone. He won't have any trouble getting the order, not in a murder case, but it might take a while, so call him right away and have him get started. Meanwhile, whatever you do, don't let on to this

Carrera woman about your suspicions. Just go back in
there and act the way you always do."

She might have been able to turn herself into Alice
Monroe for the benefit of the Clearys, but her acting skill
do have a limit.

"Try to answer the phone whenever you're around,"
Murchison says as he hops off the ledge and brushes the
seat of his pants. "If you actually talk to this guy, at least
write down everything he says. And let me know if there's
anything I can do. I'll call you this afternoon to check in.
You be careful, all right?"

She doesn't even know what that means anymore, but
she agrees. "Thanks. And thanks for coming to the wilds
of Brooklyn to talk to me. You know, you never told me
her name."

"Lindsay." Murchison doesn't have to ask who she
means. He puts an arm around her shoulder and they
watch a dragonfly, its wings sparkling like sunlit crystals
as it swoops toward the park.

forty

The study is silent, the green glass of the banker's lamp shimmering with pinpoints of sunlight. Kevin Murchison said it so calmly: "Call Russo. Have him put a tap on the phone." Simple as that. Ignore the warning, pay no attention to the threats.

She's not sure she can do that.

Maybe Antonia *didn't* make up those calls. Maybe Joanna is an expendable pawn in someone's sick game, a ready sacrifice if the police come too close.

If only she'd gotten to know Kristin better . . . she would know how to reach her, could ask for her help in sorting through this mess about Antonia and the calls and Nadia and Carl and the woman at NHP.

The brass arm of the lamp casts a slender shadow across the checkbook still lying open on the desk. One of the entries leaps out at her.

Paragon. Now she remembers. Paragon Travel, the call that came the other day.

Antonia said something about giving Charles Babcock and Kristin a trip as a wedding gift.

But the wedding has been called off, so maybe Kristin's simply enjoying her independence. Maybe she's severed her ties to Babcock and to Antonia and has gotten a job. And just *maybe* the travel agency has that phone number in their computer.

Don't they always ask for daytime numbers, so they can tell you if your flight has been canceled, the departure time changed, the passport requirements amended?

She ought to be able to invent yet another story to convince someone at the travel agency to tell her how to reach Kristin. She finds the Paragon number in the phone book, dials.

The woman who answers sounds resigned to yet another interruption that keeps her from her fashion magazine.

"I work for Mrs. Carrera's accountant, Ernest Mattucci," Valerie improvises. "I'm trying to get in touch with someone Mrs. Carrera made travel plans for. About the arrangements? The thing is, I seem to have misplaced her telephone number. I wonder if you could help me out. My boss will kill me if I don't get this information. I need a daytime phone number for—"

"Mrs. Carrera's reservations?" Desultory clicks of a computer keyboard fill the silence between the young woman's mutterings. "That's flight 3345 from JFK to Santiago, right?"

"Santiago?"

"Santiago, Chile."

Chilly. Miguel Carrera's family—the only thing Valerie knows about them is that they were from South America and had a string of coffee plantations. Was Antonia sending Kristin and her groom on a Chilean honeymoon?

Right now, anything seems possible.

"That's for Monday, April 22, at 5:15 P.M. Now, you wanted to know the price of the ticket, right?"

April 22 is only three days away. Wasn't the wedding supposed to be in May?

"No. I wanted the phone number for—"

"The adult tickets are $1,730 each. Is that all?"

"—Kristin Denby. I need that—" *The adult tickets?*

"Kristin Denby? Sorry, but I'm not running an information booth here. I don't have time for this. Listen, first you ask all these questions about Mrs. Carrera's tickets and now you—"

"What do you mean, the *adult* tickets? You said the tickets cost $1,730 each. But the check is for $3,612."

"I told all this to Mr. Mattucci. Because the child is under two years of age and will be sitting on a passenger's lap, you only pay taxes. The child needs a valid passport and if he's not traveling with both parents you need to get— Wait a minute. I better check this."

She is definitely not traveling with even one parent, at least not to South America.

The bored voice returns. "Never mind. Chile doesn't require written parental permission from the absent parent. I told him if Mrs. Carrera or her companion will be—"

"Her companion?" What is Nadia's last name?

"If they'll be traveling to, say, Colombia, maybe on a side trip, they have to process those forms through the embassy in D.C., you know? Like I said to Mr. Mattucci Tuesday."

Tuesday—the morning the accountant conferred with Antonia in the study. His unscheduled visit. The day after Kristin came by with a birthday gift, the day before she and Johnny went to the first DASH meeting, Ernest Mattucci was helping Antonia make plans to fly to South America.

"This is urgent. First of all, I need the name of the person traveling with Mrs. Carrera. And I need to get in touch with Kristin Denby immediately. You must have a number where I can—"

"You want *me* to get fired? You better call directory assistance, miss. You need to know who's traveling with Mrs. Carrera, you're gonna have to ask *her*. You want a reservation, that I can do for you, just like I did for Mrs. Carrera, right?"

No, it's wrong, it's terribly wrong. This trip isn't Antonia's wedding present to Kristin and Charles Babcock at all.

"Look, I have two other calls to take. Good-bye."

Stunned, Valerie hangs up the phone.

Antonia.

And a child under two.

Antonia did talk to someone from DASH.

Murchison said so. And with all her powers of persuasion and the lure of enormous sums of money, she might

have cut a deal. She might have bought Joanna, pai
DASH a small fortune for a little girl. Someone she ca
raise who will always be there to entertain her.

And her companion. Has Nadia been brushing up o
her Spanish lately?

Antonia can't handle a toddler on her own. Nadi
must be going along to set things up in Chile, to arrang
child care, household help. Mid-autumn in South America
Antonia will be wearing a black cashmere turtleneck an
camel-colored slacks when she settles into her first-clas
seat. A bulkhead seat, no doubt. A small child needs roon
to move around on such a long flight.

"Valerie. Oh, God, Valerie, please come up here righ
away."

Antonia Carrera, international traveler, is awake an
in need of assistance.

Slowly, deliberately, Valerie walks up the stairs. It'
not ladylike to hurry.

The darkened bedroom reeks of gardenias. She flip
on the overhead light as she enters the room. "I'm here
Antonia."

"Oh, thank God you heard me." Slumped in he
chair, Antonia pushes the hair off her face and sighs. "
was having a dream. I was in a huge warehouse and there
were stacks of wooden pallets everywhere and the first on
started burning. Funny, I wasn't in a wheelchair and
wasn't blind, but I couldn't move. My legs wouldn't obe
me and the flames started licking at my hands, and then
woke up. It was all so frightening."

"That afghan was too warm, that's all." Valerie pulls
aside the light blanket so that Antonia's hands, white and
bony, are exposed to the cool air. "I'm going to open a
window, and then I have to make a phone call."

Antonia lifts herself by her elbows, and settles back
into the seat slowly, painfully. "No, no, don't bother with
the window. I only want some company."

She can do it. She can sit here and tell another story to
pass the time. She can reassure Antonia until the woman
gets smug, complacent, maybe a little careless.

"All right. By the way, I called the agency and they're
sending someone over at eight tonight. Oh, and I forgot to

ell you. Detective Russo wouldn't say exactly what it was,
ut he told me he thought things were going to break
oon. He has what he considers the first solid lead. Isn't
hat wonderful?"

A gasp. Yes, indeed, her deft little lie has made Anto-
ia Carrera gasp, has made her hand fly from her lap to
er throat as though she means to stop herself from saying
omething. Antonia is composing herself, consciously
orking over the facts and trying to frame the questions
hat will get her the information she needs.

"Isn't that great?" Valerie continues. "Russo said
hey'd know something by Monday."

"Monday? Why Monday?"

Her delight at Antonia's discomfort is touched, fleet-
ngly, with sympathy. The woman is terrified. "I'm not
ure." She has to continue, can't leave the story so vague
nd unpromising. "He wouldn't say, but I think—" What?
What would Antonia believe, what would make Russo say
Monday? "I think it has to do with another DASH meet-
ng. He sort of hinted around but wouldn't come right out
nd say for sure."

The laugh isn't quite hysterical but it's uncontrollably
right until Antonia says, "Then they expect to find
oanna soon, do they?"

What an amazing recovery. The woman has regained
bsolute control of her voice and her face, and has done it
n ten seconds. She's sharing Valerie's pleasure at the good
ews, she's pleased that Joanna will be returned to her
ightful place soon, she's so damn convincing that Valerie
as to dig her nails into her own palms to remind herself
hat it's all an act.

"By Monday. That's what he told me. As long as I can
old on for a couple of days more, as long as I can stay
ere with you, I can wait until then."

Her sympathy toward the woman in the wheelchair
as vanished. In its place, Valerie enjoys the satisfaction of
watching Antonia twist in the breeze of uncertainty.

"Of course, my dear. You know my home is open to
ou for as long as you need it."

No talk now of sharing a life, the three of them—
Antonia, Valerie, Joanna. Antonia has repeated the offer

so many times, and, repeatedly, Valerie has refused. If she had accepted, would her daughter be sitting on her lap now?

"Thank you for your kindness. I'd better go make that call, Antonia."

"I'm still a little shaken by my dream. Do you mind staying a while longer?" Her hands slide in tight circles on the armrests of the wheelchair, then reach up to adjust the glasses that hide her eyes. "You know, you've never really described Joanna to me. How she looked when she was born. What she looked like the last time you saw her."

Antonia's request is shocking.

The woman is a marvel. There she sits in regal splendor, knowing that her plans to steal a child from her mother are in place for the final unfolding, and she's asking about how Joanna looked a week ago.

A plain Joanna, a grotesque Joanna, a heartbreakingly beautiful Joanna—which shall it be?

The real Joanna, the one who will be returned home because her mother wouldn't let herself be confused or deflected from her goal.

Valerie says: "She was one of those furry babies. That's what Esther used to say about the dark hair all over her arms and her back and the great dark thatch of it on her head. She looked a little like an unkempt old man when she was born. But then, pretty quickly, actually, all that body fuzz disappeared and her hair came in reddish, a wonderful warm chestnut color, wavy and shiny. Her eyes were these enormous green jewels, and her mouth was a classic little rosebud. It was hard to tell about her nose at first, but you know how it is with newborns, that seems to change so much practically overnight. I think it's going to end up a bit rounded, kind of like mine, rather than sharper, like Johnny's."

"What is it, my dear? You sound angry." Antonia's fine forehead is ridged with deep lines.

She can't do it, can't go on with this charade. She can't do anything rash, either. She has to keep Antonia disarmed until Joanna is safe.

"I'm just anxious. It's all getting to me. I'm sorry

Antonia. I thought I'd be able to make the time pass the way we usually do, but it's not working."

A smile lights Antonia's face and the furrows disappear. "You know, whenever you've gotten upset lately, what seems to be most helpful is a walk. And I do need a refill on my medicine. Would you do both of us a favor and take the bottle down to the Neergard Pharmacy and get me a refill? I'll be all right alone here for that short time. It shouldn't take more than twenty minutes altogether, and now that I've calmed down, I'm certain I'll be able to manage."

Yes, of course. No witnesses. No one to be present at the birth of another invented message, no one to hear the silence when the phone doesn't ring.

"Good idea. The headache medicine in the kitchen? Is that the one you mean?" Valerie's already in the doorway, anxious to escape this woman and her gardenia-scented room.

Antonia smiles her gratitude. "That's right, my dear. Thank you. You'll see, you'll feel better out in the air for a while."

forty-one

Instead of making a right turn at the corner, she dodges between two cars and crosses Prospect Park West. Antonia can't watch the street from her bedroom, can't see Valerie staring up at the windows with the purest hatred she's ever felt in her life. It's white, sharp, invigorating to allow herself such an unqualified emotion, thrilling to look at the bay window, the second-floor curtains, the glass panes in the door, and revel in the luxury of loathing.

If the phone rings, will she be able to hear it from here?

Behind the sheer drapes of the bedroom window, a dark shape appears, silhouetted like a Victorian cutout in classic profile in the center of the frame. On her own, Antonia has managed to make her way from the television alcove to the table where she keeps the portable phone and then to the window at the other end of the room.

How unladylike, to be rushing that way.

The phone is pressed to her ear. She's calling Nadia, no doubt. She's refining their plan, telling the housekeeper that everything is in order, that even the police are cooperating by assuming Joanna is deep in the bosom of DASH.

Or is Antonia busy rearranging things, rescheduling their departure from Monday to Saturday? Or even today? She could be talking to that empty-headed travel agent

right now, booking seats for three on the five-fifteen flight
this afternoon.

Russo needs to know about all this.

Her walk turns into a jog, the jog into a run. By the
time she reaches the pay phone on Seventh Avenue she's
panting and holding her side, and pawing through her
purse for a quarter. Incredibly, no one's using the phone
and she drops the quarter in the slot, punches out Russo's
number, almost groans when she hears Weinstein's voice.

"Russo or Gallagher—are they in?"

"Ma'am?"

"Russo and Gallagher." Her chest is still heaving from
the run. "Aren't they there?"

"Ms. Vincent. Are you all right?"

"No, I'm not. I need to talk to Detective Russo. Can't
you page him or something? It's important."

"What's the message?"

"Just have him call me at the Carrera house. Tell him
it's urgent. I'll be back there in about ten minutes."

"Sure, I'll page him, but I can't say when he can get to
a phone. You're sure you don't want to talk to someone
else?"

"Have Russo call me."

The phone is damp where she's been clutching it. She
slams the receiver down and swiftly retraces her steps. But
she can't go back to the house yet; Antonia would notice
that only a few minutes have passed, barely enough time
for her to reach the pharmacy. She'll stop in the park,
catch her breath, sort out her disordered thoughts.

A patch of grass, newly green and fine as baby's hair,
beckons invitingly beneath a gnarled oak. Acorn husks litter the valleys between the twisted old roots that push
their way above the ground. A breeze lifts the damp hair
off her face, and she presses her eyes shut and tries to
think.

She's lived with Antonia for four months, waited on
her, served her coffee and stories and friendship, and never
suspected the woman was capable of such treachery. Yet it
fits neatly: Antonia grew tired of her companions forever
going off to get married or to take another job. She saw

the opportunity to change all that when that call cam
from George Perry. She spoke to him the day after Joann
was kidnapped, made a deal with DASH to buy her child
made arrangements to fly to Chile with Nadia and Joanna
and pretended sympathy for the poor bereft mother th
whole time.

Her fists clench together so hard her knuckles show
white against her dark skirt. Antonia, of course, won't se
any of the signs of her agitation, but she's sure to hear it i
her voice, in the way she walks into a room. She looks a
her watch: she's been gone thirty minutes. Antonia ha
probably begun to worry about being left alone in her fin
old house for so long.

Let her.

Let her live with a gut-wrenching, mind-twisting pani
for a few minutes, the kind of panic a mother has to en
dure when she finds out her daughter is missing. Let Anto
nia Carrera feel she really has been abandoned.

The imprints on her hands, a crazy quilt of marking
left by the small twigs hidden in the grass, will fad
quickly, she knows, faster than her fury will.

She could be wrong. Maybe she's learned too well from
Lucas and Martha Starr how to build a case out of smok
and mirrors. She could be inventing another story. But i
she's making it up, then where is Joanna?

The silly tune of a commercial jingle is the only soun
from milady's chamber. Still, the house has an expectan
air about it, shades half raised, curtains parted, as thoug
it's waiting to catch a glimpse of an intriguing scene.

Valerie wanders from room to room, remembering th
stories she's told in the past seven days. Nothing about th
time before Esther's murder and Joanna's disappearanc
seems real. It's as if her entire life in this house started las
Friday.

The living room, with that slick mantel of marbl
above a fireplace cold and swept clean of ashes, the gran
piano, the white sofa and chairs—this is where she de
scribed Joanna's earache to Antonia. And in the study
sitting next to the imposing desk that hides the ledger an
the checkbook, she made up the tale of the boy in th

eather jacket and the girl with the backpack. She outlined her plan to infiltrate DASH in the dining room, reminisced about her mother in the master bedroom.

This house is a setting for fabricating lies; it's not a place to live.

She closes her eyes, pictures Joanna's smiling face.

Better.

She can face Antonia now.

Antonia is sitting in her chair beside the night table, hands on her lap, head drooping. When the light is flipped on, her head snaps up and swivels toward the sound. "Who is it?"

"I'm sorry, I didn't mean to startle you." She hates sounding like a solicitous employee, but Antonia needs to believe she's safe for a while longer.

"I must have been so wrapped up in my own thoughts, I didn't even hear you come in, Valerie. He called again. The phone rang right after you left. He said this was the last contact he'd make and that you must follow his instructions to the letter. He wants you to bring ten thousand dollars to a locker and leave it there. And then you'll get your daughter back."

The words bang around the room, slam into her chest, make her head spin.

What if Antonia isn't lying?

"What locker, Antonia? When? And how will I get Joanna? I can't believe this is happening. I was only gone for a short while. Less than half an hour."

"He said the locker is number 356 at the American Airlines terminal at LaGuardia Airport. You're to go to the first-class ticket counter and ask for an envelope addressed to you. The key will be inside. Then you deposit the money, take the key back to the ticket counter, and get on the flight that leaves at seven for Los Angeles. When you arrive in California, Joanna will be waiting for you. Don't you see, this has been about money all along. That's all, not your ex-husband or his parents or even DASH, but money."

Can she be telling the truth? Anything in the world is possible, but only one thing is likely. Antonia has devised

a plan—complicated, dangerous, urgent, a perfect way t
get rid of the one person who might ruin things. And u
less she's willing to concede her daughter's future to th
woman, she must do something right away.

"Seven o'clock? It's almost two now. How can I—'

"I've already called the bank and arranged for you t
get the cash, and I've booked you a first-class ticket o
that flight. Of course, I know I have no right to make thes
decisions for you, my dear, but I wanted to be prepare
for any eventuality. You have to decide what it is you'
going to do."

So slick.

The woman has figured out a way to get rid of he
until she and Nadia and Joanna are out of the countr
They'll disappear into South America and that will be tha
Antonia won't give up the chance to have a health
bright, beautiful child, a malleable little creature, a bit
unformed clay, a girl to raise who will always tell he
stories.

Unless the call is real . . . If it is, then every secon
she delays means jeopardy for Joanna. Ten thousand do
lars. Would someone commit murder for ten thousan
dollars?

"Of course I must go. Oh, Antonia, how can I eve
thank you?"

She shakes her head, a dignified horror on her fac
"You mustn't think of it that way. I want no thanks."

Only my baby. You only want my child.

"I'd better throw a toothbrush and a few things into
bag. I'll be ready to leave in a few minutes." She's tren
bling with the tumult of anticipation, adrenaline rushin
through her in great, jerky waves. "I'm so nervous. I'
better get going."

"My dear, the medicine—you put it in the kitchen?'

The medicine. "I forgot to tell you. The pharmaci
made a mistake on the prescription. Something about th
wrong strength; I didn't quite understand. He said he wa
expecting to get it in an hour and he'd send it over with
delivery boy as soon as he could."

Antonia frowns, then says, "Well, that's not what

nportant now. Go on and get your things, dear. The car
ill be here to pick you up in five minutes."

"Car?" Her heart is pounding.

"Well, yes, didn't I say that? I called for car service, to
ake you to the bank and then to the airport."

forty-two

This must be what it's like to be high on cocaine or am
phetamines, the drugs rich people use to convince them
selves they're infallible, inexhaustible, powerful. He
vision is sharp, her mind quick and agile, her body strong

Antonia has moved their departure up because of th
lie about Russo expecting the case to break on Monday
One story too many—with that last tale, Antonia mus
have felt the hot breath of the NYPD on her neck.

Before she calls Russo again, she has to make sur
she's right. She has to see if there's any sign that Nadi
might be going on a journey, a long one, to South Amer
ica.

She slips off her shoes and walks across the hall
pushes open the door to the bedroom where Nadia an
Carl were arguing earlier in the day. The bed is stripped
the dresser tops covered with their white scarves. An
nothing else. Not a jar of perfume, not a hairbrush, not
personal photograph in sight. The floorboards creak as sh
walks to the closet.

Empty hangers dangle from the rod.

She heads for the small, quiet bedroom at the othe
end of the hall and dials Russo's number, isn't surprise
when Weinstein answers and tells her that Russo re
sponded to his page just a few minutes ago and said he'
call in about ten minutes.

"Listen, you have to get this message to one of them right away," she says calmly. "I don't know if people say this all the time, but this really is a matter of life and death. You understand?"

"Look, I know you're mad because I—"

"Listen, Weinstein, I don't have time for interpersonal healing right now. Tell Russo *not* to call here. He must meet me in twenty-five minutes on the corner of Prospect Park West opposite Antonia's. On the park side of the street. Tell him not to go into the house. If I'm not there, he should wait for me. If I'm not there, he's to watch Antonia Carrera's house. Someone may show up there with my daughter and try to take her—"

She hears a click; her own voice sounds like it's traveling through a tinny, distorting baffle. Antonia has picked up the extension.

"Yes, I was just checking to make sure you're going to send someone with Mrs. Carrera's medicine this afternoon. Good-bye." Valerie hangs up before Weinstein has the chance to say anything.

She grabs her purse and throws a toothbrush, a pair of panties, and a clean shirt inside, looks around, snatches her notebook from the desk, and strides down the hall to Antonia's bedroom.

"I've called the pharmacy to check on your medicine. They were a little annoyed that I didn't trust them, but they promised they'd send someone over with it by three."

Antonia rearranges her face, concern sliding into gratitude, puzzlement transformed to satisfaction. "Thank you, my dear. Now, is there anything else you might need? I've checked with the bank and the money is waiting for you. You'll see Mr. Calvert and he'll take care of you. He's promised to call and let me know when you leave the bank. I've instructed the car to wait while you make that stop. Don't you let Mr. Calvert or anyone at the airline keep you waiting. You have to be polite and firm with these people."

The perfect teacher is still trying to create the perfect young woman, to replace the woman she ceased to be after her accident—and Antonia's chosen so well. Kristin Denby, whose drunken father was responsible for those

terrible scars. Valerie Vincent, whose drunken husband de
stroyed their marriage. So like Antonia Carrera, whose
drunken husband crashed that plane, stole her sight and
her unborn child, shattered her fragile body.

Antonia Carrera's been at it for years. But somewhere
along the line she's managed to forget she's not God.

Still, Antonia believes she's controlling events. And
the bank manager reports that Valerie Vincent failed to
show up, Antonia will know immediately that her selfish
plan has gone awry. And then what will happen to
Joanna?

"Thank you again, Antonia." A car horn beeps twice
and she runs to the window. On the street below, a black
sedan idles in front of the house. Showtime. "That's the
car service. I'm on my way."

As Valerie takes a last look around the shadow-filled
room, the smell of gardenias nearly chokes her. This
what she'll remember in the years to come, cloying per
fume and the darkness.

"Will you take me down in the elevator? I can do
myself, but I'll feel more secure if you're with me." Anto
nia presses the button and the wheelchair whirs forward
to the doorway, to the hall, to the tiny elevator. "You
mustn't worry about me," she says as the doors slide open
at the first floor. "The agency will have someone here in
couple of hours. They're quite good about that. The
stand by their name."

"Paragon?" Valerie's guiding the wheelchair to the liv
ing room, walking slowly so she can look around.

Antonia's head jerks back. "No. Where did you get
that name? It's called NHP. National Home Profession
als."

"Of course. That's who I called."

"Are you sure you're all right, my dear?"

"Absolutely. I feel nervous, but that will go away a
soon as I'm on the way to the airport."

The driver honks again.

"You'd better go now. Good luck, Valerie."

"Bye, Antonia." She simply can't bring herself to lean
down and kiss that dry cheek, cannot touch the woman
whose face is upturned and smiling in her direction.

forty-three

She heads down the walk toward the waiting car. The driver sets his newspaper on the front seat and doesn't turn to look at her until she's seated in back. Antonia's right—the car smells of sweat and spoiled milk and dirt that's been ground into the upholstery by countless passengers. She pulls the door shut, hard enough for someone listening from the house to hear it.

Nothing's going to happen for at least an hour. Antonia won't play it that tight. She'll allow enough time for the money to be collected from the bank and for the car to be on its way to the airport before she makes her move. She'll be waiting for a signal from the banker, maybe even from the car service dispatcher, that everything has gone according to plan.

Every parking spot along Seventh Avenue is filled, and the driver is about to make a right turn. "Just let me out here in front of the bank and circle around the block. I'll meet you in a few minutes."

She runs to the bank, pushes at the heavy glass door. It swings open, and she brushes past a knot of people standing at the automatic teller machines and heads for the main business area. The room is lined on one side with teller cages and on the other with padded office partitions. The air is chilled, the lights bright, the guard bored. "I'm looking for Mr. Calvert."

He points to the far end of the room. "Second fron the back. But he's not in. Won't be back until Monday.

This can't be happening. Why would Antonia li about *that*? "But Mrs. Carrera just spoke to him. I'm sup posed to see him right away. It's important."

The guard rubs his jaw with a hand dotted with live spots; the faint gray stubble along his chin makes an irr tating, scratchy noise. "Talk to his assistant. Seligson Anna Seligson. She's probably in his office."

Frantic, she weaves past a baby stroller and strides t the rear of the bank, her heels clicking on the polishe tiles. When she reaches the next to last office, she laugh *Norton Calvo*. It's Mr. Calvo who's not in. She continue on to the last door. *J. M. Calvert*. Too relieved to be angry she knocks on the partition. "Mr. Calvert? I'm Valeri Vincent. Mrs. Carrera called ahead to arrange for a with drawal."

Calvert looks up and smiles from behind thick glasses His hair is combed straight back, receding at the temple and he looks a little harried, a little less tidy than the ban officer who set up her checking account four months ag or the one in Taconic Hills who approved her studen loan. Valerie finds this cheering.

"Yes, Ms. Vincent. She described you very well. Re markable woman, Mrs. Carrera." Calvert reaches into hi drawer and pulls out an envelope, thick and white, an sets it on his desk. "Please, I just need you to sign this slip Right here at the red X."

He slides a form across the desk. She doesn't bother t read it, just scrawls a wiggly line at the place he indicates

"If that's all . . ." She looks at her watch. "I'm sorry I have a plane to catch. I'm in a bit of a hurry." Isn't tha how Antonia would have said it, all polite dismissal?

He hands her the envelope. "Will you count it please?"

"I really don't have the time. I'll take your word fo it."

Before he can protest, she whirls around and heads fo the door, half running.

The driver is leaning against the front fender, a ciga rette dangling beneath his mustache, arms crossed on hi hest as he watches the passing scene. He seems startled when she comes up to the car, as though he doesn't recognize her.

"Let's go," she snaps. Having ten thousand dollars in cash in her purse is making her testy.

He raises his eyebrows, then ambles around to the driver's side and slides onto the seat.

When the door is closed and he's started the engine, he says, "Go to the corner, make a left, and then stop, please."

Now the driver does turn around. His brushy mustache droops down to cover part of his lower lip and he lifts his aviator glasses. Small, dark eyes narrow and his brows knit together. "We go to the airport, no?"

"No. I've changed my mind. I'm getting out around the corner. But I want you to report to your boss that you did just what you were supposed to. That you took me to the bank and then to LaGuardia and I got out at the terminal and then you came back. It's very important that you tell him that. In fact, I want you to go out to the airport, then turn around and come back. Just as you're supposed to. Only I won't be in the car, and you won't say anything."

"I could lose my job, lady. I got two kids and a nother who—"

The sight of the hundred-dollar bill she passes him makes him falter, then he says:

"Listen, one of my kids is sick and if the boss finds out I didn't follow his orders . . ."

He shrugs, eying the money, and she knows he's holding out for more. There's no time for bargaining. She slides another hundred across to him.

He nods, folds the bills and bends down and slips them into his shoe. "Sure, I drop you around the corner and go to LaGuardia and then come back. Say you went into the terminal and I wave good-bye and that's that."

He lets her out in front of a crowded pizzeria, and she watches until the black sedan has passed two stop signs. Then she races up the block.

When she reaches Prospect Park West, the light at the corner changes and the trickle of cars pouring south toward the end of the park stops. She dashes across the street to the place she's told Russo she'll meet him.

Not Russo. She never spoke to Russo. If Weinstein didn't get the message to him on time . . . on time for what? She doesn't know, but Russo can help her find out.

The house, fifty feet down the block and across three lanes of traffic, looks so quiet, almost restful.

She's overlooked something.

The house she's staring at with such concentration is already empty. Antonia's gone, on her way to South America with Nadia and Joanna.

The anonymous caller is at the American Airlines terminal at LaGuardia checking the locker, discovering that no one has left an envelope fat with money inside, phoning some sleazy compatriot in Los Angeles, deciding what to do next with their precious little package.

She's got to stop all this wretched storytelling. She can't let her attention drift and she can't afford to make assumptions when the truth is so crucial.

Antonia has been lying.

Three stray dogs patter up to sniff at her shoes and then go trotting off. Kids on bikes holler greetings to each other and then zip past her and cut into the park. A delivery van slows to a stop near Antonia's house, but the driver hefts a large carton onto a dolly and wheels it to the brownstone on the corner.

The light changes again and traffic inches by, an intermittent stream of cars. They're all in the lane closest to the park, except for a dark sedan with a sign on the dashboard. She can't read it from here, but she knows it's a car service vehicle. The passenger in the back, a woman with dark, short hair parted on the side, the ends turned under to skim her jawline, leans forward to talk to the driver.

The driver twists around to face her, and then the door opens. The woman seems to be having trouble getting out of the car. She turns and holds out her arms. Kristin Denby reaches in to get something from the back seat of the car just as a large brown and gold UPS van double-parks, blocking the view.

forty-four

The UPS driver noses into the spot in front of the fire hydrant, then hops down and strolls toward the corner, whistling as he tucks his clipboard and a fat, padded envelope in the crook of his arm.

Each movement is an isolated torture as Kristin Denby leans into the livery car, speaks to the driver again, straightens.

Joanna is in her arms.

She's all right. Joanna is fifty feet away, and she's all right. Dear God, she's fine.

That other ticket wasn't for Nadia at all.

Kristin starts up the walk, her back to the flow of traffic. Valerie weaves recklessly between two cars to cross the street. She can't take her eyes off her daughter's face.

Joanna is smiling, looking around at the trees and the dog trotting along on the sidewalk, and then her eyes widen and she calls out. "Mommy!"

Laughing, crying, Valerie answers, "Joanna!"

Kristin pivots and stares at Valerie, disbelieving. Panic replaces the shock on her face.

Kristin Denby's unscarred, surgically perfected face . . . a gift from Antonia . . . an inspiration for Charles Babcock's love.

Valerie takes a cautious step forward. "Let me have my daughter." She reaches for her child, but Kristin dances away, clutching Joanna, sidestepping toward the curb.

Kristin's eyes are nearly shrouded by a shock of hair, her expression obdurate. "I can't do that. She's part of the bargain."

The bargain: Antonia Carrera didn't make a deal with DASH to buy Joanna for a large sum of money. She made a pact with this madwoman who's got her daughter in a vise grip. Antonia gets Joanna, and Kristin Denby gets . . . what?

HER OLD LIFE BACK.

Without having to learn to live with Charles Babcock's loving attention.

Without having to adjust to the perils of being a normal, attractive woman.

She called off the wedding, sent him a Dear John letter and a velvet box, that's what he said this morning, containing all his jewelry . . . including a pewter pin?

Joanna's head twists around, her fingers grappling at Kristin's sleeves as she searches for Valerie.

She has to make Kristin Denby doubt herself.

She has to tell her a story.

"Give me the baby, Kristin, and then you and Antonia can go off on your own. Just the two of you, without the burden and the distraction of a small child. You can go to Chile and live in one of those villas in the mountains. It's beautiful there, all those trees with their coffee berries. You could paint them. You could tell Antonia funny stories about going into the market and bargaining for sandals. Just you and Antonia, and the staff that runs the house. You could read all those wonderful books, Márquez, Allende, and poetry. García Lorca in Spanish. It sounds lovely in Spanish. You could sit on the terrace and drink coffee and tell Antonia about the sunlight in the hills. I promise I won't do anything to stop you. I'll take Joanna and leave. I'll walk away and never come back to this house and never tell anyone what happened."

Valerie inches forward, her face impassive.

Warily Kristin moves away. "Clever. You think Antonia would be satisfied with that?" She edges toward the curb, one foot about to step into the busy roadway.

Carefully, as though she's walking on glass, Valerie takes a step back, and then another. Distraction won't do it; she has to turn Kristin against the cruel, manipulative woman who's been controlling their lives.

"You should know something, Kristin. Antonia has changed her mind. She's not taking you to South America."

"I don't believe you." Still clutching Joanna, Kristin spins around and heads toward the cement flowerpots at the foot of the walk.

"It's true," Valerie calls, a step behind. "She's changed the plan."

"Antonia!"

Kristin's shriek cuts the air, and Antonia's face appears behind the glass, her ear turned toward the street. Her graceful fingers hold aside the curtain as though she can see what's happening in front of the house, and then the drapes fall shut.

Joanna has started to cry, her little arms reaching over Kristin's shoulders.

"She wouldn't. Antonia! You didn't do that! You're not backing out of this, are you?" Bright splotches burn Kristin's cheeks as she shouts at the window. "She didn't change anything. Get away from me. Don't make me run across the street . . . all that traffic . . . I know what Antonia wants."

The driver is out of the car, one foot on the curb, looking from one woman to the other as though he's watching a tennis match.

"It's what she used to want. It's no good, Kristin. Please, just give me my daughter."

Is Kristin Denby capable of hurting Joanna to protect herself?

"I'm going inside now. With this little girl. I need her."

Kristin's words glitter with cool resolve.

What you need is the rest of this story, to help you understand what you're really going to do.

"Antonia told me why she changed her plan. She knows the police are ready to arrest you. They found . . ." *Lie. Make her doubt herself.* ". . . someone who saw you wearing that pin, the one you dropped at Esther Klein's. You know, the pin with the lady sitting in the moon, the one Charles Babcock gave you. The police know your name, Kristin. And Antonia knows they know."

Joanna has stopped crying, but she's squirming, trying to twist out of the arms locked tight around her.

"Antonia knows if you're found together she'll be an accessory to murder, so she's going to take Nadia to Chile instead of you. Don't you see? When you get to the airport, there won't be a ticket for you at all. Nadia and Carl will be waiting with their passports and their bags, and you won't be allowed on the plane."

"Nadia?" Her braying laugh is cut short by a snort of derision. "That's ridiculous. Nadia hated it whenever Antonia sent her to my apartment to stay with this kid. I told Antonia I couldn't be with a child all day and all night, but Nadia said she wasn't going to do it anymore. Nadia's not going to Chile." But her eyes flicker with doubt.

Kristin Denby has swallowed the story, and now she's trying to digest it.

"Oh yes, she certainly is. Antonia said she'd be too vulnerable with you around, that you were too volatile, that she feared you were unbalanced. She's been planning this since Wednesday. Ernest Mattucci changed those reservations, and Nadia and Carl are going in your place."

Joanna's green eyes blink rapidly as she reaches up to smear the tears on her cheek.

"Antonia's going to pretend, all the way to the airport, that everything's fine. But you wait. When you get there, you'll see, there won't be a ticket for you. So give me Joanna. I'll go away, and you can disappear, far away from all this."

Valerie stretches out her arms and moves cautiously toward her daughter. Kristin looks up at the window again, then takes another step back, away from the house, closer to the car and the confused driver.

Make her talk. Distract her.

"That's real gratitude, isn't it, after you went to all this trouble, even committing murder to give her what she wants."

Kristin sidles toward the curb; a car rattles by, and Joanna turns to look at it, wriggling in Kristin's arms. Valerie stands still, waiting for Kristin to move away from the roadway.

But she steps off the sidewalk, stands between the livery car and the UPS van. "You don't *really* know anything, do you? I needed to show Antonia you weren't so perfect. That you'd lied to her. That you couldn't be trusted. I knew you had a secret. I followed you home one night, waited outside that apartment. And you rewarded my patience by coming out with your baby."

"It's all right, Kristin. I won't touch you." *Speak gently, slowly.*

But Kristin is oblivious. It's her turn to tell a story, and she won't be interrupted. "When I first told her you had a child, she didn't believe me. She got all cold and hard. 'Valerie wouldn't lie to me. I don't believe you. There is no child.' So I offered to bring her proof."

"Proof that I had a baby? What would that do except get me fired?" Valerie backs away.

"Exactly. And then Antonia and I could resume our lives together." Kristin shakes the hair out of her eyes and steps onto the sidewalk again.

"So you killed Esther?"

"It was . . . the stupid baby-sitter wouldn't believe me that I was going to bring the child back. She kept asking me dumb questions—who was I, what was I doing? Like Antonia, sucking off my life so she could *own* me. Except that old lady couldn't give me anything I wanted in return. No pretty clothes. No quiet room. Only the baby."

From the corner of her eye, Valerie sees a figure approach. Brown pants and shirt: the UPS driver. Cameron Zax. Why does she remember his name? "Wouldn't Joanna's birth certificate have been proof enough? It was right there in Esther's house."

"I was ready to settle for that, but that damn babysitter wouldn't listen to reason, kept trying to grab the papers out of my hand. Clawing at me, shouting questions. The next thing I knew, I was holding a broken cane in my hand, she was lying on the floor, and someone was banging from downstairs. Banging on the ceiling with a broom or something."

Kristin's chest is heaving, her eyes wild as she looks over her shoulder again at the brownstone. Valerie blows her daughter a kiss, is rewarded with a tentative smile.

"So I ran away." Kristin is tiring, her voice quavering. This story's almost over. "I went back to my apartment and watched television. Thank God. Because I turned on the news broadcast and saw this kid with my pin, and I knew if I didn't get it back, someone else would see it and know."

Antonia didn't have to see to know. The announcer had described the pin perfectly—a pin that Antonia must have realized instantly would link Kristin to Esther's murder. A pin that Kristin had surely placed in Antonia's hands hours after Charles Babcock presented it to her so Antonia could feel the delicate tracery of the woman's flowing dress and the lovely curve of the moon . . .

"So you went to the police station," Valerie says, "with all those papers you still had and you walked away with my daughter and your pin. And then Antonia phoned you from East Hampton. As soon as I left, she called you and proposed a deal."

Kristin picks up the thread, as though it makes no difference which of them is talking because the story is all that matters. "I could hear it in her voice: she was hooked on the idea of a child. You ever get the top-button lecture from Antonia? God, how she loves to think she's responsible for creating me. As though I was nothing before she took charge of my clothes and my hair and my goddamn reading list. Think of what she could do with a baby."

"So now you expect to get away? You're looking at a life sentence for murder and another fifty years for kidnapping, Kristin, especially if you try to run now. Give me the baby." She takes a step forward, her eyes on Joanna's face and not on the young man circling around behind his van.

Don't look at him, Joanna. Just keep watching Mommy.

"Prison? Maybe that would be good. I might like the kind of jail where I'd be left alone. Anyway, that's not going to happen. You don't want to take the chance I'll tumble and drop her, now, do you?"

The woman is consumed by a madness so reckless it takes Valerie's breath away. She must keep talking. About what—the weather in Chile? The price of baby food?

Joanna is staring, questions in her eyes.

I love you, Josie. Stay quiet for a while longer, sweetie.

The UPS driver steps from between two parked cars and touches Kristin's shoulder. She spins around, her face white.

"It's only me, Kristin. Cameron. Cameron Zax, remember?"

She bolts toward the walk clutching Joanna, then stops to shrug off Cameron's touch. "Leave me alone," she shrills. "Go away!"

Cameron Zax raises his hand and smiles. "Kristin, oh, beautiful Kristin," he croons sadly. "Don't do this. Please don't do this."

Kristin whirls again, and now Valerie can hear it, an insistent tapping on the window. Antonia is trying to get her attention, and Kristin fumbles in the purse hanging at her side.

She's looking for the key.

"Here, let me hold the baby while you find the key." Cameron Zax keeps his hands in his pockets but he's a step closer now.

Kristin is wavering, Valerie can see it in her eyes. She's running her tongue over her lips, shifting Joanna against her hip. And then the frantic tapping on the window glass begins again.

It's time.

She sprints ahead, grabs Kristin's arm, and reaches out for Joanna. But Kristin dances away, edges toward the house. She's wild-eyed, stumbling backward. Instinctively Valerie puts out a hand to steady her. Kristin shakes it off, staggers a few steps closer to the house.

Valerie lunges forward, bracing herself for the struggle. Kristin swerves away, both arms clasped firmly around Joanna. Joanna's mouth quivers and her legs flail out, her body wriggling in the too tight embrace that's

keeping her pressed against Kristin Denby. Her frightene
whimper becomes a noisy sob.

"Stop that!" Kristin looks down at the terrified chil
her face contorted with fury. "Stop screaming in my ear!
Now.

Valerie grabs Joanna at the waist, tugs her free in
single powerful movement, feels Kristin falter and the
stumble as the child is torn from her arms.

Joanna buries her face in Valerie's shoulder, her littl
body tensed, legs pulled up, arms clasped around Valerie'
neck.

"Josie, oh, my baby. Joanna, oh yes, it's all right."
She's kissing her face, touching her lips to the salty tears
her hands pushing the curls out of the crying child's eyes
the smell of her overpowering and wondrous.

A small crowd has gathered, the limousine driver, tw
women with bulging shopping bags, a kid on a skate
board, and they all turn at once as a dusty car squeals to
stop behind the UPS van. Detective Gallagher flies fron
the driver's side into the crowd as Mitch Russo runs to th
door of Antonia's brownstone.

Valerie backs down the street, hugging Joanna and
whispering to her, easing away from the crowd, away
from the possibility that her daughter might get hurt in th
turmoil.

Russo presses the buzzer, then stands back and aims
powerful kick at the etched glass. It shatters with a horri
ble crash, and then he reaches past the glittering spikes
turns the knob and is gone, swallowed up into the house

A piercing scream cuts through the commotion on th
sidewalk. Valerie clutches Joanna, turns, then gasps in hor
ror. Teresa Gallagher unwraps her arms from around Kris
tin's legs and pushes herself to a standing position. Kristin
is lying on the sidewalk near the iron fleur-de-lis fenc
surrounding the now fading tulips. A stream of thick rec
blood seeps from between the fingers she holds pressec
against her face. As she pulls her hand away, Valerie stares
transfixed at the ragged cut that slices across the woman'
face from her cheek to her mouth.

A knot of people cluster on the sidewalk, obscuring
her view. Sirens blaring and red lights flashing, three blue

and white police cruisers pull up, and when the crowd parts to let the uniformed officers through, she can see Kristin Denby struggling to stand. Cameron Zax is on one side of her; Teresa Gallagher's hand is locked onto the arm that's holding up a handkerchief, bright crimson as her blood soaks through the white square.

They both have what they wanted.

She has her daughter, her beautiful, frightened, healthy daughter. And Kristin Denby will have her scar back.

forty-five

"If you change your mind, Cissie says to tell you we've got plenty of toys, if you don't mind her playing with bucket-loaders and a beat-up old Fischer-Price workbench. The hammer's a little chewed up where David tried to pound down the hinge of an old iron gate." Russo leans back against the tree, examines a battered bottle cap lying atop a twisted root, smiles.

Joanna wriggles in Valerie's lap, squirms to a standing position. "Look, Mommy. Doggy." She giggles and claps her hands, bends forward and puts her hands on her chubby knees.

"It's a squirrel, sweetie. Squirrel." The skin on the back of her legs is so soft, her hair a shining tumble of curls. Joanna Claire Vincent, animated, curious, happy, is enchanted by the squirrel's dark, darting eyes and twitching tail, enjoying the creature's antics from a shaded patch of Prospect Park. This is a gift, an amazing, precious gift to be here with her sharing such a supremely ordinary activity.

Teresa Gallagher rubs at her back, tosses an acorn a few feet from the squirrel, and then hunkers down to study something in the grass.

"I really do appreciate the offer, but we're going back to Taconic Hills. I have to convince a certain history professor to give me an extra week to finish a paper, and then

Joanna and I are going to spend at least a month barefoot."

"Yeah, well, Cissie kind of knew that's what you'd say. I guess you're not too unhappy to be leaving Brooklyn."

It will be a while before she'll be able to pass Esther Klein's apartment without feeling grief, even longer before she can look at Antonia's brownstone, at the gaslamp out front and the bay windows, without reliving the past week. And she'll never be able to walk by the house a few blocks away, where Kristin Denby has kept Joanna hidden in the garden apartment, without wondering how it was she didn't know her daughter was so close during the whole terrible time.

"Actually, if we could do a little selective bulldozing, I'd love this neighborhood, the park, the old houses, all the shops on the Avenue. But I'll be glad to get back home."

"You're leaving right away? You got someone coming to pick you up or what?"

She's so full of energy she could almost walk the ninety-five miles up the parkway to Taconic Hills. "I guess we'll take the train and have someone come get us from the station." A one-way ticket, back to her own real life.

A train ticket—she reaches for her purse, pulls out the big white bank envelope, peels off four hundred-dollar bills. "I almost forgot about this. The ransom money, I guess Antonia would say. You'll find nine thousand four hundred dollars in this envelope. I gave two hundred to the driver who was supposed to take me to the airport, and Antonia Carrera never paid me for this week, so I'm taking it in cash. You know a place in the neighborhood where the four of us can have a terrific, hideously decadent champagne lunch?"

Russo's eyes crinkle into a smile. "You better watch out. They're sure to ask for proof of age for our little beauty here. Yeah, sure, Aunt Sonia's, over on Eighth Avenue." He strips two more bills from the thick bundle. "But this lunch is on Mrs. Carrera."

Teresa Gallagher kneels in front of Joanna. "Close your eyes, honey, and hold out your hand."

Joanna's head tilts; her nose wrinkles and she shakes her head and takes a step backward until she tumbles into Valerie's lap.

"It's okay, Josie. Cover your eyes and hold out your other hand. Teresa has a surprise for you." Valerie wraps her arm around the little chest, pulls her daughter closer, feels the little body fit into the curve of hers like a miracle. "Here, like this." She extends her own hand.

Joanna covers her eyes with her fingers and holds out her other hand. Teresa Gallagher places her closed fist on the upturned palm, then opens it one finger at a time. "Okay, now you can look." She lifts her hand slowly, gently.

A ladybug, bright orange with two large freckles on its back, crawls along Joanna's palm toward the smooth, tender skin of her wrist. "Tickles, Mommy," she giggles. "Tickles."

about the author

MARILYN WALLACE's first novel, *A Case of Loyalties*, won the Macavity Award for Best First Novel in 1986. Her second, *Primary Target*, was nominated for an Anthony Award. *Lost Angel* is her sixth, and she is also the editor of the *Sisters in Crime* anthologies, which have won Anthony, Macavity, and American Mystery Awards. She lives in New York City, where she is at work on her next suspense novel, *Current Danger*.

If you enjoyed LOST ANGEL, you will want
to read Marilyn
Wallace's next novel of psychological suspense,
CURRENT DANGER.
Look for it in hardcover from Doubleday
coming soon at your
favorite bookstore.

Haunting novels of
psychological suspense from

MARILYN WALLACE

A Single Stone
"Riveting and original." —Cosmopolitan

A child is found dead in Linda Orett's hometown, murdered under the same circumstances as Linda's own daughter three years ago. Now, Linda plunges back into a chilling world where no one can be trusted—not the police, not her husband . . . not even herself.

___29833-X $4.99/$5.99 Canada

So Shall You Reap
"Wallace proves she is the peer of Mary Higgins Clark." —Carolyn G. Hart

Sarah Hoving has a happy life in peaceful Taconic Hills. But celebrating the town's bicentennial, the murderous events of two hundred years ago begin to recur. As the past takes on a horrifying life of its own, Sarah may be the next victim . . . or even the killer herself.   ___29736-8 $5.50/$6.99

The Seduction
"A compelling psychological thriller." —The Sun, Baltimore

Someone's courting Lee Montara and her sister Rosie. The sisters watch and wait, determined to confront the stalker. They have a gun. But only he knows where his dance of seduction will lead.   ___56840-X $5.50/$6.99

Lost Angel
"Wallace . . . steadily ratchets up the suspense in this . . . gripping tale." —Publishers Weekly (starred review)

Five months ago, Valerie Vincent did the only thing a desperate mother could: she took her infant daughter and fled without telling a soul where she was going. But suddenly it looks as if she didn't run far enough. . . .

___56839-6 $5.50/$7.50

Ask for these books at your local bookstore or use this page to order.

Please send me the books I have checked above. I am enclosing $_____ (add $2.50 to cover postage and handling). Send check or money order, no cash or C.O.D.'s, please.

Name _____

Address _____

City/State/Zip _____

Send order to: Bantam Books, Dept. MC 41, 2451 S. Wolf Rd., Des Plaines, IL 60018
Allow four to six weeks for delivery.

Prices and availability subject to change without notice.   MC 41 12/96